Helix - Ascension

by

Michael Davies

Helix – Ascension

For information address
michaelxdavies@gmail.com

First Printing 2020

ISBN: 978-0-6485470-1-3

Published by The Mickie Dalton Foundation
NSW
Australia

Other Works by Michael Davies

The Nightmares of God
The Janus Conspiracy
Accounts of a Killing
A Friendly Killing
Dreamkill
Ready, Steady, KILL!
Helix Dreams
Helix – The Second Renaissance

For the Young Adults (12-18)

The Many Worlds of Mickie Dalton
The Many Galaxies of Mickie Dalton
The Many Universes of Mickie Dalton
The Strange World of Mark and Anna

For the 8-12 age group

The Julie Malloy Gang and the Smugglers
The Quest for the Locket
The Secret of Yuri Kirilenko
The United Nations and the Extra-Terrestrial
The Secret of Charlotte's Cello
The Star of the Yshan Kings
The War of the Yshan Empire
The Star of the New Yshan Empire
The Saga of the Yshan Kings
The Red Fog of Time
The Mysterious Recorder and The Door to Elsewhere
Prisoners of the Picture
A Step Back in Time
What Can't be Seen Can Exist
How I Spent My Evening

For the Little Ones (3-5)

Mary's World

And in non-fiction

The Business School Approach to Writing Your Novel

Acknowledgement

This is the third book in the Helix trilogy and the second written in collaboration with my friend and colleague, Greg Dickson. As with the second book, *"Helix – the Second Renaissance"* Greg and I spent several working sessions over some months, brainstorming the ideas that built the story. Greg would come up from Sydney to my place on the mid-North coast, work flat out for over two days, developing the ideas on the white board and then head home, leaving both of us exhausted and exhilarated by what we had created. Then I had to get to work and write the results! It could not have been written without this collaboration.

Many thanks also to Greg's partner, Penny who read the completed draft and saw the errors, the inconsistencies and the weaknesses and advised on the corrections.

Finally, sincere thanks to my oldest friend, John Read for his advice on quantum science matters and the invaluable links to articles on the subject.

Prelude – June, 2030

"These episodes confirm what we have been thinking for some years," Garry said. "This whole ability to look back through our timelines has been artificially implanted in humans and we know this happened some seventy thousand years ago in Neanderthal Man and then again in Cro-Magnon Man about forty-five thousand years ago. But we still have no idea who it was that gave us this ability."

Silence rang around the table and then it was broken by Ben Fuller.

"That would be me," he said.

The room was frozen. Everybody stared at Ben, nobody seemed capable of saying anything.

"Ben?" Mary finally spoke. Her voice was weak and shook slightly. "Ben, that's not a funny joke."

He smiled at her. "Not a joke, Mary. Not me personally, of course, but several long-ago ancestors."

Silence fell again as everybody tried to absorb the shock. Mark Craymer sat back in his chair, his arms folded across his chest in some form of protection. Salmaan Basrai, the statistician was wide-eyed, his complexion an unhealthy grey. Jennifer Chang leaned on the table, her elbows supporting her and her hands over her mouth. Annabelle Calvert was white-faced, her eyes wide as she stared at Ben. Alana didn't move, but her eyes studied Ben with cold attention. Garry and Mary looked least affected, but both had gone very still.

"You'd better explain, Ben," said Garry after a few moments. "Who or what are you?"

Ben turned his smile onto him. He looked like a college professor running a tutorial with a group of students.

"Not of this Earth, as you have already realised," he said.

"So from where, then?" Garry's voice seemed under control, but the rigidity in his body indicated severe tension.

"Elsewhere," replied Ben.

"Where elsewhere?" snapped Mary, shock making her irritable.

"That I can't and won't tell you. If I did, astronomers all over the world will show serious attention to the region and it won't help because whatever they see will be several hundred years out of date."

"This really should be insane," said Garry. "Ben, we've known you for some years, you've been an invaluable member of our group. There is absolutely no reason to believe any of this."

"None at all," agreed Ben. "But…?"

"But somehow I do," said Garry. "And I think everybody else does, too."

In various ways, from small nods to muffled sounds, the rest of the group showed agreement.

"So you had better explain everything," said Garry.

"It's what was said in the scroll," said Ben. "There are a number of intelligent races in this galaxy at various levels of growth. Three of them are at a similar level of technological development. Humanity is one of those."

He paused and looked around the listeners as they absorbed this information.

"One of you will have to grow into the future leadership

and mentorship of all the less developed species. In time, one of you must take over from us."

"And who is us?" asked Mary. Tension showed in her harsh, strained voice.

"You won't know that until you are appointed guardians," said Ben.

"And just how did you get to have this exalted role?" asked Mary. Her anger was becoming evident. Ben looked at her.

"Why so angry, Mary?"

"At university I knew who the professors were," said Mary. "I knew their backgrounds and qualifications, I could look them up in public records. In ASIO I knew who the top people were, the ones defining and arranging my life, I knew what training and qualifications they had. When I worked for them or studied under them, it was my choice to do so. But here you are, Ben, telling us you are somehow our supervisors, mentors and perhaps authorities over the human race. We know absolutely nothing about you and we obviously have no say in your appointment. Are you also responsible for our discipline? What punishments do you impose for our failings? Who are you to judge us? Who the *hell* gave you this power over us?"

Mary was almost trembling with anger.

Startled, Garry looked round the table. He could see in several faces the reaction to Mary's blast and some echoes of her fury.

"It's a fair question, Ben," he said. "Can you answer it?"

Ben was silent for a moment.

"Civilisations have risen and collapsed around the galaxy," he said finally. "Many species have developed technology, become the dominant one on their world, risen to great heights of genius. They developed machines to build amazing structures, science to explain the beginnings of the universe and weapons that could obliterate their world and its inhabitants. What they didn't develop was the wisdom and maturity to manage their technologies. They collapsed and died."

The room was so silent Garry could hear the breathing of each of the people there.

"There was one species that was on the ascendant path of technology," continued Ben. "But there were the usual problems, pollution, wars, social unrest, the same stories that were common to almost all the technological species. They lived in constant fear of conflict, disease, possibly even global nuclear war, just as this human race has lived for a century or more."

He was silent again for almost a minute. Nobody moved, sensing that the key part of what he was telling them was yet to be told.

"Then one day, a brilliant scientist began exploring the nature of DNA, something that had been discovered a few decades earlier. And yes, DNA and its characteristics are common to all the intelligent races. As his team of researchers became more and more skilled in what they were doing, as they developed astonishing technologies to help them, they found that their DNA held the visual and sound records of their lives and then also the lives of each of their direct ancestors. They found they could explore the history of their species and this helped them learn everything about themselves. But they also asked the question of why did they have this ability? It wasn't necessary for survival, it didn't help them become and remain the dominant species on their world."

"Just as we have asked," said Mary, her anger fading in the increasing fascination with what Ben was saying.

"Exactly the same. And they came up with the same conclusion that you did, that the ability was installed in their people by some external force for some specific reason. They were correct, just as you are correct."

"And what happened?" asked Garry.

"Their world changed," said Ben. "They became thoroughly knowledgeable about their histories and with that, their understanding of the forces that they had allowed to act on them increased. They transformed from a large number of different groupings, all at war with each other to some extent, to a single group of cooperative people who knew that there could be no more lies, no more subterfuges, no crime, only people with extraordinary gifts of creativity."

"We're not there yet, not by a long way," said Mark Craymer, the first words he had spoken since Ben's revelation.

"And you may never get there," said Ben. "But soon after that moment of discovery, somebody appeared among them who told the people involved in these discoveries something of interest."

"As you have appeared among us," said Mary.

"Yes," said Ben. "He told them of the many civilisations that had reached a similar stage of technology and destroyed themselves. He told them of one civilisation that had somehow avoided that self-destruction and grown so much that it could travel between the stars and had seen how close to suicide the other civilisations were. It learned to become helpers and mentors to these civilisations but without revealing themselves because that could cause massive stress and fear."

"And those mentors and helpers are your people?" asked Mary.

"No," said Ben. "Those people knew that they would one day die out as all civilisations do and they were looking for somebody who could replace them. My people are the ones they found as potentially able to do that."

"Good grief!" said Mark. "Just how long ago was this?"

"Our discovery of the DNA implants occurred nearly two million years ago," said Ben. "We picked up the baton from our mentors about one and a half million years ago when the last of them died out as they had forecast."

Silence fell round the table as they absorbed this.

"Ben, something here doesn't ring true," said Mark after a minute or so. "When we played golf that day and you showed the telekinesis abilities, you seemed astonished by it, just as anyone else would have been. Why? If you are as advanced as you say, your people must have had this ability for centuries, maybe even millennia. So why did you reveal this in our game? Why reveal it at all?"

Ben smiled at him.

"Because I was genuinely astonished," he said. "I had no idea I had the ability. My people have never shown anything like that, nor have any other intelligent races."

Mark looked unconvinced. "Are you saying that your work with human DNA gave you the ability?"

"It would appear so," replied Ben. "Somehow, spending all those hours studying human DNA, I was taught how to do it. Honestly, Mark, I was as gobsmacked as I seemed. This is a completely new development."

Silence fell again for a few moments before Garry broke it.

"So now what?" he asked. "Will you start some sort of training program to raise us from this primitive state to somehow being able to mentor alien species?"

Ben shook his head. "No need for the sarcasm, Garry. I understand your resentment, all of you, but that's not how it's done."

"So why don't you explain how it's done?" said Mary. Her anger had not faded completely.

Ben looked thoughtful. "One of the basic realities of achieving change is that the person or group being changed must *want* that change. It cannot be imposed successfully by an external authority, not permanently, anyway. My having told you all this is about as far as I go for now. The rest is up to you."

"And can you suggest how we will do this?" asked Mary.

"It won't be easy. As I said, the whole world must want the changes that will be required for you to grow to maturity. But you have made a good start. This foundation is already perceived as a world influence by most countries. You must use that good will. Go to the United Nations and tell them what I have told you. Talk to world leaders everywhere. Explain how maturity comes from knowing where you came from and how you have developed to this stage. Encourage the spread of this technology, refine it until every home has access to learning about their ancestry. Some great strides are being taken already."

"Such as?" asked Garry.

"The great fortune that your friend, Eamon Jackson, now Pope Leo XIV has established a relationship with another great religion and set in motion a gradual decline of religious forces that's a significant step towards maturity."

"That's going to take many years, maybe centuries," said Garry. "And other religions are not yet showing any inclination to follow them."

"You have the time," said Ben.

"Really?" said Garry. "Is there some point at which you sit in judgement over Humanity and decide our future?"

Ben looked sadly at him. "You're still angry, I can see. So I must tell you something. Such a judgement has already been carried out once. It took over a hundred years and ended just a decade or two ago. We looked at Earth's history since the start of the twentieth century."

"And?" Garry's voice was harsh.

"You failed," said Ben.

The silence in the room could be felt.

Garry broke it after nearly half a minute.

"Why?" he asked. "And what does this mean for us?"

Ben looked at him. His expression was sad.

"There are many factors on which a species is evaluated," he said. "But the overall question we have to ask is whether the species has the characteristics needed to act as mentors, guides and teachers to the less developed ones.

"I said we have looked at you for many centuries before deciding that Humanity had at least the potential for the role and that's why we implanted the DNA recording ability. You have displayed many positive characteristics, many negatives and for the last century or so, the evaluation has been intensive as you found yourselves on the shortlist."

"And this where we failed?" Mary's voice was cold, almost contemptuous.

"Still angry, Mary?" said Ben. "I can understand that. But bear with me, please."

He looked round the table. All the faces showed varying degrees of shock and anger.

"Yes," he said. "As Mary asked, this is where you failed. The last couple of centuries have had more wars than any other species we are evaluating. The level of cruelty, inhumanity and lack of concern for others has been quite frightening. The numbers of mass killings by various political authorities of all shades of philosophy, added to the greed that has seriously damaged the planet, all this was enough to remove you from the shortlist."

"So where does that leave us?" asked Mark. "Do you and your mentors now fly away and let us continue the process of destroying ourselves?" His expression was one of somebody who had just witnessed a disgusting sight.

"We wouldn't do that under any circumstances," said Ben. "We haven't been all that successful in preventing the ugliness, but we're still hoping that the ability to look back through your own history will give a boost to self-understanding and improvement."

"Jesus Christ, Ben," broke in Garry. "This makes you sound like the most sanctimonious prick of all time. Do you realise how you are bloody *preaching* to us?"

Ben nodded, his face calm.

"I do understand why you see it that way. But it's the role we were asked to take on and we accepted. I can only report what we have seen."

"So that's it, is it?" said Mary. "We are doomed to remain as the poor students while somebody else is promoted to teacher, guide and mentor? I'd be interested to hear just what this other species has that made them fit for the job."

"Nobody has been nominated for the job, as you put it," said Ben. "But will you give me a few more moments to finish what I was saying?"

"Is it worth it?" snapped Mark.

"I think so," said Ben. "Let me tell you some other things we saw that make a difference to our conclusions."

"A difference?" Alana had remained silent till now, but her anger was still obvious.

"Yes, a difference," replied Ben, smiling at her. Her face remained hostile.

"Two things we have found about Humanity that gave us some doubts about the earlier decision," Ben continued. "The first was this astonishing factor of telekinetic powers. We have never seen this in any other species among those we know about. And that includes my own. When it showed up in me, I was utterly shocked. Somehow, the human DNA has a teaching capability that we could never have foreseen and that makes you unique. I can't imagine just how it might be transferred to another species or how they would use it, but we are encouraged that to date it has been used for perfectly benign, creative applications."

"And the second?" Alana still looked cold and angry.

"The second reflects one of the main things we look at. A seriously indicative factor in a species is how it treats helpless animals. A second one is how it treats its criminals. Humanity does not rate well in those. A third is the creative ability in the arts. We know of several species that display no such creative talents at all. They are very dull people and could never function as teachers and guides."

He paused and looked round the table again. Some of the hostility appeared to have eased.

"But in you, we have seen the astonishing artistic, musical and dance techniques, even in pre-Christian millennia. Nobody else has developed such features so early in their growth. Those talents vanished for many reasons and remained largely hidden until what you term the Renaissance occurred. In reality, the first Renaissance was what you have been finding in early millennia. The developments of the middle ages are really the Second Renaissance. The fact that humanity could have a second such flowering of the arts, medicine, politics and learning is astonishing. And now you have done it again. You are into your Third Renaissance."

He paused, looking round as if checking for reactions.

"And that was enough to convince us that Humanity did have the potential for massive growth and maturation. You have been returned to the evaluation list."

The reaction to Ben's words was severe, almost as severe as hearing of Humanity's failure. There was no celebration, no calls for drinks, nothing of that kind. Instead, all of the Second Foundation reacted as if given a reprieve from a death sentence, almost collapsing in their seats as if like marionettes with their strings cut. Annabelle was weeping into her hands, Mary was staring at her fingers as if studying very vein and muscle. Alana was still studying Ben like a scientist examining the effects of an experiment. Garry had his chin in his hands, his elbow on the table, looking into some unknowable distance. All of them seemed incapable of speech.

"So now what?" asked Garry after a few minutes.

"Now you must use your role and your position as the focus of everything that has happened since Garry's people discovered the technology. You should probably start as many of my ancestors did, meeting with the influencers, the leaders and trying to teach them about this and why Humanity must change and mature. Maybe start with the United Nations and some very specific world leaders who have the perception to accept the reality. It will not be easy and you will face opposition and blank refusal to believe. It will take generations. But the signs of potential are there. The probable merger of two of the main religions in the world and their changing focus on humanitarian acts rather than dogma is a positive sign. Get them on side, their assistance will be critical."

"How long have we got?" asked Garry.

"About two hundred years," said Ben. "And you will need every minute of it."

Chapter One

The UN Building, March, 2031

"I must again express my opposition to this entire waste of time!"

Mikhail Gryzlov spoke calmly but the anger in him was evident. His English could have been that of any highly-educated Englishman and indeed, he had received degrees, including a doctorate in International Business from Durham University. In his fifties, he was a tall, slender man who wore his tailored suits with complete elegance.

"The Security Council has no business listening to wild, bizarre claims about aliens mentoring the human race and humanity being somehow trained to take over the role for the galaxy," Gryzlov continued. "This is the sort of nonsense for devotees of *'Star Trek'* and similar fantasies."

"The Council agreed to this meeting because the Prime Minister of the United Kingdom asked for it and submitted considerable evidence for the requirement."

Daniel Baxter spoke firmly, no trace of the irritation that might have been caused by the constant objections from the Russian that had been voiced over the two weeks of debate leading up to this meeting. "The four other permanent members of the United Nations Security

Council voted in favour and the Russian Federation is thus bound by the agreement."

"Then let the minutes record my absolute opposition," said the Russian.

"Your opposition is noted once more," said Baxter. "So now, let me introduce the two members of the Australian arm of the organisation known as the Karen Petrova Foundation. The Foundation is well known throughout the world for its work in pharmaceutical advances beginning with its founder, Doctor Karen Petrova and continuing with the British firm, Life Technologies. The Australian operation, Blueprints is highly regarded for the development of DNA-associated technologies, especially the ability to look back through our DNA records at earlier times."

"We are all aware of the work of both organisations."

Dominique Galtier was a very ordinary looking woman of middling height, grey hair tied in a bun, slightly overweight and needing a cane to walk because of the loss of her right foot in an accident in her early teens. Only when one looked at her large hazel eyes that could almost pin a person to the wall did her astonishing intelligence show itself. Her grasp of international affairs and her fluency in six languages were legendary as was her double doctorate in Quantum Physics and Mathematics.

She smiled. "Their reputations speak for themselves," she continued. "If they say they need to address the United Nations, then it is essential that we listen."

"Thank you, Madame Galtier," said Baxter. He looked round the conference table, looking each of the four others directly in the eye. "Does anyone else wish to say anything before we start?"

Teng Wah Li smiled and shook his head. Unusually tall and heavy-set for a Chinese man, his build showed his ancestry from the northern regions of China. His full head of hair was jet black.

"I want to hear what these two say," said Rosalie Jackson. Her mid-Western accent was barely noticeable. Dressed in a perfect trouser suit in light tan, the bright red fingernails were a sharp contrast.

Attention swung to the two remaining persons in the room. Ben Fuller spoke for them.

"My name is Ben Fuller," he said. "I am a member of the Australian arm of the Karen Petrova Foundation. Doctor Petrova, as you all know founded the internationally famous research company, "Life Technology" and its associated company, Blueprints. My associate here today is Alana Shimova. Her credentials have already been presented to you."

Ben paused and looked in turn at each of the Security Council members. He saw that he had their entire attention, but the hostility in the Russian's face was still obvious.

"What you will hear from us today may well defy belief," said Ben. "But I ask that you hear us through to the end because we will later present absolute proof.

"The very first fact that you must accept is that there are other intelligent species in the galaxy. A few are more advanced technologically than humans, most are not."

Mikhail Gryzlov sat back in his seat and folded his arms across his chest.

Ben smiled at him. "You may choose to protect yourself against this fact, Mr Gryzlov, but you cannot hide from it for long."

"How do you know this astounding fact, Mr Fuller?" asked Dominique Galtier. Her face was alive with interest.

"Because I am one of them, Madame."

The silence in the room was almost physical.

"Then what are you and where are you from?" asked the French woman.

"There is no point in giving you those details, Madame Galtier because they will provide nothing to the discussion."

"Then what are you doing here, assuming that we are to believe your claim?" The American, Rosalie Jackson spoke with a rasp in her throat through tension.

Ben nodded with a smile. "That goes directly to the heart of the matter, Mrs Jackson and that one I will answer. Some background first.

"There has long been a huge worry among the people of this planet that you could destroy yourselves in one way or another, from nuclear war through poisonous, life-ending pollution. It is a valid worry and I can tell you that such catastrophes have happened among other intelligent species. They have done exactly as Earth has done, develop to the point where technology has exceeded wisdom and they have destroyed themselves. Earth is dangerously close to that position."

"And you are here to stop that happening?" The tension remained in the American's voice.

"Not really," said Ben. "We would not interfere if you persist in that path and we really do not have the ability to prevent you destroying yourselves."

"What then?"

"What we have done is give you a tool that may help you avoid the problem yourself. You all know very well now that the human DNA provides the records of your own life and all your ancestors. That has made massive changes in culture, especially in the arts, diplomacy, religion and almost everything else. That was our sole contribution."

"You did that? You implanted that ability in humans?"

The Chinese Council member spoke at last. His English was flawless without accent, as was so often the case with

Chinese educated at British establishments. He showed no expression.

"We did, Mr Teng."

"When?"

"When we first detected intelligence in Neanderthal man, about seventy-five thousand years ago, then again in Cro-Magnon man when it emerged about forty thousand years ago."

"Why that particular mechanism?"

"Because that mechanism achieved two things, Mr. Teng. First, it gave you the chance to learn your histories without any political or racial bias and that is essential for you to know yourselves. Second, the removal of all privacy has led to a completely open society, another essential factor. The secondary effect of causing the sharp decline of religious dogma and bigotry is also essential."

"Essential for what?" Madame Galtier had been intently following very word.

Ben looked at the British member, Daniel Baxter, who nodded.

"I would like you to watch the short video," said Baxter. "It is a recording of a meeting that took place in 1875 between the Prime Minister, Benjamin Disraeli, the Home Secretary, Richard Cross and a man known only as Harrington. It was seen through the DNA of the Prime Minister's secretary who took the minutes."

He pressed a button on the table in front of him and a screen on one wall came alive with the meeting where Harrington had informed Disraeli and Cross of the need for Britain to take a lead in international affairs and guide the world to a new level of maturity.

The screen went blank and silence returned for a few moments.

"That could easily be forged," said Gryzlov. He was still sitting back in his seat, arms folded defensively across his chest. "Your Hollywood people could easily create such a scene."

"But for one problem," said Teng Wah Li. All faces turned to him.

"A similar event happened to my predecessor some years ago. I was just a junior assistant to our Foreign Minister when a woman formally requested a meeting with our top officials. She was able to get consent and she told us almost exactly, word for word what that man Harrington said to Disraeli. We never released the details to the world."

"We have similar recordings from thousands of years in the past," said Ben. "Our agents have been trying to guide humanity ever since civilisations developed but we have largely failed."

"But failed in what?" asked Madame Galtier.

"As we have been telling you, there are intelligent species around the galaxy. Few of them have reached the level of technology that you have achieved, though some have exceeded it, including my own people. Too many have destroyed themselves like young people have destroyed themselves throughout history because of a lack of mentors. It is clear that the less developed species need mentors. My people have been in that role for millennia but we will die out in the future. We must be replaced."

"And you think we on Earth can become that replacement?" Some of the tension had left the American's voice.

"Not necessarily," said Ben. "You are one of several species we are evaluating. I must tell you that for a time, humanity was considered to have failed, but then you displayed some characteristics that called for reconsideration. But no future mentor has yet been selected for advanced training."

"Those characteristics being...?" The Frenchwoman looked curious.

"Mostly, the ability to create a new Renaissance in all those forms that you have and do it three times," said Ben.

"Prehistoric, Middle-ages and the present, I assume?"

"Yes, Madame. That and the extraordinary telekinetic abilities that some humans have developed to varying degrees."

"And why is that a factor?" asked the American woman.

"Simply because it is unique," said Ben. "It has not occurred in any species we have ever encountered or been recorded by our predecessors."

"I still don't believe a word of this nonsense," broke in the Russian. He finally leaned forward on his seat, placed his elbows on the table. "You said you could prove all of this fantasy. How?"

Alana broke her silence.

"I think we will take you travelling," she said.

Chapter Two – Northern Finland

"This has been like some Magical Mystery Tour," said Daniel Baxter. "Helicopter from the UN Building, US Military jet to Helsinki and now this second chopper flight to... where the hell are we, anyway?"

"Well into untravelled territories in the north of Finland," said Alana. "Shall we get out and let the flight crew go back home?

In silence, the members of the UN Security Council climbed down the steps of the massive helicopter that had brought them from a military base near Helsinki. When they were a few minutes away, the machine lifted off and vanished into the low clouds to the south.

"I'm ashamed to say I'm feeling frightened," said Dominique Galtier. "Here we are, miles from anywhere, no signs of civilisation and I'm cold. I feel a terrible urge to run away as fast as I can."

"Me too," said Jackson. "I'm feeling terrified."

"I'm the same," said Baxter. "I'm shaking."

"Yes," said Teng. "This is not rational."

"All of us are feeling the fear," said Ben. "That includes Alana and me. But it's deliberate."

"Deliberate? How?" Baxter stared at him.

"You'll all be in shelter in a few minutes," said Ben. "Then it will become clear."

He made no signal or movement that could be seen, but a green glow appeared a few metres in front of them.

"What the hell is that?" demanded Mikhail Gryzlov. He had not spoken a word since leaving the UN Building in New York. Other than indicating a choice of meal on the military jet, served by a young man in US Army uniform with sergeant's stripes on his sleeves, he had been silent, his face expressionless.

"A doorway," replied Ben. "Would you like to enter?"

"A doorway to what?" asked the American, Rosalie Jackson. "There's nothing there."

"It's a spaceship," said Alana. "And like all good sci-fi spaceships, it's cloaked. Nobody can see it and that fear we are all feeling is a deliberate transmission from the ship. It keeps anyone who might wander around up here from getting too close. Please, let's get inside."

With varying degrees of reluctance, the entire group moved through the green glow and found themselves in a large, circular construction with a dozen armchairs set around several coffee tables. The walls were a pleasant light blue with a black band about a metre wide and a metre above the floor stretching round the entire circumference with a few breaks at intervals that could be doors.

"This is a spaceship?" said Teng Wah Li. He had been sociable during the long journey, talking animatedly to Ben and Alana, asking numerous questions about the information Ben had delivered to them. "It's more like a conference room. Where's the flight deck? Does it have a crew?"

"No crew, no flight deck," said Ben. "This ship is entirely automated."

"What about windows?" asked Jackson. "If we're about to go into space as you say, I'd like to see the view."

The council members were stunned into silence as the

black band became alive with a view of the Moon. The craters were huge and the Moon's horizon filled a third of the panels

"Good God!" shouted Baxter. "We're near the Moon? When did we take off? I didn't feel a thing! Shouldn't we have been strapped into our seats, or something?"

"Gravity engines," said Ben. "They apply equally on every atom in their sphere, so you don't feel acceleration. If you had, we'd all have been squashed flat against the wall."

He turned and looked at the Russian.

"Now, Mr Gryzlov, do you believe a little more of what we have been telling you?"

Surprising all of them, Gryzlov smiled. "Yes, I do," he said. "So, where are we going?"

"A small tour of just a few of the species we've been reviewing over the years," said Ben. "There'll be no contact and nobody will realise we're there, but this is just to give you a little idea of what's involved."

"This is simply astounding," said Baxter. His face was pale and a slight tremble was visible in his hands. "Suddenly we're in a spaceship with engines of some unimaginable technology, we passed the Moon in just seconds and now you're telling us we'll be visiting a planet of another star?"

Ben nodded with a smile. "Yes, Daniel, that is exactly what I am telling you. The point of this trip is to prove to you that I am part of a species much more technologically advanced than yours and so I hope you will believe all the other things I've been telling you."

"I've no doubts about any of that now," said Baxter. He sat down heavily in one of the armchairs. "Does this ship serve drinks? And how about food? How long will we be on this trip?"

Gryzlov also took a seat. "You've convinced me too, Ben. And I'd like to know about food and drink and perhaps all the other facilities we will need. Mind you, right now, my insides are still churning with that departure. Just a drink would be a life-saver."

Ben pointed at a panel in the wall.

"Touch that," he said, "and you will find that we have loaded all the food and drink you will need. Please help yourselves."

The two men rose from their seats and moved to the panel. As it opened, a line of bottles was visible with glasses alongside. Teng and Jackson exclaimed with pleasure and they all busied themselves pouring a selection of drinks.

"A question," said Madame Galtier. "This is a huge galaxy, about a hundred thousand light years along its longer axis, quite a few million suns in there. How do you know when an intelligent species has developed and how do you find them?"

Ben nodded in appreciation of the question.

"It's a good point and we're really not sure of the mechanism, but somehow we get a mental trigger when a species reaches a particular level of intelligence. Should humans ever get to take over our role, we will teach you how to detect this signal, just as our mentors taught us."

"Interesting," murmured the Frenchwoman.

"What's happening out there?" broke in Baxter. "We seem to be well past the Moon."

"How fast are we moving, for God's sake?" asked the American, a slight note of hysteria in her voice. "And how *far* are we going?"

"That was my other question," said Galtier. "We can't travel faster than light, so how are we going to get to another planetary system?"

"You are correct, nothing can travel faster than light," said Ben. "But several scientists have proposed that there may be ways round that. They've suggested wormholes, hyperspace, bending space among them and one of those is right. We are accelerating at an astonishing speed and we will reach some ninety percent of light speed over the next three hours. At that stage, we get a sort of sideways kick into another dimension which we can call hyperspace. Completely different laws of physics operate, distance becomes irrelevant. On this trip, we will travel four hundred light years in just a few minutes. May I suggest that you look in that direction, which is our direction of travel. No human has ever seen this sight before."

They all turned to look where he was pointing.

"Ah!" said Galtier. "Blue shift!"

Unlike the others, she was showing no shock or tension, but seemed fascinated with observing the developments.

The stars in front of them had all developed a strong shade of blue.

"We're moving at a significant fraction of the speed of light towards the source of the light coming from the stars," she said. "That moves the spectrum into the blue. And if we look behind," she turned to the opposite side and the others followed her, "the stars behind have shifted into the red. It's how we tell that galaxies are moving away from us as the Universe expands."

She looked at Ben. "This is amazing! I never thought I would see this to such an extent. And will we see the light of the universe gather in a disk in front of us as we near the speed of light? Physicists have proposed that this will happen."

"And they had it right," replied Ben. "Keep watching."

For the next hour, the group watched in silence as the stars ahead became a deeper shade of blue.

"What's happening?" said Teng, pointing at the sides of the panel.

To left and right, darkness was spreading from the side as if a black curtain was being drawn from each side.

"Just as we thought," murmured Galtier, a small smile on her lips.

As the curtains were further drawn across the view ahead, a curve developed in them and slowly they realised that what they were seeing was that that the blue stars were now all in a dense disk that was slowly shrinking.

"At this speed, all the visible light in the Universe is being gathered in front of us," said the Frenchwoman. "It will be interesting to see how small it gets. Ben, does it vanish as we are kicked into hyperspace?"

"It does, Madame."

They watched in silence as the blue disk ahead shrank further until no stars could be identified and the disk was just a solid, bright blue.

And then it winked out. All the viewing panels were pure blackness.

"This is frightening," whispered Jackson. "Where are we?"

"Outside the Universe," said Galtier. She seemed to be the only calm person in the room, other than Ben and Alana. "Or maybe in another Universe," she added. "How long, Ben?"

"Just watch," he replied.

Barely three minutes passed as the tension in the room grew and then with an explosion of light, the screens all round were filled with stars.

"We have travelled over four hundred light years," said Ben. "In about thirty minutes, we will enter orbit around a planet that contains a humanoid race that we have watched for a few hundred years."

"Are they one of those in contention to replace you at some point?" asked Gryzlov. He had not spoken since he had asked about food and drink but had watched with intense concentration throughout the journey up to and through hyperspace.

Ben shook his head. "Not at all. They have proved to be an intense disappointment."

"In what way?" asked the Russian.

"They have reached a level of technology that equates perhaps to seventeenth century Earth," said Ben. "No machinery, though their science is starting to develop. But they have no history of art of any sort through their entire history. There has never been a picture drawn or painted, never a sculpture, no form of dance or music has ever been identified, no works of fiction. Their cities are nothing but uninspiring, featureless collections of cubes. There are no parks, no statues. There is no sport, nothing of any form of entertainment. We call it the Dull Planet. We decided to abandon them as mentor prospects many years ago."

"How very sad," murmured Jackson. "No art, no sport, no entertainment? What will happen to them?"

"We think that they will become a technological race," said Ben. "But never to reach space-faring stage because they are simply without curiosity. We and our successors will probably do little but watch them."

Silence fell again as a small planet appeared in front of them. The distance decreased as they watched and with no obvious transition, they were in orbit.

Below them, the planet seemed quite Earth-like. Several continents could be identified and there was a line of smaller islands all round the equatorial belt. White clouds obscured some of the land and the larger part of the surface was filled by blue ocean.

A small sigh came from Teng.

"To think, we are the first humans to look at a new world which has a civilisation living there. How very like Earth it looks."

"Will we visit?" asked Jackson.

"No, we must not go outside," said Ben. "We did not have time to immunise you against local bugs, nor to clean out your Earth-bound bugs, so the risk of infection to both of you would be severe. No, we will hover above one of their larger towns, nobody will see a cloaked ship and we will watch the locals from our cameras."

Another thirty minutes passed as the ship moved lower and lower over a large land mass until they were suspended above a town that looked, as Ben had described, just a series of cubic blocks arranged in neat rows.

"Streets are unpaved," said Baxter. "Some sort of large animals drawing wheeled carts. They look like oxen."

"They do seem to be similar to Europe about the seventeenth century," said Gryzlov. "The buildings are stone."

"But as Ben said, no parks, nothing that looks like a town square, no statues," said Teng.

"And nothing resembling a church," said Gryzlov. "And that's certainly very different from old Europe."

"No evidence of any religion or any spiritual practices," said Ben. "But then, no wars of any kind, little or no travel beyond their immediate areas. They are fascinating to sociologists, but to me, honestly, this is the most uninteresting species of all those I have encountered."

"So why did you start the tour with this uninteresting planet?" asked Daniel Baxter.

"Mainly to prove to all of you that I have been telling you the truth. I am part of a species that is massively ahead of humanity in the technological sphere. This trip was mainly to make that point. I hope you can accept the other elements as a result. We have a mentoring role to try and steer intelligent races to find their full capabilities and some day, far into the future, we must find our replacement."

"Are we to see another example?" asked Teng. "And how long do you plan to keep us away from home?"

"One more," said Ben. "And you will sleep in your hotel

rooms in Helsinki tonight before flying back to your home countries in the morning."

"And how much of the galaxy will we have covered in these few hours?" Dominique Galtier seemed enthralled by the events of the day.

"Four hundred light years so far. Another one hundred and ten light years on the next leg and then the return home will be a final four hundred and fifty light years."

"All in a single day," murmured Gryzlov. "I look forward to telling that to my government. The reactions will be... *interesting*, shall we say?"

"This has been a staple of sci-fi writers for decades," said Baxter. "It's been the common way of overcoming the difficulties of inter-stellar travel when the speed of light is the limit."

"I've been a sci-fi addict all my life," said Galtier. "How fulfilling to see yet another forecast come true."

"And we seem to be on the move already," said Baxter and pointed at the screen. The stars were already turning a light blue and the first signs of the concentration into a disk were just evident.

"We seem to have accelerated far more quickly than last time," said Baxter. "Why is that?"

"Earth's solar system has hundreds of telescopes looking out," said Ben. "Hitting near light speed early would have distorted the images of any telescope looking in this direction and caused serious questions. No such limitation here in a less technological system."

"And what will we see this time?" asked Rosalie Jackson.

"The other end of the spectrum," said Ben. "Possibly the leading contenders for the galactic mentor role so far. Technologically, they are well ahead of Earth, they have space travel within their own solar system but not beyond. They do have a gravity drive of a primitive level so they can travel at great speed, but they have not discovered hyperspace."

"Humanoid?" asked Galtier.

"Only partially. You will see when we take station above one of their towns. Again, you cannot go outside for the reasons as before, but even without that problem, you would find it dangerous. It's a high gravity world, very dense and so immensely rich in gold, diamonds and similar products. They will find it valuable when they finally encounter other intelligent species and begin trading. But if you went outside, not only would the atmosphere density prove lethal, you would be unable to stand upright in the gravity and you would sustain severe damage to your internal organs."

For the second time, the travellers saw a planet below them. This was far less like Earth, being mainly land masses with much smaller ocean expanses.

"All very flat," said Gryzlov. "No major mountains that we've seen."

"As I said, it's a very high gravity world, more than twice the force of Earth. The early mountain ranges gradually flattened over the millennia."

Silence reigned as the ship moved over one of the continents, gradually losing height and finally hovered a few hundred metres over a major city.

"You said this is a space-faring world," said Baxter. "Can they not detect us?"

"Not at all," said Ben. "The cloaking technology is very advanced."

"An attractive city," remarked Jackson. "I see some parks, much less of a grid-iron design, but no tall buildings. And... hey, is that a sports stadium?"

Beneath them, the structure looked like any major football stadium on Earth. The field was oval, surrounded by rows and rows of seats.

"They have a game called *'Protaskorp'* which actually resembles the Australian Rules form of football," said Ben. "But it's played with a spherical, metal ball that weighs about ten kilos."

"Good grief, what manner of life form can do that in a high-gravity world?" asked Galtier.

"Look! People!" shouted Jackson and they all stared at the sight on the screen. Their viewpoint from high up made it difficult to judge the scale and size of the people they saw, but the crowds resembled any similar population on Earth.

"We'll go lower," said Ben and the ship descended until it hovered over a huge building.

"Three arms! Good lord, they have three arms!" said Teng. "It looks like the right arm is massive and they have two much smaller left arms."

"And a terrifying head," said Galtier. "It looks like a wild boar. Quite frightening."

"They are a large, intensely strong species," said Ben. "If we could get close, you would see that an adult male is usually well over two metres tall. The right arm developed as a fighting weapon, while the two left arms have hands that are capable of very fine movement and manipulation. It has proved to be an excellent form for technological development."

"But what makes them a leading contender for Galactic mentorship?" asked Teng.

"As you saw, they have sports," said Ben. "They also have a wonderful artistic culture, mostly shown in art, sculpture and music. With that size, dance is less developed, almost unknown. They have conquered their natural aggression and channelled it into some intensely competitive and violent sports, having not had a war for some centuries. And you might be amazed to find that they have a highly sophisticated sense of humour. There are many other factors that indicate wisdom and maturity."

"This is all quite overwhelming," said Jackson. "To be honest, I'm exhausted and quite wrung out."

"Hardly surprising," said Ben. "And that's why this is just a short, introductory trip to show you the reality of what is facing you. Time to go home, I think."

Once more, the entire group stood, enthralled as the ship accelerated to near light speed, entered the mathematical mysteries of hyperspace and re-emerged into the familiar solar system that included Earth. As Ben had promised, they were back in Helsinki by evening.

"You're undoubtedly all ready for your beds," said Alana. "I certainly am. But we have one more thing to discuss before we head home. Let's meet here after breakfast."

General sounds of agreement ran round the group and they headed for their rooms. All the Council members sent brief messages to their home governments reporting on the events and then retired to bed. None of them slept soundly after the astounding experience they had just gone through and when they met for breakfast, the faces and body language showed serious fatigue. Almost with amusement, they all agreed that they'd all had little sleep and most of them had denuded the room's store of alcoholic beverages.

When they had finished, Alana rose to her feet.

"We have a short bus trip. Would you all please come with me?"

* * *

"This is a secure room," said Daniel Baxter. "The British Ambassador here at the Embassy has made it available. I guarantee there are no hidden microphones and nobody can hear us in any way possible."

"Do we need this level of security?" asked Teng. "What are we about to discuss?"

"We are going to decide on the next step for Humanity," said Alana. "Now that you have seen the reality of what we are looking to do and become, is there any doubt that we as a species wish to proceed?"

A moment of silence hung in the air then all the members of the Security Council shook their heads.

"How could we not want to continue?" asked Dominique Galtier.

"Then let us proceed," said Ben.

Chapter Three – The Second Foundation, May, 2032

"Things have moved rapidly," said Garry to the Foundation members. "Ben's Magical Mystery Tour, as one of them called it certainly convinced the members of the Security Council of the reality of the task ahead of the human race. Alana, will you carry on?"

"The Council members agreed to take the full story back to their governments," said Alana. "They have reported back that all five countries fully endorse the program we agreed on in Helsinki."

"And what about the rest of the world?" asked Mark Craymer.

"The British Government has taken responsibility for advising all other governments of what is planned," said Alana. "For now, information will be given only to Heads of State who will inform their inner cabinets under intense security and penalties for leaking information. It is Ben's opinion that the world is not yet ready to learn the whole story. Of course, the Australian government is fully informed of what we are doing and is totally supportive. Australia is playing a global leadership role in this world-shaking development."

"And the next step?" asked Mark.

"We set up an apprenticeship college here in these

grounds," said Alana. "We will seek out an initial intake of trainees from around the world and the governments of all countries will nominate their very best and brightest young people."

"Will they be told exactly what is facing them?" asked Robert Swann.

"It's a critical point," said Alana with a nod. "It's up to us to determine this. Initially, they will be pledged to absolute secrecy as they will be joining a project of international importance."

"That would be essential," agreed Swann. "And I suggest they be advised they will be out of circulation, unable to leave for at least a year unless they are somehow deemed unsuitable at some stage."

"So just what will the training be and for how long?" asked Annabelle Calvert, the historian.

"As I said, that's what we will determine in this group, as advised by Ben," said Alana.

"And the building?" asked Salmaan Basri.

"You will recall Sir Connor Shackleton who did such a great job designing this building," said Garry. "We contacted his company and although Sir Connor has retired, one of his close colleagues will take on the project of designing and building an ultra-secure building for both college facilities and residences for the first students."

"And he will need to be advised by me about some very special facilities," said Ben.

"Such as?" asked Mark.

"Something we will bring from my home," said Ben with a smile. "It might blow your minds, but it's essential. When it's installed, we'll have an introduction."

"How will you bring it in?" asked Mark, his face reflecting high interest.

"Very carefully," replied Ben and laughed.

Chapter Four - RAAF Base, Williamtown, March, 2033

"Not exactly a dark and stormy night," said the Air Commodore. "I've dreamed of something like this since I was a kid and it was always accompanied by thunder and lightning and storm clouds and stuff like that."

"I'm sorry it's so ordinary," said Alana with a laugh. She and the Air Commodore had hit it off immediately as one-time fighter pilots. "If I'd known, I'm sure they could have arranged a suitably dramatic arrival."

He echoed her laugh. "Well, it's dark anyway and to be honest, this is still pretty earth-shaking."

"You're certain the grounds are secure?" asked Garry.

They stood in a group by the staff car that had brought them out to the edge of runway. Behind them and on each side, several armed men stood silently.

"In Britain, the Royal Air Force has its RAF Regiment to protect Air Force assets," said the officer. "We've got Number One Security Forces Squadron, commonly known as 1SECFOR. This is their home base and believe me, they're every bit as nasty and crude as their Pommy equivalents. Isn't that right, Andy?"

"Bloody oath, sir," replied one of the dark figures to their right.

"That's Squadron Leader Garry Belmont," said the Air

Commodore. "Short on words, but believe me, with Andy's blokes patrolling the perimeter, not even a small wombat could get in tonight." He took a deep breath. "Hello! Something's happening." He raised his binoculars and looked at the middle of the field where a green glow had appeared.

Behind him, Squadron Leader Belmont spoke into a microphone, his words inaudible to Garry and Alana. Three sets of headlights flickered into life from a hangar across the field and a large truck followed by two four-wheel drive vehicles drove towards the green glow. As they arrived, the glow widened into a vertical square.

"A ship has just arrived?" The Air Commodore's voice seemed quite calm. "And you said that's a doorway? The rest of the ship is cloaked?"

"Correct," said Alana.

The two smaller vehicles stopped and disgorged a dozen armed men who lined up on either side of the green glow of the doorway while the truck backed up to within a few metres. A bulky object appeared, resembling a metal crate about a metre on all sides, hanging suspended a short distance above the ground. It moved out of the doorway and into the truck.

"They have anti-gravity?" said the Air Commodore. Only a slight hoarseness indicated the shock he was experiencing.

"They do," said Alana.

"And what is that thing?"

"Ben won't tell us yet," replied Garry. "But he said it's harmless and educational. There's no reason to doubt him."

"I wish he'd come with you," said the officer. "I'd like to be able to tell my grandchildren one day that I'd met a real live alien."

"He keeps a low profile," said Garry. "Until the entire story can come out, it's safer that way."

In the middle of the field, the green glow subsided and vanished. Nothing else seemed to happen.

"It was a spaceship capable of inter-stellar flight," said Alana. "And it just left."

"So there's not a bloody thing the fighter squadrons here could have done about it, eh?" The officer's small laugh seemed a little strained.

"Not a thing," agreed Alana. "One day I hope we can show you more of what's going on and you can meet an alien. And I'll tell you more about those ships."

"I'll look forward to it," replied the Air Commodore. "Andy's men will now escort you and that whatever-it-was back to your place." He stepped back and threw Alana a full salute. "Colonel Shimova, Garry, it's been an honour, a privilege and highly educational to meet both of you."

"Thank you, Air Commodore," said Alana. "We're all grateful for the help. We should be able to have you come and visit us in about a year."

"I'll look forward to it. Andy?"

He climbed back into the staff car as another vehicle drew up. Andy opened the door for Garry and Alana and copied the senior officer's salute as he closed the door.

A few moments later, back in Garry's car, they joined the convoy of the truck and an increased escort now of four vehicles with armed troops and drove back to the Foundation offices. At the rear of the new building that had grown during the last year, they watched in silent fascination as the large crate floated out of the truck and into the loading bay. Not one of the men watching spoke a word. A few minutes later, they drove out of the grounds and headed back to the RAAF base.

Chapter Five – The Apprenticeship Begins – May, 2033

"We have twelve starters," Garry said to the Foundation group. "Several countries nominated their brightest and best young people and they were subjected to some intensive screening by Ben and Alana before we picked the final twelve. We have people from from the USA, Britain, Uzbekistan, Nigeria, India and Australia. All of them are aged between eighteen and twenty-five."

"Can you go over the required qualifications for these young people?" asked Mary. "I know we've covered this before, but I'd like to review just what made them so special?"

"Mainly huge emotional strength," said Ben. "They will face shocks like nobody has faced before when they first see alien species. It will be far greater than the Security Council members experienced when they came on the short trip, because they didn't leave the ship and didn't get anywhere near the physical reality of being on an alien planet."

"That won't be immediate, though, surely?" said Mary.

"No, not for some months," said Ben. "There will be a long, hard training program first, though we will take them on a similar trip just to see what another world looks like."

"And what other qualities were required?" asked Robert Swann.

"Empathy for those unlike themselves," said Ben. "In vast quantities," he added with a smile. "And an interesting fact associated with that, not one of the people we interviewed was a member of any religious grouping."

"All atheists?" asked Swann.

"More agnostic," said Ben. "They didn't specifically believe there are no gods, they simply didn't know, having seen no evidence either way. It's the open-mindedness that will help them over their training period."

"And do they fully understand what they are training for?" asked Annabelle Calvert.

"Not yet," said Ben. "During their initial evaluation processes, they knew they had applied for a position involving international development and that they would be away from home for at least a year, more likely two. A complete briefing will be one of the first things they get."

"So now that they are safely set up in the college building with their accommodation, what next?" asked Mary.

"The classroom," replied Ben. "Hours and hours of classroom training before they get their first field trip."

"And who will their teachers be?" asked Mary.

"That will be a surprise," said Ben, a small smile showing briefly.

* * *

The atmosphere in the small auditorium was electric. The multi-nation group of young people were like any similar group attending their first lecture at University but there was an extra component to the tension in the room as none of them knew just what they were to be taught and where their training would lead. But they were all aware that they were an elite group who had come through intensive selection procedures.

Some instant friendships were formed.

"Gernardy Volkov," said the tall young man with an early-growth of black beard to the slender girl on his right. "From Tashkent, Uzbekistan."

"Olivia Grey," she replied. "Taree, New South Wales."

"Just up the road from Sydney, if I've studied my map of Australia properly?"

Almost as if they had been friends for years, they chatted easily for a few moments.

"Any idea just what we've signed up for?" Gernardy asked.

"Not really," she said. "But it sounds interesting, international, some travel."

He nodded, just as the lights in the auditorium faded and the platform at the front became a little brighter. Without warning, a man appeared standing in the middle of the platform. He looked to be in his forties, clean-shaven, tall, slim and with a full head of black hair. He had not walked on, simply appeared and the gasp from the audience reflected the collective astonishment.

"Good morning, my name is William Kennedy," the man said. "And no, you did not see me walk on, because I didn't. In fact, there's nobody here. I'm a projection."

He smiled as a murmur of astonishment ran round the room.

"What's more, this projection is three-dimensional and not one of you here could identify it as such, however closely you looked. In fact, why don't a few of you come up here, walk around me and look for yourselves?"

"This I have to see," said Olivia and stood up, closely followed by Gernardy and they walked down the steps to the front in company with every one of the class members.

They were the first to reach the image of the man and stood less than a metre from it. Kennedy smiled at them, looked them straight in the eye and spoke softly.

"Pretty good, eh?" he said.

Gernardy stared at him. He examined him carefully as others came near and he could see nothing to suggest the man before him was anything but a solid human being. He caught Olivia's eye and she nodded.

"Nothing to say this is an image," she said. She reached out and tried to touch Kennedy's shoulder but her hand passed through the image. She drew her hand back sharply.

She and Gernardy moved back and returned to their seats in silence, but Gernardy broke it when they had sat down.

"There's no technology like that anywhere on Earth," he said quietly.

"I agree. Which makes this whole thing triply interesting," she murmured back.

Gradually, all the students returned to their seats with very little discussion. Kennedy smiled again.

"I imagine all of you have had the same thought," he said. "You've all thought that this is not a technology existing anywhere in the world."

Olivia looked at Gernardy. "Clever boy," she muttered.

"You'd all be quite right," continued Kennedy. "This technology comes from a very long way away, many light years in fact."

Gernardy took a deep breath and looked around the room. Every face was staring intently at the man on the platform with varying degrees of shock, sometimes excitement.

"Let me tell you more," said Kennedy. "There are a number of intelligent species around the galaxy at varying levels of technology, a few ahead of you, including my own, most of them some years behind. There have been more, but a common pattern with intelligent, technologically advanced species is that they destroy themselves, just as many people believe Earth is doing to itself. Several have already done so."

The silence in the room could be felt.

"When my species was approaching technological development, we were guided away from self-extermination by another civilisation that had taken on the role of mentor. Instead of killing ourselves, we were able to grow to maturity and take over that mentorship role when our own teachers disappeared. My people are seeing that our own time is coming and we must find our successors over the next few hundred years. We are looking at possible replacements and humans are one of them. Your training is part of the process, while others will be trying to guide the people of Earth to maturity.

"Over the next few years, you will see and do many astounding things. Some of you may not succeed in developing as we need for you to become mentors and you can leave the program at any time. We will be bringing in others to train over the years."

He looked round the room.

"Your first two or three years will be an apprenticeship, learning from more advanced students who classify as Journeymen, a level to which you will rise as you develop. They will actually be members of what you would term alien species.

"I will leave you now as I know you will need time to absorb what I have told you and try to adjust yourselves to the requirements of the next year and beyond. May I add, this first year is simply the introduction. If it proves not to be what you want, you can leave then. Things will get even more intensive, astonishing and challenging after that. So until tomorrow morning at nine o'clock."

Kennedy vanished with the same shocking suddenness with which he had appeared.

It was several minutes before sound reappeared in the room as twelve stunned young people recovered enough to return to the present world.

Chapter Six - The Apprenticeship – August, 2033

"This has been like drinking from a fire hydrant," said Gernardy. "I never knew there could be so much to learn and how much we've covered since we started."

"I think we're all exhausted," said Olivia. "Who could have known there are over a dozen intelligent species in the galaxy?"

"And we've had a decent grounding in the histories of each of them, the geography of their planets and actually seen videos of the people," said Gernardy. "At school, we spent four years learning about just parts of our world, the history and geography. Now we've done more than twelve times as much in four months."

"No wonder we all look so buggered," said Olivia. "Look at us!" She gestured round the lounge where another six students sat in various poses of exhaustion. "And the others are asleep!"

"They'd better wake up soon," said Gernardy. "Kennedy said we've got something special today."

As he spoke, the remaining four students entered the lounge. Within a few seconds, the image of William Kennedy appeared in the room. Having seen this on a daily basis for the last few months, nobody was surprised any more.

"Good morning, everybody," he said brightly and

received a low murmur in response. "A real change for you today," he said, smiling at the obvious fatigue in the group. "Follow me."

He turned and led the way out of the lounge, down the corridor and to a door that none of them had ever seen open. This time, it opened as they arrived with no obvious sign from Kennedy and they walked in to find themselves in a large hall, big enough to hold two hundred people but without any features at all. There were no windows, the walls and the floor were a single light green colour and although there was no obvious source of illumination, the light was like the outdoors on a bright day.

"Interesting technology," murmured Olivia. "And look, the door has vanished."

Gernardy turned and saw that the door through which they had just entered had faded, leaving only the same featureless green as the rest of the wall.

"This is the simulation room," said Kennedy. "You will all spend a great deal of time here over the next year. Let me show you what it does."

In a soundless flicker, the room changed to a scene that appeared to cover a far larger area than the room. It was a village scene, small huts lined one space, fields stretched into the distance. Gasps and exclamations of shock ran round the watchers. The realism was complete, just as the image of Kennedy had seemed perfect even on close inspection. There was even a smell, something like horse manure.

Several people were in the scene. They were dressed in clothing that would have suited peasants of an earlier century in England, rough cloth, no colour other than grey and black and the women's dresses reached to their ankles.

"This is just a holographic image," said Kennedy. "So nobody can see you. It is life on a world over two thousand light years from Earth. This reflects the technological age of this society, something equivalent to eighteenth century Earth."

"Is this a society that may one day become a mentor?" asked one of the students.

"Most unlikely," said Kennedy. "It misses some of the essential qualities of a possible mentor, particularly the strength of its arts capabilities and it has little inclination to curiosity, science or any form of technology. It's a stagnant society, though that may change. It's one we will simply keep under observation and that responsibility may become one of yours at some stage."

"All these people look like humans," said Gernardy. "Are all intelligent species physically similar?"

"Most do tend to be humanoid," replied Kennedy. "It's a physical state that has been shown to be most conducive to automation, technology and transportation. But there are many differences in the several species around this galaxy."

"That raises an interesting point," asked another student. "Just how many species are there in this galaxy that could one day become dominant, intelligent and capable of civilisation?"

"Several hundred," replied Kennedy and smiled as a collective gasp ran through the group. "But only a dozen or so have attained sufficient levels of technology and civilisation to require full-time attention. There have been hundreds more, but they have died out from the common failings of mass suicide from war, pollution and catastrophes such as asteroid collisions. However, let us stay with this exercise for now."

He began to walk out into the scene and waved to the group to follow him.

"You can walk among them," he said. "The system is programmed so that the individuals you see will avoid walking into you or letting you touch them. Try it and see."

A few of the group tried to approach holographic images, but the images seemed to walk away in a natural manner as the apprentices came near.

"As you see," said Kennedy. "But this is just a simulation. Let's go and have a look inside one of the houses where a family lives."

The scene flickered and became the interior of a hut, dark and primitive. A woman sat on a bench nursing a small infant, two children looking about eight or nine years old sat on the floor playing with wooden bricks.

"Just like any society of this cultural age on many planets," said Kennedy.

After twenty minutes of further wandering around the simulated scene, the images vanished and the apprentices found themselves back in the light green-coloured room.

"Much of your initial training will be here," said Kennedy. "Only after you have become familiar with alien scenes, alien people and alien environments will you travel to see the realities."

"How will we travel?" asked Olivia. "Do we take a spaceship ride?"

A hum of interest ran round the room.

"That's a matter for another lesson," said Kennedy. "You are a long way from being prepared for that experience. Now, go and have lunch, meet back in the lounge in one hour."

The group walked out, most of them silent as they tried to absorb what they had just seen.

Chapter Seven - The Human "Mule" Development – June, 2034

"We have been unsure of inviting the Petrova Foundation to talk to us," said the President of Lithuania. Irena Zemaitaitis was a tall, willowy and elegantly dressed woman in her fifties and she spoke excellent English with just a light accent that Penny could not identify.

"But once we had been given a briefing by the British Foreign Secretary about your address to the Security Council, we knew that we would have to meet," she continued.

"It was certainly a shock to all of us," said the Prime Minister a heavy-set but younger man. Penny and Avram knew that Viktoris Nekrusias had been an Olympic weight lifter, winning a silver medal at the 2032 Games.

"We were all delighted to receive your invitation," said Avram. "Penny and I were two of the very first people to join the company then known as Blueprints and we have experienced almost all of the astounding developments since those early days."

"So there really are intelligent species in the galaxy and one of them is part of your team?" asked the President. "Can you see any differences in him?"

"None at all, Madam President," said Penny. "He had joined the Foundation in Australia while most of us were still working in England and it was an astounding shock when Ben finally revealed himself."

"So would you tell us again, just what is happening with this new knowledge and what part are we expected to play?" said the Prime Minister.

An hour later, the discussion ended with both the Lithuanians looking excited, exhausted and overwhelmed, all at the same time.

"This is all truly amazing," said the President. "I don't know how our people will react when this has been opened up to the world. We had some serious troubles back when the Churches were faced with the new knowledge about the origins of Christianity and you may know that the Orthodox Church has still kept itself apart from the main churches."

"But it seems to be settled now," continued the Prime Minister. "So I hope you will take this opportunity to see something of our beautiful city of Vilnius."

"We wouldn't miss it for the world," said Penny.

"It's a homecoming," said Avram. "One thing I discovered as I researched my own DNA is that several ancestors came from here before emigrating to Israel in the nineteenth century. They were mostly from Vilnius but some of the family lived in Klaipeda and Palanga."

"Then I do hope you will visit all of them," said the President with a warm smile.

"We intend to," said Avram. "But this evening we want to see your beautiful Cathedral."

"Then we will say good afternoon now and see you again tomorrow morning," said the Prime Minister and the meeting ended with warm smiles and handshakes all round.

"It's quite beautiful!" exclaimed Penny as they stood in the square near the Cathedral.

"A real mixture," said Avram. "The main part could be a Greek temple, all those white columns and statues on the top, but that dome at the far end, something more Turkish or Middle-eastern about it."

"But I love this huge tower at the front," said Penny. I wonder if we can get up inside?"

For thirty minutes, they strolled round the Cathedral, almost alone in the square.

Then the situation changed.

From the far side of the square a large group of men appeared. They carried clubs, some posters in a language neither Penny nor Avram could read and they began shouting. The sound was hostile like the appearance.

"Oh-oh," muttered Avram, "we need to get out of here."

"I'm not sure we can," said Penny, looking behind her where more men had appeared.

"Let's just stay still and hope the cops will arrive soon," said Avram. "I don't know what this is all about, but let's hope it doesn't affect us."

"Some of those people are carrying crosses and crucifixes," said Penny, anxiety making her throat tight. "This is probably one of the groups opposing the new church doctrines."

The mob surrounded the cathedral and some of them began spraying crosses on the white walls, sometimes slogans in what Penny assumed was Lithuanian. Then one group saw her and Avram and advanced on them. Their expressions were not friendly.

"Stay still," muttered Avram. "The cops are bound to know about this soon."

Penny was silent. She was staring hard at the men now surrounding them. Their faces were angry, and clubs were raised in a threatening manner. The situation was frozen for several minutes.

Penny found herself extending her mind out to them. She felt the anger almost as a physical sensation and with her mind, she seemed to touch the coloured, furious flow of rage. The collective minds seemed like furious, jagged blades of bright red and dense black. She had no idea what she did, but she knew she did something, almost the sensation of moving a light object with her mind that she had developed and practiced since first discovering the ability.

She watched the colour of the flow lose its brilliance and fade into a light stream of gentle blues and silvers. As it did, the anger of the mob declined to nothing and suddenly smiles appeared in the faces across from them. The clubs were dropped, in the distance, the crosses were laid to the ground and the crucifixes were lowered.

"What the hell's happened," whispered Avram.

Penny was breathing hard. "Whatever it was, I know I did it," she gasped.

Before anything else could be said, police sirens sounded and several police cars appeared in the square. A number of uniformed men strode rapidly towards Penny and Avram and they stopped in astonishment.

"English?" snapped one.

Avram nodded.

"You are not hurt?" The officer's accent was strong.

"We are not hurt," said Penny.

The police officers moved among the crowd, talking to many of them and the mob dispersed quietly.

"Come," said the officer. "I take you to your hotel."

* * *

"I don't know what happened," said Penny to the laptop screen. She and Avram sat together on the lounge in their hotel room and the screen showed Garry, Mary and Ben in the conference room in Australia.

"But you know that you did *something*?" said Garry.

"I'm certain of it," said Penny. "Somehow, I saw the anger, I felt it and then I touched it and it all calmed down.

It was as if I touched a switch, or something."

"Well, thank God you did," said Mary. "There have been reports all over the world about some religious fanaticism still showing in those who will not and cannot accept the new conditions. The violence has been severe, many lives lost."

"Ben, you're looking shaken," said Garry.

"I have never encountered anything like that, anywhere, in any species," said Ben. "The ability to affect the moods and attitudes of any single person in such a way is totally unknown to us. To do it with a crowd of some hundreds is almost inconceivable."

"So how has Penny suddenly acquired it?" asked Mary. "And will other people find they can do the same?"

"I have to believe it comes from the DNA influence," said Ben. "Penny has been one of the very first to be using the scanners, but if she had developed this, I'm pretty sure others will follow."

"As if being human hasn't changed enough," said Mary. "This is something we never saw coming. God only knows what it means for the future."

Garry suddenly laughed.

"What's so funny?" asked Mary and the others looked puzzled.

"It looks like we've borrowed something else from Isaac Asimov," said Garry, struggling to keep his voice steady.

"You'd better explain," said Penny.

"As we all know, Karen was a close friend of Asimov's," said Garry. "And it was his suggestion that she establish a new operation and we have come to refer to it as the Second Foundation, because of Asimov's famous *"Foundation"* series of books. And I suspect Karen placed us here, at the other end of the Earth from England in a sort of acknowledgement of Asimov's Second Foundation being set up as he termed it. 'At the other end of the galaxy'"

"Aha!" exclaimed Mary. "I think I see where you're going with this."

"You may recall that the one thing that totally screwed up that brilliant forecasting system that Asimov called "Psychohistory" was the arrival of a mutant, a man they called "The Mule" who could influence the emotional state of other people."

"Good grief," said Avram. "I remember reading that series. And you think Penny has somehow developed something like that talent herself?"

"It does seem like it," said Garry. "The question is, is Penny the only one who has this mutation or are others going to appear out of the woodwork?"

"And has it resulted from the work all of you did with DNA from the beginning?" said Ben, his face alive with interest. "If it is, we can be sure others will appear. Again, the human species seems to have come up with something unique."

"I'm not sure I like this," said Penny. "I know it saved us back at the Cathedral here in Vilnius, but the idea of such a talent scares me. I just don't know how it could be used. What if somebody finds they have it and causes people to be violent and hate-filled?"

"That is certainly a worry," said Ben. "We will have to watch events and see if such a Mule talent could be causing them."

"And one more thing," said Penny. "Please don't ever call me a Mule or a mutant. That would be offensive and I might not like it."

"Given the talent you have displayed," said Garry, "I'd say if somebody offended you, they'd have huge cause to regret it."

"You'd better believe it," said Penny.

Chapter Eight – A Galactic Intelligence – February, 2035

Sometimes, the members of the Second Foundation found time to relax and discuss ongoing matters.

This blistering hot late summer day, Garry, Mary and Ben found themselves sitting by the pool that Garry had decided was a vital addition and had installed a few weeks earlier.

"Ben, one thing that has puzzled me over recent months," said Mary, "is how your race, now our mentors, ever discover newly sentient, potentially intelligent species."

"Indeed," said Garry. "From what I recall, the galaxy is about a hundred thousand light years along its long axis. I've read that it could contain as many as four hundred billion stars and maybe a hundred billion planets. How do you monitor such incredible distances?"

Ben looked thoughtful and took a few moments to pour himself a glass of cold beer from the cooler by the seat.

"Probably a good time to tell you a new secret about the Universe," he said.

"Good grief, Ben, is this another bombshell like when you announced your identity?" said Garry.

"I think so," replied Ben. He smiled at the other two. "So I really have your attention now?"

"Yes, I would say so," said Mary. Her rigid attitude indicated she had understated the situation.

"We began to think that our galaxy is more than just a collection of billions of stars, planets and assorted dust. Our own mentors had never told us any of this, it's something we concluded a few centuries ago when something triggered the idea."

"What idea and what triggered it?" asked Garry.

"Twice in our history of being mentors, we somehow learned that a new species had evolved on a planet in an unexplored region of the galaxy," said Ben.

"How did you learn?" Mary leaned forward in her seat, staring at Ben.

"That's the problem. We had no idea. But when we sent a ship to have a look, we found a very primitive race of hominoids, very like ourselves and humans, roughly at the stage of development of Cro-Magnon humans here on Earth."

"When was that discovery?" asked Garry, his attention as intent as Mary's.

"About twenty thousand Earth years ago."

"You said it happened twice," said Garry.

"I did. The second species appeared in our awareness some five thousand years later. Again, we went and had a look and found much the same, a hominid species at a similar level of development as the first. A different sun, a different planet, about forty thousand light years between the two."

"But you said that you "somehow learned" about these two new species. How did you learn?" asked Garry.

"That's the issue," said Ben and took a deep drink from his mug. "We have no idea."

"What?" Mary and Garry expressed their shock at the same moment.

"Really, we have no idea how we learned," said Ben.

"But over a few years, we began to realise that many of us somehow knew about the first species, it was almost common knowledge, but nobody knew how they had learned of the fact."

"Curiouser and curiouser," said Mary.

"Indeed," said Ben. "It was a rather impossible thing we had discovered without thinking about it. The Red Queen in "Alice" would have been proud of it! It would have been one of her six impossible things she could think of before breakfast."

"And what have you concluded?" asked Mary.

"After years of discussion, philosophical mind-bending and massive debates at all levels, we concluded that the galaxy is actually some form of entity with some level of sentience."

"Good God!" exclaimed Garry.

"It gets better," said Ben. "We can't conclude that the galaxy is a self-aware intelligence, but somehow, there is a totality about it and somehow it concluded that we as Mentors had to be made aware of these developments."

"This is truly bizarre," said Garry. "Where are these new species now? How far have they developed?"

"One of them appears to have stagnated," said Ben. "They have remained at about the level humans reached some thirty thousand years ago. They have language, some primitive tools but they remain at the hunter-gatherer stage."

"And the others?" Mary looked curious.

"Potentially a worry," said Ben. "They have evolved unusually rapidly, now they are at perhaps Elizabethan stage in England. But they are violent, very warlike, far worse than humans were at that stage."

"Have you implemented the DNA memory facilities in them."

"Yes, we did, a few thousand years ago. Of course, they have not yet developed the technology to discover it. But our general belief is that they will continue to develop, far faster than humans did and may well be another of those species that destroy themselves when technology exceeds wisdom."

"How long?" asked Garry.

"We estimate two hundred years," said Ben. "If that does happen, it will almost certainly happen before they develop space flight and certainly before they discover inter-stellar capabilities such as we have."

"Have you left observers on that planet?" asked Mary.

"Not for now," said Ben. "We drop in and have a look every few decades, but we haven't seen any need for possible intervention so far."

"If humans do become the Galactic Mentors," said Garry, "they may become something we have to deal with at some future time."

"Very possible," said Ben. "Let's not worry about it for now."

"In that case," said Mary, "can we address another topic that has intrigued us for some time?"

"What's that?" asked Ben.

"Your management organisation," said Mary. "Specifically, how are the mentors organised, who assigns them to their positions, who dictates what they do and even more specifically, who do you report to? Who is your boss?"

Ben looked thoughtful for a few moments. "There's rather more there than I should be telling you at this stage," he said. "But let me give you an outline. First, the management. When our own Mentors vanished, they had already nominated a number of individuals who had the ability, wisdom and intelligence to form an overall management group. They were approved by the nations' leaders on my world."

"I assume this took place after they had nominated your species to be the new Galactic mentors?" said Garry.

"Correct," said Ben. "Apprenticeship and Journeyman programs just like the one that started here a couple of years ago had been running for a few hundred years, so we had many well qualified people to be assigned to species that we judged ready to be monitored. That committee developed policies for each planet and the lead mentor on each planet followed those, directing teams of other mentors, each with journeymen and apprentices covering a specific region of the planet."

"A pretty standard management operation, then?" said Mary.

"Very much so," agreed Ben.

"And judging by your work with us, does that mean you are the lead mentor for Planet Earth?" asked Mary.

Ben nodded.

"And just what are those policies?" asked Garry.

"Quite open," said Ben. "Once a species has been considered to require development and support in its growth to maturity, all we do is facilitate developments where we see them required. Common elements are the growth of education throughout the planet, development of the arts because they always provide strong maturity and any assistance we can give in times of crisis."

"Would you try and stop a war?" Mary asked.

"That's always too big an undertaking," said Ben. "And the sad fact is that war often stimulates growth in some areas like technology, medicine, society and more. And when a nation moves towards war, the drive is simply too big for anything we could do to stop it."

"That's sad," said Garry.

"But reality," said Ben.

"And the way you have been so closely involved with this foundation for so many years, is that the standard? Is this how the lead mentors work on all planets?"

"No, my work has been unusual," said Ben. "There is something different about the human species that has interested us. You have already displayed some unique qualities, such as the telekinesis and the recent example of Penny changing the attitude of the mob in Lithuania, nothing like this has been seen in any other species. I have been instructed to watch it closely."

"That's interesting," said Garry. "If we do eventually become nominated to take over from you, how will it happen?"

"We can't force you to take the role," said Ben. "If we get to that stage, the first thing will be for your representatives to meet with the Committee to see if you want the job. If you do, there's a lot of education to cover, such as the handling of the spaceships, various technologies we have and lots of other matters."

"How long will it take before we reach that point?" asked Garry.

"At least two hundred years," said Ben. "That would just be for the initial stages. Taking over the full duties could take another thousand years.

"So it won't be the current Foundation people who get to meet your committee?" said Mary. "That's a shame, I'd like to meet such a group."

"It might be possible to arrange it anyway," said Ben. "But there's a lot to do before then."

"In that case, we'd better get down to it," said Garry. "Let's go in for lunch."

Chapter Nine – May, 2035

"Has anyone seen Ben?"

Mary looked across the dining table at Garry, Penny and Avram. They all looked up from their lunches with expressions of curiosity.

"Actually no, not for a few days," said Avram. "I thought he was somewhere overseas?"

"He's not scheduled to be," said Mary. "But he said he had a couple of personal things to do and might take a day or two off, but that was a week ago."

"Have you tried calling him at home?" asked Penny.

"No answer. I was thinking I should drop round there today."

"Let's all go," said Garry. "I need to pick up a bottle of scotch and a breath of fresh air would be good. I've been head down, bum up over reports all morning."

"As soon as I've finished this Risotto," said Penny. "Let's take Mary's Subaru."

"Somehow it feels empty," said Mary as she drove her car into the driveway of Ben's house.

"He could be out or just in the garden," said Avram.

"No, it's that odd sense of nobody there," insisted Mary as they climbed out of the vehicle. "Anyway, let's try. I've got the key to the house if necessary."

"Let's see if anything is visible inside," said Garry and walked to the front window. He leaned against the glass and then jumped back with a grunt. "That hurt!" he said. "It felt like an electric shock."

"Ben must have some way of discouraging visitors," Mary said. "Are you okay?"

"I think so," said Garry, rubbing his forehead. "Are you going to be able to open that door, though?"

"A good question," she replied. She opened her handbag and extracted a key on a wooden carving. "Well, Ben gave me this key," she said, examining it with care. "It looks normal enough. Nothing for it but to try. But let's try the doorbell first."

Reaching the front door, she pressed the doorbell and they heard the musical notes of a waltz from inside the house. A few moments passed, and Mary tried again with similar results.

"Hang on a second," said Garry and walked round to the garage next to the house, returning a moment later. "His car is there," he said.

"I've got an odd feeling about this," Mary said and in some trepidation, slowly moved the key to the keyhole. "So far, so good," she said and inserted the key with no obvious effects, opened the door and led the way in. The hallway was cool but bright from the windows in the adjoining front room and the sun shining in through the open door.

"I'd say Ben has some sort of force-field around the house," said Penny. "Nothing obvious until somebody tries to force an entry."

"And the key has a cancelling effect," added Mary.

"I'll check the garden," said Garry and walked through to the back of the house and the others each took a glance in one of the rooms.

"Nothing there," said Garry a few moments later as he returned. "We'd better look upstairs."

The four walked up in single file and reached the landing.

"I've never been here before," said Mary. "Which is Ben's bedroom?"

"The front," said Garry. "I came here when he first looked at the house."

Penny was nearest the door to that room and she opened it and walked in.

"Oh my God!" she shouted, her voice high-pitched with shock.

The others rushed in to see an awful sight.

Ben lay motionless on the bed. He was fully dressed, his arms by his side. His eyes were open, staring at the ceiling.

"Ben's dead," said Penny and burst into tears.

In the stunned silence that filled the room, only Avram broke the stillness as they stared at the body on the bed.

"That doesn't look right," he said and bent down over Ben. He checked the pulse, put his ear on Ben's chest and then carefully examined the white face.

"This isn't Ben," he said.

"What?" Mary exclaimed.

"Not only is this not Ben, it's not a human being," said Avram. "This is not human flesh and while there's no pulse or heartbeat as you'd expect in a corpse, there is a hum of some sort of energy in the chest."

"Avram, what the hell is this?" asked Garry, the dismay in his face slowly being replaced by curiosity.

"I think I know," said Mary. The others stared at her.

"When we went travelling to other planets, Ben took us in a ship," Mary continued, still gazing fixedly at the shape on the bed. "That's because we have no other way of interstellar travel. But remember when he said he would go home to seek advice from the mentors, he just left. He didn't call a ship, nothing. He just went."

"You mean... you mean he can travel in some other way, just his... what, his soul, his spirit, his consciousness, what?" Penny looked as white as the body on the bed.

"I think so," said Avram. "I suspect the body we see here is some sort of human clone, something grown from cells for use on another planet and his consciousness, or whatever it is somehow inhabits this when needed. His real body is somewhere back on his home planet."

"Let's get out of here," said Garry. "We don't know when he'll need to return and I don't think I want to watch what happens."

In silence they left the house and drove away.

"It makes sense," said Avram at one point. "If our people are going to live among other species, they'll need to look like them. And not all are as close to human form as a couple of those we've seen so far. This will have to be the way we go, we leave our bodies behind on Earth and we inhabit a cloned body of the species we'll live with."

There was silence in the car for a few moments.

"That's going to be difficult for many people," murmured Garry. "I'm not sure I could handle that."

"Maybe that's part of the training," said Penny. "Gaining a mental attitude that lets you cope."

Silence returned to the car.

* * *

Two days later, Ben walked into the office.

Mary saw him walk into the lobby in her security screen and felt a small shock run through her. She knew she was about to learn something fundamental. She touched some keys on her keyboard and spoke softly as Penny, Avram and Garry acknowledged the contact.

"Ben's here," she said. "Come to my office."

They arrived a moment later and took seats, saying nothing. All of them looked tense. A minute later, Ben walked in, studied each of them with care and then took a seat.

"So you know," he said.

"Only a part of it," said Garry. "You have some means of travel between interstellar systems without any physical support. And this body you have is an artificial creation. Is this how we will work on other planets with other life forms?"

"Yes, it is."

"That's terrifying," said Penny. "It was bad enough going by spaceship, that was a huge shock. But this... this astral travel or whatever it is, it's so far outside my comprehension, I can't take it in."

"You must have realised from the first time you saw different life forms that something like this had to happen," said Ben. "How else will you be able to live among aliens if you don't look like them?"

"I suppose,' said Penny. "But I doubt all our apprentices will be able to handle the idea."

"There will certainly be some drop-outs at that point," said Ben. "It takes a special kind of mentality to accept the reality."

"But you have been back and forth a few times," said Mary. "Will our people be able to do the same, assuming that we do eventually reach that stage?"

"Of course. Everybody needs an R&R break back home every now and again."

"When do our trainees first face this?" asked Mary.

"Some time yet. There's a lot of training to cover first."

"Ben, I have to ask," said Avram. "This human form you have, is this your own? Is this how your people look?"

"Not entirely. At some stage, we will invite you to meet us and then you will see."

"When I examined your body," continued Avram, "it was not human flesh, but something provided energy from inside. But now, if I examined you, I have no doubt I would see human flesh. Ben, what goes on in this transfer process?"

"It's complex. When we create a physical form that will house a consciousness, we grow it mostly from cells of the species. But we also add some materials that will preserve the body until a consciousness takes over and we also add an energy source that acts as an artificial heart until then. But when the consciousness enters the body and takes control, the remaining materials all convert to the natural flesh of the host and the natural heart takes over from the energy source."

Avram looked stunned. "Did your people develop this technology?"

Ben shook his head. "No, we were given it by our predecessors who also gave us the space travel technology. Should you eventually become mentors, we will pass both technologies and some others to you."

Avram leaned back in his seat looking thoughtful.

"Something puzzling about that," he said. "Many times during our early research in DNA records, we found individuals who appeared to have no ancestors. As you know, there are two dots right at the start of the DNA history track which are the records of each parent. But we found some tracks without these dots. Were these not actually humans, but the cloned bodies you created?"

"Correct," said Ben. He shifted in his seat as if uncomfortable. Avram noted it with interest.

"But quite a few of these "no-dots" as we termed them were two or three generations back from the original DNA donor," he said. "So they had procreated descendants. Surely your clones would have been sterile?"

"Oh dear," said Ben. "Avram, you've identified one of our worst mistakes. You are quite right, these artificial bodies should have been sterile. In every other species they are. But somehow, a few human clones were able to procreate. It seems to be another of those areas where humans have been different from other species, just like your telekinesis and emotion-control talents that a few of you have found. It's been corrected, but only recently."

"I suppose it could be comforting to know that even a technologically superior race like yours can make such mistakes," said Avram.

"Not to us, it isn't," said Ben.

"Ben, something else," said Penny. "And this scares me. When we do a transfer of consciousness, does it always work? Can it fail?"

Ben went very still. "I have to admit Penny, on rare occasions, a transfer has failed."

"And what happens then?"

"I don't know. I've had my own nightmares of being lost somewhere in a timeless void, I don't know if I'd be still conscious and aware."

"That's not comforting at all. What will you do if the receiving body fails to get the transmission?"

Ben hesitated. "It's happened three times that I know it."

"And what did you do?"

"We had no alternative after waiting a few days but to terminate the original body."

Nothing more was said and the meeting broke up in a strained silence.

Chapter Ten – June, 2035 – Shostakovich

Garry spent little time in the DNA research group area these days. The routine had developed well. The geneticist researchers were mostly spending their time looking back through human history, working with historians and linguists to discover the clear evidence of historical facts and events, tracing the movements of human groups around the world and tracing the evolution of languages.

New discoveries were still being made, some of them filling in the gaps, sometimes shocking the experts with the extent to which they'd assumed facts that were now shown to be wrong.

But for once, Garry was in the area when something new, wonderful and quite unexpected happened.

"I'd been looking back through the timeline of one of my friends in the orchestra," said Lorrie. "His family were able to leave Russia in the sixties and then came to Australia."

"And what happened?" asked Garry, intrigued by Lorrie's obvious excitement.

"Suddenly, we were looking through the eyes of one of his Russian ancestors and seeing a musical score. It was obviously hand-written, rather untidy and there were many scrawled comments. Neither of us speaks Russian, but what we could obviously see was that this was a major work for both chorus, soloists and orchestra. Let me show you."

She clicked on the screen of her monitor which was filled with a complete page of musical notes on several staves.

"I'm pretty sure the top staves are for soprano, alto, tenor and bass soloists," said Lorrie. "Then the next four are for the chorus of those voices, then the rest appears to be the music for the individual instruments. There's a title on the first page and some more comments, but as I said, neither of us speaks Russian and we cannot make out what it all means. At one point while we looked through this, the observer writes a letter to somebody, but we can't identify who it is."

"This is good timing," said Garry and picked up the phone, dialled two digits and waited while somebody answered. "Galina, we need your specialist help," he said. He paused, hearing the response and laughed loudly. "No, Galina," he said. "We do not need you to kill somebody! Come down to Lorrie's desk, will you?"

While they waited, Garry studied the images on the screen. He had never learned to play a musical instrument so the composition was quite incomprehensible to him. Much of it was blurred by the many hand-written comments in Cyrillic script all over the pages.

There was a stir when Galina Volkova entered. She had a similar effect that Karen Petrova had always caused, everybody turned to look at the tall, athletic woman who walked in. Garry knew that Galina was in her late thirties but her clear skin and bright eyes indicated a much younger person and she walked with the fit, aggressive stride of a top athlete. Her marriage to Bill Askins had generated much interest and delight in the whole company.

"So," she said. "Who needs the services of Galina Volkova?"

"Good morning, Galina," said Garry. "How many people have you killed this month?"

"None so far," she replied and looked at her watch. "But it is only the third day, I have plenty of time to meet my quota of three."

She looked down with a severe stare at Lorrie who had burst out laughing.

"Be careful, young lady," she said. "Do not laugh at Galina Volkova unless you wish to be the first of my quota."

Ripples of laughter spread from the desk as Lorrie tried hard to suppress her giggles.

"I promise, no laughter," she gasped.

"Good," said Galina. "Now how can I assist?"

"This," said Lorrie, her calm restored. "It's a musical score for soloists, chorus and orchestra, full of comments in Russian and obviously fairly old."

Galina stared at the screen for a few moments.

"Get me a chair," she said and when one was placed for her, sat down before the monitor and continued a silent study.

"Yes," she said after just a couple of minutes. "It is a score for major work. The Russian words for Soprano, Alto, Tenor and Bass are the same in English, the instruments *'skripki'* which is violins, *'truba'* is trumpet and so on. But what is most interesting is the title. This is a Requiem Mass and it appears to be from a long time ago, at the latest, early or mid-twentieth century. It is interesting that the words are in Russian instead of the traditional Latin. I do not know of any Requiem Mass composed by a Russian in that era except for Koslovski. Let me go to the last page."

She pressed buttons and eventually the final page was displayed.

"Nothing there," she said.

"There's a letter," said Lorrie. "Would you look at that?"

"Of course," said Galina and waited while Lorrie displayed the hand-written letter.

Silence held the group while Galina read through the letter. Finally, she sat back with a sigh.

'It is addressed, 'Dear Dmitri' and it's written by somebody very knowledgeable about music," she said. "And he is also well aware of the culture and politics of that time. He says that this work is too dangerous to publish because Stalin would send him to a Siberian prison if he knew of it. He reminds Dmitri that he has already been denounced by Stalin on multiple occasions for his other works and another offence would merit a life sentence. He strongly recommends that Dmitri destroy the score. It is signed by Sergei Prokofiev and dated 1950."

She looked round the group.

"Prokofiev was a very famous composer. There can only be one man to whom he has sent this. This unknown Requiem Mass is by Dmitri Shostakovich. Nobody in the whole world has ever suspected that Shostakovich composed such a work. We must have a great expert examine this material."

She sat back and the silent group around her saw tears flowing down the perfect skin of her cheeks.

*   *   *

Two weeks later, the Foundation received another famous visitor, a rising star of composers in Australia and a noted concert pianist.

"Elena Novikova," said Galina as she held the door to Garry's office for a small woman to enter.

Garry rose to his feet. "Miss Novikova, we are so honoured to see you."

"Elena, please," she said. "And you do me great honour in asking me to examine this astonishing find."

The three of them took seats around the coffee table.

"I have heard so much of your work," said Garry. "I am always astonished at the range of your compositions, from works for piano solo, music for trios and quartets, music for movies, ecclesiastical compositions."

The composer shrugged her shoulders delicately.

"I am fortunate. But I really do want to see this Requiem Mass. Do you have a piano available?'

"We do," said Galina. "Once you said you would come here, I bought a grand piano, a Steinway of course. We have a music room and it's reserved for you."

Garry raised an eyebrow. "You bought a Steinway just for Elena's visit? I hesitate to ask how much that cost."

"Then don't," replied Galina. "What else could we do when Australia's finest composer comes to visit?"

Struggling not to laugh, Garry rose to his feet.

"We have printed out the entire score of this amazing work," he said. "Let's go and see what you think. I hope you won't mind if others come along?"

"Of course not," said Elena with a smile.

"This is pure magic," said Elena seated at the piano. She had read through sections of the score before playing a note but then played several long extracts of both the choral parts and the orchestral ones.

"He has done what Bach did with the *"Saint Matthew Passion"* and Dvorak did with his Requiem Mass. He has created a short, simple piece of great beauty, opened with it and then repeated it in various forms throughout. This is the theme."

She played a few notes and though simple, it was quite beautiful and the effect was obvious on the group of listeners.

"And then this," she continued. "This is astonishing. It is a standard piece in a Requiem Mass, termed *'The Sanctus'* but what he has done is unique. He gave this small part to the Alto chorus which I have always loved for its cool, beautiful tone. Let me sing it in English."

She began a piece on the piano and softly sang along with it.

Holy, holy, holy,
Lord God of Hosts.
Heaven and earth are full of Thy glory.
Hosanna in the highest.
Blessed is He Who cometh in the Name of the Lord.
Hosanna in the highest.

Everybody was affected by the extraordinary beauty of the music and several of the listeners had tears in their eyes.

"Now imagine that with the alto chorus," said Elena. "I think it would send shivers up my spine. This is stunning. We must get a professionally structured score printed and then arrange a world premier of the piece at the Sydney Opera House"

Six months later, the Sydney Symphony Orchestra played the world premier of the Shostakovich Requiem Mass with the massed voices of the Sydney Philharmonia Choirs. The standing ovation lasted for twenty minutes and even after the end of the performance and the departure of the audience, many hundreds of people stood in the forecourt of the Opera House, unable to leave the scene. Many of them unashamedly still displaying the tears that had flowed throughout the evening.

Chapter Eleven – The End of Religion – August, 2035

"It's been far too long, old friend," said the Archbishop of Canterbury.

"Sixteen years," said the Pope as they shook hands and beamed at each other as old friends do.

"No difficulties getting here?" asked Peter Collins, taking his seat in the armchair in the lounge room of his house.

"None at all," said Eamon Jackson. "Just like last time, your government facilitated my arrival at a small airfield, no customs or immigration officials and a car to bring me here. It's one of the small perks of being the head of even a small state like the Vatican."

"I'm so delighted you came," said Collins. "Apart from the fact that I enjoyed our last meeting, so much has happened since then, we really needed to have this discussion. I know we've communicated by emails and phone calls to coordinate some of our developments, but there's nothing like a face to face meeting."

"It has been amazing," said Jackson. "What we set in motion then has taken off like wildfire. Religion has almost entirely vanished from public life, particularly in the western world and our church services have become almost entirely group discussions and reviews on how to continue fulfilling the charitable needs of our populations. I see that much the same has happened with you."

"It certainly has," said Collins. He got up and moved to the sideboard, poured two cups of coffee and handed one to Jackson before resuming his seat. "Any religious notes now tend to be comparisons between what those young radical rabbis were teaching two thousand years ago and what's happening today. What we are doing now and what we are becoming seems far more like the philosophies of those young men and I believe they'd be very happy with it all."

"I find it interesting what's happening in schools and universities," said Collins. "In both, Christianity and all that it involved has mostly been moved to a field of comparative religious studies where students study all the other religions, both present and past..."

"Mostly past," said Collins with a laugh. "We're seeing Christianity now as on a par with the old Roman, Greek and Norse mythologies. Studies now are of the origins, developments, myths and eventual deaths of them."

"Which are fascinating," said Jackson. "I remember such studies in my early days and wondering if Christianity would one day be merely another one of the many mythologies that have passed into history."

"So are we both wondering if it is time to consign our creeds entirely to this repository?" Collins looked thoughtfully at the other man.

"I believe it is. So how shall we go about it?"

"How strange it is to be at this turning point in human history," said Collins.

"And it's happening with just two old men sitting comfortably in a luxurious lounge with good coffee and an excellent lunch to come." Jackson smiled, but his face reflected severe concentration.

"The history books will make much of this scene," said Collins.

"Probably! But here's my first thought to open this debate. I propose that we formally drop the names of "Catholic" and "Anglican" as well as "Church." Maybe we should now be known as organisations dedicated to good works, which is what we have become anyway and should always have been."

"That is certainly what we have become," agreed Collins. "And perhaps that is a good name for a new organisation. Perhaps "The Good Works Operation" could apply?"

"I rather like it. And no more Popes or Archbishops, no bishops, cardinals, no such clerical ranks, no more robes and coloured decorations."

"We would probably still need some sort of ranking, if only to allocate duties at various levels," said Collins.

"Then why not just Level 1, Level 2, etc?' said Jackson.

"With a Managing Director replacing us?" Collins looked immensely amused at the idea.

"This really is just the organisation of any charitable organisation," said Jackson. "Will our people be capable of making such a transition?"

"Most will, I believe," said Collins. "What we have seen in recent years is the easing of relations between churches and sectarian charitable organisations as our business models have become so similar. We're all now aiming at the same things, helping the poor, feeding and clothing those who cannot, assisting the sick and the differences between us are fast disappearing."

"All of which, of course are just the traditional teachings of Christianity," said Jackson. "We're just going back to basics. Will all our people be able to handle this without the trappings of religion?"

"Some will not, but those will be assigned to genuine pastoral care in the field if they choose, but it will still be difficult."

"So then we should begin executive searches for people capable of heading up global organisations such as ours."

"Which leads to the key question. One organisation or two?" asked Collins

Do you think a merger would work at this stage?" asked Jackson. "I'm not sure yet that it would."

"No, I agree, that's a bit too early. But after a few years when the two operations are working in identical fashions, a merger will be almost automatic."

Jackson nodded. "Then here is what I suggest. Begin the searches worldwide for Managing Directors of global charitable organisations as ours will become very soon. When we have found both, you and I resign, or should that be abdicate? Leave the new directors to their jobs and we start our own new careers."

"Of course, I will have to clear this with the King," said Collins. "He is the Head of the Anglican Church, so this must be done with his approval."

"Is he likely to object?'

Collins shook his head. "Above all else, the King is a very pragmatic man. I believe he understands world trends as well as anyone could."

"King Henry the Eighth would be crabby about his descendent killing off his personal creation like that," said Jackson.

Collins laughed. "But what will happen with the other religions? The Eastern Orthodox Churches have shown little sign of joining us, Islam is uncertain, there remain Hindus, Sikhs, Buddhists who have their own philosophies, Judaism remains somewhat smug about the whole thing."

"The other religions will join us in time, I'm certain," said Jackson. "But one thing that please me immensely is the number of atheists and agnostics who have joined our congregations. They have seen the elimination of religious dogma and found an organisation that shares their own views.

"That is certainly a wonderful development and we have seen it also," said Collins. "As to the other religious groups, I don't think we can do anything but leave them to reach their own decisions. But I do think that our two churches doing what we propose will eventually have its effect on the many millions of people of assorted faiths."

Peter Collins, the last Archbishop of Canterbury stood up and went back to the sideboard. He pulled out a bottle of scotch and poured two small glasses.

Eamon Jackson, the last Pope stood up and joined him, taking one of the glasses. They touched them together.

"To the end of religion," said Jackson.

"May it rest in peace," said Collins.

They swallowed their drinks.

Chapter Twelve – Tracing History – August, 2035

Garry turned from his computer monitor as he sensed a presence at his office door.

"Galina!" he exclaimed with delight. "We hardly ever see you here these days. Have you come to kill me?"

"Not this time," she said with a straight face. "But I really do feel like killing somebody, I assure you."

Garry had always been amused at the way Galina never showed any sign of humour in her immobile face and yet it was obvious that she was laughing internally. He moved to an armchair and waved her to the other one.

"What's the problem?"

"This," she said and slapped the book she was carrying down on the coffee table with some force.

Garry turned it to read the title.

"The World's Greatest Pharmacist," he saw. The second line was more informative. *"The Life of Karen Petrova."*

"It is absolute garbage," said Galina. "Karen would never have approved it."

"What specifically is wrong?"

"Several lies. The writer said Karen stole some of her drug compounds from other people. He also said that her marriage to Hector was a sham, an arrangement between them to finance her research and make millions."

"Good grief! That's bullshit! Anybody who knew her knew how happy she and Hector were and nobody has ever claimed that they originated any of the drugs Karen developed."

"You know that, I know that, but this lying turd is trying to tell the world otherwise."

"Who is this bloke?" asked Garry.

"His name is Gilbert Halliday."

"It's a pity we don't have any of Karen or Hector's DNA. We could soon put an end to this nonsense."

"We do," said Galina.

"We do? Where?"

"At Life Technology in Reading. You need to call your friend there, that Greg person. He knows that Karen had stored some things in her personal research laboratory, but he doesn't know what. As you know, she had already stored the information on modifying DNA with him before. A long time ago she told me that she would store DNA of both of them and told me to wait until accessing it was critical."

"And now it's critical," said Garry.

"Very."

"I wonder if Karen will ever stop surprising us with information that she had hidden way and reveal just when we need it," said Garry.

"I'm pretty sure that Greg has kept some secrets waiting for the right moment to reveal them," said Galina.

"I agree," said Greg. "So here's what we do now. First, we have our legal wallahs call the publishers and tell them one humungous lawsuit is pending unless they pull this off the shelves. Second, we find a top biographer and commission him or her to write an authorised biography of Karen and her ancestors with our full support. We finance it fully and the writer goes to England and accesses the material."

"That sounds like a good start. Can I then kill this Halliday thing after?"

"Restrain yourself, Galina. It wouldn't look good on the corporate record."

"Maybe I can just rough him up small amount?"

"Not even that, young lady. Now, go to the gym and beat the living crap out of a punch bag."

"Spoil sport," she said and got to her feet. As she closed the door behind her, Garry could swear he saw a tiny grin on her lips.

* * *

October, 2035

"This is earth-shaking," said Garry. A month had passed since Emily Wiltshire had been commissioned to write the authorised biography of Karen Petrova. The assignment had obviously thrilled the young woman, a journalism graduate from Sydney University. "Let me read her email to you."

The conference room was silent. Avram, Penny, Bill, Galina and Alana sat round the polished executive table. Garry unfolded the printed email and began reading.

"Dear Garry,

"I have been in Reading for ten days and I have some extraordinary news for you. Greg has been thoroughly helpful, I have an office and full access to Karen's personal laboratory. The DNA of both Karen and Hector was well labelled and easily identified and I have made a start by looking at Karen's early childhood which appears to have been a very happy one, largely shielded from the worst aspects of Stalinist rule in Moscow because of the high status of her parents.

"But on the second day, Greg came to me and said he had actually been given some detailed instructions by Karen, many years ago. It included the instruction that should anyone ever be assigned to doing what I am doing, they should be told about the small container kept in the company's deep freeze at a safe site in a secure building in Reading. There was a letter to him about this container and he had been told not to read it until I had been informed about it.

"I have included the letter with my own, but let me tell you the stunning information it contained.

"The frozen contents of the container are the eggs and sperm from Karen and Hector. As you know, they never had children during their lifetimes but they always felt that any children of theirs would be remarkable, gifted and valuable to the world. You have the authority to check the legal issues and if you can get approval, you are to see how best to produce a child with the materials provided."

Garry put the paper down and looked around the room. Every one of them displayed some degree of astonishment but one or two faces also showed delight. The silence lasted nearly a minute before Galina broke it.

"I know that they always wanted children but felt that with the lives they led, they might not be able to give them all the attention and caring that children need. It was a serious problem for them."

"We have to use this," said Alana. "Can you imagine the sort of children those two would produce?"

"It's a wonderful idea," said Penny. "The idea of having a couple of sprogs and offshoots of those two is incredible! But what are the legal issues? Who can authorise a pregnancy to be initiated? Who would carry the child or children to term? Who would then be the parents?"

"Some of those questions we can answer," said Bill. "Galina and I are absolutely ready to have another child now that our son is turning three. Both of us would give the world to have one of Karen's children."

"Yes," said Galina. Small tears glistened in the corners of her eyes. "If we can get legal assent, I will bear this child and Bill and I will be the legal guardians of it."

By now, everybody in the room was smiling with delight.

"Garry, get the finest legal minds we can find to start this process," said Alana. "I for one cannot wait to meet a junior Forbes-Petrova and see what they become."

"Are we all agreed on that?" asked Garry.

"You don't need to ask," said Avram. "Of course we are."

"Meanwhile, I know we look forward to seeing Emily's reports on Karen's life history," said Garry.

"It's more than her life history, isn't it?" asked Avram. "The biographer is going to look at her ancestry as well?"

"Oh yes," said Garry. "Same with Hector. I'm pretty sure both have extraordinary lives behind them."

"Should be fascinating," said Avram.

January, 2036

"An interesting report from Emily," said Garry to the group around the conference table. "The possibilities she is hinting at could be even more shattering than the news of Karen and Hector's potential children."

"What developments with that situation?" asked Galina.

"Excellent timing, Galina," said Garry. "I got the news this morning. We had contacted a high-quality solicitor on that subject a few weeks ago and I got his letter this morning. He says that the field of Family Law has become much simpler in the last few years and he will be able to make a good case to permit a third party to receive a fertilised embryo and carry it to term. Equally simple, the mother will be deemed the natural mother and her partner will be permitted to adopt the resulting child as his own."

"Oh my!" said Galina and took Bill's hand. "When will this be done?"

"The paperwork has already been lodged," said Garry. "Considerable influence has been brought to bear on the system and the names of Petrova and Forbes carry vast amounts of weight. I expect you can plan on going to England in just a few weeks."

Murmurs of pleasure and approval ran round the room.

"I am so looking forward to meeting a child of Karen's and Hector's," said Penny. "Maybe two of them. They will have awesome parents in Bill and Galina."

"And so to Emily's report," said Garry. "Stand by for some more tremors!" He unfolded the page in his hand.

"Garry, greetings from Reading.

"As you authorised, I have hired twenty research staff and trained them in the use of the DNA scanners. They have been assigned to the painfully slow and detailed task of going through the family histories of both the Petrovs and the Forbes'. One of the more eager beavers jumped well ahead and spent over forty-eight hours at the monitor looking back to the beginning of the Forbes line and it's probably no surprise to learn that the Forbes ancestors came to England with the invading forces of William the Conqueror in 1066. A young man named Gilbert de Fournier, a relative of the

noble family in Poitiers fought in the Battle of Hastings, demonstrating such bravery that William awarded him lands in the region now known as Lincolnshire.

"Fournier stayed in England and married a local woman named Anna, building a mansion and setting up home near Lincoln. He adopted the family name of Forbes to minimise the stresses between Normans and Saxons in the area.

"Anna died in childbirth only five years later and after a short period, Forbes went travelling. As a man of extreme wealth and connections, he found open doors everywhere. In the year 1080, he arrived in Kiev and was made welcome by Roman Svyatoslavich, known then as "Roman the Handsome" who was prince of Tmutarakan in Kievan Russia. There was an endless round of parties in that society and Forbes was invited to one at the royal palace. I have recorded the episode from Forbes' point of view and the images have been sent to you. I've linked in the translation software so that the speech will be in English."

Garry touched the switch on his desk and the monitor came to life with a colourful scene of a gathering of nobility.

"Just look at that crowd," said Alana. "Even after viewing scenes from thousands of years ago, it's still almost impossible to believe that we are looking at a gathering of European heads of state in the Eleventh Century."

"Let's listen in," said Mary. "This is incredible."

June, 1080, Kiev

"Good evening, Sir Gilbert, welcome to my home."

"It is my great honour, Sire. I bring you greetings from King William of England who wishes you to know of his friendship and support."

"Then I am honoured also," said the Prince. "You will understand that I must be the perfect host of this gathering and so I can spend little time with you, but let me introduce you to one of my staff, Count Vladimir Monomakh who will ensure you meet the people of my court."

Forbes bowed and turned to see a tall, slender, middle-aged man. They introduced themselves and found it easy to talk to each other.

"Sir Gilbert, I would like you to meet a cousin of mine, Lady Tatiana Petrova. You will find her unusual because she devotes much of her time to studies and not the pursuit of feminine interests."

The Count beckoned to a young woman a few metres away and Forbes drew a short breath. She was beautiful, petite, perhaps as tall as his shoulder and her perfect, cream-coloured skin was like alabaster.

Forbes took her hand and bent over it, taking the courage to give the delicate fingers a small kiss. He sensed the reaction in her.

"My lady, this a great pleasure."

"Mine too, Sir Gilbert.

"Your cousin tells me you like to study the natural world?"

"That does not dismay nor frighten you, Sir Gilbert?"

Almost reluctantly, their hands separated.

"Indeed not, my lady, this intrigues me. What field of study interests you?"

Seeing a couch come free, they sat down, well aware that their knees were almost touching.

"Medicine," she said. "It saddens me that people should get sick and die or remain sick for the rest of their lives. I feel certain that there must be a way to prevent such horrors."

"My lady, that intrigues me," he said. "If only that I too have some convictions that are not widely known. I look at people, at children and their parents and wonder why does a child look like its parents? What mysterious cause is there? Why do some siblings resemble each other so closely while others show no similarities at all?"

She took a sharp breath. "Now that is truly an interesting topic. Perhaps when they..." she blushed and dropped her head to her chest.

Forbes laughed. "My lady, I understand. But yes, perhaps when that sinful deed occurs..." He watched her face and saw a flash of a smile cross it and thought she was the most fascinating, beautiful woman he had ever met. "Perhaps then, something is transferred between the parents, some sort of information from both man and woman that shapes how the child will look."

"This sound logical," she said and laughed, her face still red.

"What have you found about disease?" he asked.

"Not much yet," she said. "I have found some papers in the church that describe some mixtures, but the priests are very frightened and reluctant to let me see more. Only my position in society lets me see some small examples."

"And what have you found?"

"There have been some findings in the past. Some plants were considered to have curing abilities. When I can, I walk into the gardens and woods with one or two of my ladies in waiting and pick what I can. I crush them, smell the liquid that comes from them, but I have found nothing of value so far."

"Such activities would have you burned as a witch in England," he said gravely.

"Again, my place in society protects me," she said.

They were interrupted by the return of Count Vladimir.

"I must take my cousin away to meet others," he said.

Forbes and Tatiana stood up. Instinctively their hands touched.

"I must go," she said, her eyes fixed on his. "I wish it were not so, for you and I, we could change the world."

"We may well do so, anyway," he said. "When I see your courage in breaking so many social barriers, it makes me even more determined to devote my life to studying the question of how children resemble their parents."

"I know you will," she said, tears appearing in her eyes. She turned and walked away.

March, 2036, The Foundation Office

Garry resumed reading from the email.

"We haven't yet traced who Tatiana was, but we have found some writings that indicated a royal personage did conduct experiments on plants. We'll keep researching, but there is some suggestion here that she was a remote ancestor of the Petrov family, though we have no proof of that. It could be just our fond imaginings! However, we will follow through more of the Petrov line and see if Tatiana appears anywhere."

Silence reigned for a few minutes as Garry folded away the letter.

"Good grief!" said Penny. "How extraordinary."

"I look forward to hearing the results of further research," said Bill.

August, 2036, The Foundation Office

"As you all know, Galina and Bill have gone to England," said Garry. "All the legalities have been settled and Galina is about to have an embryo implanted in the next few weeks. The process of unfreezing the ingredients, fertilising an embryo and checking Galina for all the physical requirements will take a little time, but we should be able to welcome a pregnant Galina back home before the end of the year."

Smiles and murmurs of delight ran round the room.

"And on a related topic, we have another email from Emily in Reading," said Garry and smiled at the stir of interest round the conference table. "Her staff have now all been taught how to record scenes of interest and link in the translation software and she sent me this one last night. But let me read you her email first."

"Dear Garry and all at the Foundation:

"My people here have been going slightly berserk tracking down Karen's ancestry after finding the example we have sent you from nearly a thousand years ago. We are all quite stunned by this and look forward to hearing your reactions.

"This latest recording dates from 1831 and takes place at the Coronation of King William the Fourth. We have determined that the four people involved are Neville Forbes, a wealthy businessman and amateur scientist from Lincoln, his daughter Alicia, Major Gregori Petrov, of the Russian Infantry of the Guard, First Brigade and another Russian officer, a Lieutenant from his uniform, but we have not found anything more on him.

"I have recorded the critical scene, starting with the entry of guests into Westminster Abbey, following a coach procession from St James Palace."

September 9th, 1831, Westminster Abbey

The scene was from the viewpoint of a woman, judging by the odd glimpse of a full skirt as she walked along. It could also be seen from her occasional sideways glances, that she had her arm in that of an older man on her right.

They walked into the imposing entrance of the Abbey and an usher in ceremonial dress escorted them to seats in the long rows that faced the middle of the Abbey.

"This is very exciting," said Alicia to her father. "I got a little glimpse of the King and Queen climbing into the Royal Coach, but we should get a really good view this time."

Lines of people continued to enter and were ushered to seats. Alicia looked up as a tall young man walked up to her.

"Good morning," he said. "Major Gregori Petrov of the Russian Infantry of the Guard. Will you permit me to sit next to you? Our Russian contingent has rather overflowed our seating."

Neville Forbes rose to his feet and leaned over Alicia to shake hands with the Russian.

"I am Neville Forbes. This is my daughter, Alicia. You are most welcome, Major. What is a Russian officer of an elite regiment doing here?"

The Major smiled. "The Emperor of Russia and King of Poland, Tsar Nicholas commanded me to represent the Imperial Russian Throne at this joyful event," he said.

"Surely, not you alone, Major?" said Forbes.

"Quite so, Mr Forbes. I am merely one of a party of senior officers and statesmen. You can see them over there." He pointed at a group of about a dozen men, some in full, colourful military uniforms. "But I must be honest sir, when I saw your daughter in the procession here, I could not resist this rather impudent act of joining you."

Forbes laughed. "Yes, I have been told that Alicia is an outstanding beauty and she is most sought after by the eligible bachelors of England. But I must believe that your behaviour will be impeccable in this Abbey, so please do join us."

The Major sat down next to Alicia and smiled at her. From the way her vision was focused on him, Alicia was fascinated by him and the watchers in Australia could see why. He was an impressively handsome young man, perhaps in his thirties and his uniform enhanced the good looks significantly. It was a dark grey, close-fitted tunic and trousers, a double row of buttons down from a high collar to the waist and epaulettes on each shoulder. It set off an excellent physique underneath.

"I hope you will not mind my sitting with you, Miss Forbes?"

"Indeed not, sir." There was a catch in her voice.

("She's sure got the hots for him," said Avram.

"And why not?" replied Penny. "That's one seriously sexy hunk of manhood."

"Shhhhh... said Alana.)

"Where does the Forbes family live?"

"We have owned lands in Lincolnshire since the Conquest of 1066," said Alicia. "My grandfather built a lovely new home near Lincoln, the previous one was over eight hundred years old and tending to fall apart."

"And how do you spend your time in Lincolnshire?"

Neville Forbes broke in. As Alicia looked at him, he was smiling, seemingly not concerned that his daughter was so engaged with the Russian officer.

"I import tea and other spices from India and China," he said. "We own five ships and they are constantly at sea. I'm building another one in Portsmouth."

"This is impressive."

"As is your English, sir," said Alicia. Her eyes were focused firmly on the Russian.

"I thank you, Miss Forbes. My parents insisted I learn as a child and it is a useful skill for a soldier who must travel the world. Everywhere I go, I meet your countrymen and it enables an easier friendship to speak in their tongue."

"Your parents showed great wisdom, Major."

("I think he's moved a bit closer to her," said Penny. "I wonder if Daddy can see?"

"She's not objecting," said Mary. "This is a situation of the mutual hots, I would say.

"Quite right," said Garry. "He's practically drooling."

"Shhhhhh," said Alana.)

"Indeed they did, Miss Forbes. Both parents are scientists. They have been fascinated for years at the possible medical capabilities of plants and the conduct many experiments, mixing various leaves, seeds and other vegetation."

"That is most interesting," said Forbes. "My family has also shown intense scientific interest, but in different areas. Alicia has maintained the interest in the strange way in which children seem to inherit the looks and characteristics of their parents. I added a fine laboratory and library to our home and Alicia spends much time in there."

The conversation was interrupted by the orchestra playing the music of Handel as a procession began from the front door, along the middle of the Abbey towards the altar at the end. The congregation rose to its feet as the King and Queen walked slowly up the aisle.

The next half hour was a blaze of colour as the King and Queen Adelaide were crowned and then the procession returned. When the royal party had left the Abbey, there was a massive stir of movement as the guests also left.

"Mr Forbes, Miss Alicia there will be carriages back to St James Palace. Will you join me? I know that my man has reserved one for us."

"Your man, Major?" asked Forbes.

"I have an aide-de-camp with me, a young lieutenant. He stayed outside but he will have ensured we have a carriage," said the Major.

"Impressive again," said Alicia and received a glowing smile.

("Be still, my heart," said Penny. "That is one gorgeous man."

"I think I hate him," said Avram.

"Well, apart from all the hormones flooding Westminster Abbey, it looks like have a third example of the two families being scientifically advanced for the age, one in genetics, one in pharmacology," said Garry. "Let's see what they talk about in the ride back to the palace.")

A young man was holding the pair of black horses in front of a black carriage with the Imperial Arms of Russia on the side.

"You brought your own carriage?" said Alicia.

"The Emperor insisted," said Gregori. "The Imperial House of Russia must be properly represented at the coronation of a British monarch."

"We have our town home quite close, so we did not bring our carriage," said Forbes. "We would be delighted to accept your kind invitation."

"Indeed we will," said Alicia, her cheeks pink.

(They'll be needing a hotel room soon," said Penny. "Shhhhhhh," said Alana)

They climbed aboard and the other officer took the front and drove the horses, joining the procession back to St James Palace.

"I am impressed that a young woman shows interest in the sciences," said the Major.

"I have always encouraged her," said Forbes. "I do not believe that the only role for women is to marry and bear children."

"I wish we could work together. We could change the world," said Gregori.

"I too could wish that," said Alicia, her voice just a whisper.

("They're holding hands," said Penny.

"And Daddy doesn't seem to mind," said Bill.

"He's a Forbes," said Galina. "They do seem to be a remarkable family with very modern outlooks. But did you notice that comment about changing the world? Each of these recordings, that comment has been made. It's uncanny.")

The ride to the Palace continued with the young couple obviously taken with each other and the elder Forbes showing nothing but approval.

August, 2036, The Foundation Office

Garry returned to the letter.

"We tracked the next four days with Alicia and she persuaded her father to invite Major Petrov to the family home in Lincolnshire. Although the three of them (we haven't found out yet what happened to Forbes' wife) spent quite a lot of time talking about the sciences that would one day become pharmacology and genetics, Alicia and Gregori also managed to spend some time together over the next four days. There were some highly passionate moments and massive grief when the Major had to leave to return to Russia. We haven't found out what happened after, whether they met again, but Alicia

did devote her life to further studies of family physical similarities and wrote some interesting papers on possibilities. We are reconstructing one that seems to forecast the discovery of DNA."

They looked up as the door opened to the conference room.

"Ben!" said Garry with pleasure, "it's great to see you back!"

Warm applause rang round the conference table as Ben walked in.

"Sorry for the absence," said Ben, taking a seat to Garry's right. "Organisational matters back home for a week."

"Nothing serious, I hope?" asked Mary.

Ben shook his head. "Just bureaucracy. All settled now."

"Your timing is excellent," said Garry. "We've been doing some research into the histories of the Petrov and Forbes families, mainly to do a proper biography of Karen and Hector, but we've found some amazing stuff."

"Oh, really? Will you fill me in some time?"

"Indeed, starting right now. We had sent a researcher to England when we discovered that Karen had left DNA samples in the laboratory of the original company, so we've been able to look back through the centuries. The researcher, Emily has been sending us recordings of past meeting between the two families."

Ben sat back in his seat, looking apprehensive.

"Something wrong, Ben?" asked Alana.

"Er... no, not at all."

"We've seen two previous meetings," said Garry. "This morning we received a new email and recording, and we're all eager to see this. Let me read the email first to explain what they found in Reading."

He opened the page and began to speak.

"Dear Garry,

"More news from Reading. We are gradually learning our way round these systems, but as you will know from your own research, tracing families is a hugely complex and cumbersome business. Starting with just one pair of parents, each next level doubles the number of timelines we have to follow. The first process is to follow the father's line back for five generations, then the same with the mother's and this has provided huge amounts of data. Selecting what is of interest is equally tricky, also. Although you sent me here to research Karen's life and that of Hector, that is a far simpler task and four of the staff are fully engaged in that. The rest are looking back through the family timelines.

"We are coming across some fascinating episodes, much like the one of the meeting in Kiev between the first Forbes and Tatiana, which perhaps triggered a drive to research in genetics and pharmacology.

"And here is another one, an episode of another meeting where a woman called Amanda in the Forbes ancestral line meets a man in the Petrov ancestral line. As far as we can identify from the comments made by these two and comments overheard from others, this took place in 1876 at a celebration of the opening of the Mason Science College in Birmingham."

Garry hit the switch and all heads turned to the large screen on one wall.

Birmingham, 1876

The room was full of colour. From the viewpoint of the

observer, it was a ballroom with a mix of women in period dresses and men in severe black clothing. The women's dresses were hugely complex, lots of ruffles and the emphasis seemed to be at the wearer's rear.

An occasional downward look by the observer revealed that she was dressed in much the same way. She was scanning the crowd and making occasional comments to her female companion. When she turned to look at her, the other woman was older, more middle-aged and dressed in an equally ornate style.

"What an exciting evening," said Amanda. "So many beautiful people all in one room."

"Indeed," said her companion. "It's nice that your father has allowed me to be your chaperone for the evening."

"Aunt Maude, I insisted! I know that he is not really comfortable with my work in science, but he bowed to my wishes and let me come here. I'm sure there will be many interesting people to meet."

"I'm sure," agreed her aunt. "Oh look, there's cousin Geoffrey over by the punch bowl talking to a young man. I'll try and attract his attention."

"Oh yes, please do!" said Amanda. "And make sure he brings that young man with him. He looks most interesting."

Aunt Maude laughed. "He is certainly very handsome," she said and began waving.

It took only a moment for Cousin Geoffrey's attention to be gained. He smiled, waved back and said something to his companion. Both men started walking over.

Amanda's gaze was fixed intently on the new arrival.

"Cousin Maude, how lovely to see you here," said Geoffrey.

"Hello, Geoffrey, you know my niece Amanda, I think?"

"Of course, always a pleasure. May I present to you Mikhail Petrov? He is visiting from Moscow."

("Good grief!" exclaimed Alana. "Another Forbes-Petrov meeting! What an extraordinary coincidence!"

"Quite bizarre," said Garry. "I'm beginning to have some questions about this.")

Birmingham, 1876

It was clear from the image that Amanda's full attention was focused on the face of Mikhail Petrov. He had taken her hand and bowed low over it, but it seemed to the observers that they had not broken the contact.

There was a soft chuckle heard from Aunt Maude.

"These two seem to have found some mutual interest, Cousin Geoffrey. We cannot leave them alone, but why don't we sit at this table? You and I can occupy one end and the young ones the other end. It is short enough that they are not strictly alone."

All four seated themselves and Amanda found herself quite close to the handsome young Russian.

"What brings a beautiful lady from a noble English family to the opening of a science college?"

"How do you know of my family?"

"Your Aunt's cousin told me. He said he would want us to meet because of our similar interests."

"Then you must tell me also, what brings a young Russian man from Moscow to such an event?"

"Tsar Alexander asked me to come. He has great interest in science and he knows of my work in medicine. He thinks Russia may learn some useful things here."

"You know the Tsar? You must be a very important family."

"The Petrovs have something of a reputation in Russia. My father was highly regarded for his research into use of plants for curing the human diseases and I have maintained his fascination. So now you can tell me why you are here."

Amanda's eyes had drifted down to the table and her hand was only a small distance from Petrov's.

"There have been people in my family who have had similar interests," she said. "My grandfather was a keen researcher into the same topic and my uncle William had a particular fascination with the question of why children usually look like their parents. He was curious about what mechanism could achieve this. We talked many times about it and I took up his passion when he died last year."

"Have you found anything? This sounds incredible."

"Uncle William believed that when a couple... er.. marry..."

Petrov's hand moved slightly and their fingers touched.

"Do not be embarrassed, Miss Forbes, I know what you mean. And it seems most probable that the parents do pass something of themselves to the future infant. Some of my ancestors have wondered about the same thing."

"I have collected many pictures painted by competent artists of parents and children," said Amanda. "When they appear to resemble each other, I have carefully made measurements of the faces, the space between the eyes, the size of the noses, for example and I have found many commonalities in those faces. There must be something that the parents pass to their children."

"I wish we could work together, Miss Forbes. I believe we could change the world."

("Whoops!" said Alana. "There's that 'change the world' comment again."

"I'm past believing all this is coincidence," said Garry.)

"I believe so. How long will you be in England?"

"Just four more days.

"You will spend them here at the College?"

"If you will be here, then I cannot be anywhere else."

They were interrupted by the other couple and the two were separated.

August, 2036, The Foundation Office

Garry picked up the letter again.

We stayed on Amanda's timeline and found that she and Petrov did spend more time together at this celebration. But they never met again after that.

We then dug further. It appears that Amanda continued her studies and got further in as photography was developed, commissioning many portraits of parents and children. She was unable to publish her works because of the social constraints of the times. She did marry five years later and produced a son she called Michael. We will review his timeline at some point. Her husband, a doctor died shortly after that and she retreated into research, having no further social contacts.

Work continues.

There was silence round the table for a moment.

"It looks like genetics was a theme from the early days with Forbes family members and pharmacology the same with the Petrov line," said Avram.

"Is this just coincidence?" asked Penny.

"Hard to see how it could be anything else," replied Garry. "But it intrigues me. Still, let's just leave Emily and her team in Reading to work on and if they find anything else along these lines, we may have to investigate further."

"That's just incredible," said Avram. "Ben, just to fill you in, we've now seen three occurrences where a Petrov met a Forbes where there was intense physical attraction and discovery of mutual interests in the sciences, especially genetics and pharmacology."

"Yes," said Ben.

"Yes? That's all you have to say?" asked Alana. "You find nothing peculiar in these meetings of the two families over the centuries. We've seen three, there could be many more."

"There are," said Ben.

"There are? Ben what do you know about all this?" Garry stared at Ben, some anger in his face.

"It's one of the functions of mentors," said Ben. "We have some technologies that forecast the physical and mental make-up of individuals, the results of meetings between them and also the desirable traits in people who can advance the maturity of a society."

"You mean you've been some sort of global match-making operation for a thousand years or more?" asked Penny, bursting into laughter."

"Not entirely. Notice that none of these meeting between a Petrov and a Forbes resulted in actual marriage. It would have been interesting to see what would have happened if they had."

"So what *did* they achieve?" asked Avram.

"The objective was to ratchet up intense interest in the fields of genetics and pharmacology among people we saw to be highly influential," said Ben. "Those meeting that you saw resulted in considerably increased investigations, research and learning in those individuals and in others too. If not for certain cultural or political issues, any of them might have ended up in a marriage that could have had the effects of the marriage between Karen and Hector."

"And you said that you and your predecessors engineered these meeting?" said Garry.

"Mostly done by apprentices. A regular assignment was to engineer such a meeting."

"And will some of our apprentices do this on other planets in other societies?" asked Garry.

"Most likely," said Ben.

"Ben, you said you had a system that identified candidates for such meetings," said Avram. "Tell us more about that."

"It's something we developed over a few hundred years," said Ben. "We can identify people of unusual talents, track them and their developments and identify when meetings will have the right stimulation effect. It's not always just two people, it can be several, it's not always related to the sort of physical attractions that you have seen in your examples and it can also be applied to forecasting the movements of large numbers of people in a society."

"Sounds bit like Asimov's *"Psychohistory,"* said Avram.

Ben laughed. "It is," he said. "One of our apprentices had been working with this system many years ago and joined a class of Asimov's at his university. Once, during a tutorial with the great man, he touched on the subject of forecasting such movements and responses and this is what triggered the idea in Asimov's mind."

A burst of laughter came from Alana. "I wonder what Galina's uncle would have thought if he had known his great idea came from an extra-terrestrial," she said, wiping her eyes. "He'd have been absolutely thrilled, I'm sure."

"But Ben, this has serious implications," said Mary. "If you can influence societies this way, why have you not prevented wars and tyrannies and horrors like Nazism? You could have saved us so much grief."

"For two main reasons," said Ben. "The first is that the forces that lead to wars and tyrannies and similar horrors are simply too great for us to affect. They are the result of huge masses of minds working together. It's like single man standing on the beach trying to stop a tidal wave."

"And second?"

"Even if we could, we would not. One thing history has shown in all times and on many worlds is that such conflicts are a key part in the growth and maturing of a society. Horrible as it may be, these events cause the acceleration of technology, science and education and much of this is a huge benefit at a later stage. That's providing they survive the war, or course. Some civilisations have not."

"That sound dreadful, but I can see the logic," said Alana.

"I can give you an example," said Garry. "As you know, I had lens replacement surgery some years ago when I developed cataracts in both eyes. I went from near blindness to perfect vision in two quick operations. But that process of inserting new plastic lenses in my eyes resulted from the second world war. Pilots would get plastic shards embedded in their eyes when their canopies were shattered by gunfire. The surgeons noticed that the plastic did not develop cysts as would have developed with other foreign bodies. That led to the lens replacement surgery like I had. How many millions of people would have gone blind with cataracts without that procedure?"

There was silence round the table.

"I think I see," said Avram, breaking it. "The mentors aim to develop a society where wars and tyrannies have become obsolete, rather than try and force the removal of them."

"Exactly," said Ben.

"I look forward to seeing how our first apprentices develop under the training they get," said Alana.

Nods of approval ran round the table.

Chapter Thirteen – First Apprenticeship Mission
May, 2036

"This is the point at which we expect that several of you will drop out," said the holographic image of William Kennedy. He looked around the twelve apprentices seated in a single row before him. None was aged over thirty and all had been in the program from the beginning, three years earlier.

"Over fifty-three people have entered this program since it started," Kennedy continued. "You here are the most senior and you will soon move on to more advanced training. But for many reasons, this exercise today is the one that causes more anxiety, fear and other debilitating emotions than any other."

The expressions on the faces before him reflected moods varying from anxiety to interest to a firmly imposed neutrality.

"You all understand what this is about," Kennedy continued. "Should Humanity be appointed the mentors to replace us, many of you will have to live for extended periods among the species you will be observing and influencing. You have all taken trips to observe some alien species who might one day be the subjects of your care and you have all spent a lot of time in the holodeck suites becoming familiar with some alien scenery and life."

He looked around the apprentices carefully.

"But today, we will make one holodeck identical in all respects to an alien planet. You have seen it before, but today we will make the gravity, the atmosphere and all other environmental factors the same as on the original world. And now the hard part."

He paused.

"You have already been taught that you will actually inhabit the bodies of the species involved. Your consciousness will be transferred to a life form that has been grown from the cells of the species and once the transfer has occurred, you will become that species for as long as the connection is maintained."

There was dead silence in the room. Several faces in front of him had become deathly pale. One of the young women raised a hand.

"What happens to our own bodies?" she asked. Her voice was harsh with tension.

"Your body stays here, fully monitored, every life sign perfectly controlled. There is absolutely no physical difference between your normal self except that your consciousness is elsewhere."

"And our... consciousness somehow travels hundreds of light years in a few seconds to a manufactured body and takes over it?"

"That's about it," said Kennedy. "However, in this case, the new host body is here in this building."

"Here?" asked Gernardi, a man in his late twenties with jet black hair and a three-day growth of beard.

"Yes, we've grown three possible host bodies over the last few weeks from cells flown in from the species' home planet."

"And how does our consciousness know which body to enter?"

"Good question. When the host body is fully grown, a power source is implanted in it to allow it to survive after it has been disconnected from the growing vat. That power source is programmed to respond to your mental configuration and we have recorded those of all of you. You will automatically be drawn to the host body prepared for you."

"Good grief!" whispered another woman at the end of the row.

"It is hard to grasp, there's no doubt," said Kennedy with a smile. "And without doubt, it's the most demanding part of your future jobs."

"So who is going today?" asked another apprentice, a woman with long red hair down her back.

"We programmed the three hosts with the configurations of Olivia.." he pointed at the red-haired woman, "Ellard.." he pointed at a man who had not yet spoken but had sat expressionless throughout the session so far, "and Gernardy"

"The remaining nine of you will observe the entire process here and I expect that some of you will find it disturbing," Kennedy continued. "A few more things before we start. You three have not been prepared with language or cultural norms as yet because there is no certainty as to which species you will be assigned for your later training. So you will not meet any others in this exercise. This is just for familiarisation and it will be stressful enough as it is. Nor will you be able to speak to each other because the vocal cords of this species are quite incompatible with any Earth language. But we will be monitoring you and if you find you cannot cope with what is happening, you will be returned immediately. Now, let us see what this is all about."

He made no obvious sign or movement, but the far wall became transparent. On the other side was a scene that seemed quite Earth-like, with a grass field, some trees along one side and the sight of a river further away.

But in front of the observers were three bed-like structures on each of which a figure lay.

"Oh my God, it's the three-arm species we saw," said Gernardy. "We're going to become those?"

"Yes, you are," said Kennedy. "Now, Olivia, Gernardy, Ellard, would you please go next door where you will be prepared for the exercise?"

Olivia and Ellard walked as indicated, looking frightened, but Gernardy seemed quite composed, even eager to face the procedure and strolled in a relaxed manner to the indicated door.

They walked into a room that looked like any hospital ward, six beds along two walls. They were greeted by two middle-aged women wearing standard nurses' uniforms.

"Hello," said one. "I'm Stephanie, this is Jessica. Each of you take a bed, lie out and relax. We're going to give you a pill that will take all the tension away from you, because we don't want you arriving in a strange new body already stressed out."

Silently, the apprentices did as they were asked and each of them was given a small pill with a plastic cup of water.

"Lie back," said Jessica.

"Aren't we going to be wired up to something?" asked Ellard.

Jessica smiled. "Nah, we don't do that stuff. These beds have complete monitoring capabilities without any wires. Just lie back, relax and watch what happens. It might be scary but it's also fascinating."

*　*　*

Gernardy opened his eyes.

The sky above him looked normal, but as he adjusted,

he realised there was a light green hue to it. He shifted his head to one side, noting how different the muscles in his neck felt. He decided to sit up and moved to grasp the side of the bed with his hands and realised with a shock that ran through him like a jolt of electricity that such a movement was nothing like he expected. His right hand put a firm grip on the side of the bed, but he felt helpless to move the left arm. He stared down and saw why – he had two left arms.

My god, this is real, he thought. *I really am in an alien body.*

He concentrated on the left arms and slowly got the feel of being able to move them to his command. He found that he didn't need the left arms to get upright. As he pushed with his right arm, he sensed the enormous power in the limb and he lifted himself upright with ease.

Cautiously, he swung his legs to the side, becoming more confident in the strange body with every second. He stood up and looked around, immediately seeing two other occupied beds just a short distance away. As he moved to them, both stirred. He watched as they went through the same process of growing awareness, experimental movement and adjustment.

The two bodies were not identical, he realised. One was smaller, less bulky and muscled. *Good god, it's a woman,* he thought. *It must be Olivia. And in this body, I can sense the reaction to the opposite sex! This is incredible!*

Olivia was the first to stand up. They stared at each other and then touched hands in recognition. The contact was with the upper left arm of each of them and Gernardy realised that somehow they knew a convention of greeting. The massive right arm was for combat and emergencies, the smaller left arms were for social contact. Without thought, both of them had automatically followed this rule.

The brief moment of comprehension was broken as Ellard stood up. Even with alien movements and facial expressions, the wild panic in him was obvious. He stared around him, looked down at his body and his arms began flailing in terror. Then he collapsed to the ground and a loud cry began, full of fear and it became a human-like scream, muffled as he tried to bury his face in the grass.

It lasted only a few seconds. Abruptly the sound ended and the body became motionless.

They've recalled him, though Gernardy. In soundless communication, he looked at Olivia and both seemed to understand what to do. They bent down and lifted the lifeless body with extraordinary ease, Olivia at the legs, Gernardy at the shoulders. Both of them had developed good control of all three arms and they carried the body to one of the beds, laid it out and stood away.

He looked at Olivia and understood the message. They began to walk around the area and examine the vegetation, the river and the smell and colours of an alien world. It was so real that he tried to pull down a cluster of nuts from a bush. But as he reached for it, his hands went through the image and he had to remind himself that this was all a holographic simulation.

An hour later, the world around him flickered and he found himself lying on a bed back in the hospital ward.

"How was it?" asked Jessica, the nurse.

Carefully, Gernardy tested his two equal arms and sat up.

"Bloody amazing," he said.

Chapter Fourteen – Alien Arrival - September, 2036

"It delights me that our association with the Second Foundation has lasted almost from the beginning!" Penny sipped at her glass of wine in the lounge of the Foundation building. Another few people sat in similar situations, relaxing at the end of a day of hard training.

"It's always a thrill," said Avram. "You and I were almost the first ones hired by Garry. Only Bill was already there."

"You have one up on me," said Ben Fuller. "I'm not related in any way to the man who first announced himself to you, but at least we retained the tradition of keeping the name."

"It's a wonderful thing to be part of," said Penny. She had changed little from the slender blonde girl that Garry had interviewed many years ago, though the maturity and strength in her reflected in her features.

For an hour, the three of them chatted with the ease that many years of friendship had given them.

"We keep growing," said Avram. "Since we started the apprenticeship program three years ago, we've grown to over sixty apprentices in training here. Garry says he's quite stunned by this."

"And they're starting to spread out," said Ben. "We've got our people placed in six different worlds now and they're learning fast."

He stopped when a small chime echoed in the room. Several faces looked up, but resumed their conversations when Ben took out his communicator. He put it to his ear and listened in silence for a few moments.

Penny and Avram stared at him as the shock in his face grew, his eyes wide and a tremble became evident in both hands.

"Acknowledged," said Ben and put the communicator away. He stared back at the other two.

"Ben?" asked Avram. "Something wrong?"

"Yes," Ben said. He looked round the room but nobody was paying them any attention and nobody was within earshot. "I think you'd better call in Garry and Mary."

He stayed silent for the few minutes it took for Avram to call for the others and when they arrived, bringing Alana with them, they took seats and looked at Ben with curiosity.

"A problem, Ben?" asked Garry.

"One of our ships was visiting one of the other planets," Ben said. "The people there are still some centuries behind Earth and they are unlikely to progress rapidly. We were just having a periodic check-up, we didn't have mentors in place."

He stopped and poured himself a glass of beer from the bottle on the coffee table. The trembling in his hands had increased.

"Our ship's crew found there was another spaceship there and a military presence had been established just recently."

"Good grief!" exclaimed Avram. "Presumably that's the warlike Species Twelve we've been watching?"

The reference was to a known species that had been

developing rapidly and was closely watched by the Mentors because of its aggressive and rapid technological development. Space travel had been developed a decade earlier.

Ben shook his head. "No, they may have developed some exploration of planets in their solar system, but nothing close to interstellar travel."

"Then who?" asked Alana. Her worry was growing as she saw the anxiety in Ben.

"Remember how we have told you that the galaxy appears to be rather organic?" said Ben. "How we have somehow been given a signal, nobody knows how, that a new species has developed that should be examined?"

"Yes," said Garry. "You told us it seems to happen when a species reaches something like our Neanderthal ancestors."

"That's how it has always been," said Ben. He was staring at his glass and his voice had coarsened with the tension he was feeling. "But when we examined this new species that had clearly invaded the primitive one, we saw that they had interstellar travel and an obvious aggressive military bent, we saw a problem."

He looked up and stared at the others.

"We never had any notification about them. They have just appeared, fully developed, at a level of technology superior to Earth's. And we have absolutely no idea where they came from."

"Oh dear," said Mary after a full two minutes of silence as she and the others tried to absorb the information. "This is rather troubling."

Despite the shock, Ben smiled briefly

"Australian understatement, eh?"

"Indeed," she replied, not smiling. "This has never happened before?"

"Never. We have always known about a new intelligence emerging early in its development."

"What will happen?" asked Garry. "Is this a call for some form of armed intervention?"

"Not a chance. That's completely beyond our belief structure and policies."

"So what then?" asked Mary.

"I need to go away for a couple of weeks," said Ben. "My group will have to discuss this and see if we can work out the full situation and what we can do about it. But the biggest problem is the mystery – where did they come from and how come we didn't know about it?"

* * *

Two weeks elapsed before Ben returned and the same group as before met, this time in Garry's office and away from other ears.

"This has caused a lot of soul-searching," said Ben. "It's a problem the mentors have never encountered before."

"How?" asked Garry.

"Two problems, actually. The first is the issue of where the hell this species came from without our ever knowing about it until it was at this high-technology state. As I said, in the past, in those very few occasions when a new species emerged, somehow we got a signal from the galaxy itself. We still don't know just how that happens, but it has. This time, we didn't. The group finally decided the only solution was that the species didn't originate in this galaxy."

"But that doesn't make sense," said Mary. "You said they've acquired inter-stellar travel technology, but not inter-Galactic, surely?"

"That's the problem," said Ben. "As far as we have been able to analyse their technology, it's conclusive, they could not have reached here from anywhere within this galaxy."

"So where, then?" asked Avram.

"From another galaxy or another dimension," said Ben. "Neither seems remotely possible."

There was silence in the room as the others tried to absorb the implications of this bombshell.

"I can't even begin to comprehend how that could be," Garry finally said.

"Nor can we," replied Ben.

Silence ruled for another few seconds.

"You said there were two problems," said Alana.

"The second one is what to do about it," said Ben.

"Surely you have the technology to force them to withdraw, defeat them militarily?" said Alana.

"Undoubtedly," said Ben. "But the history of numerous civilisations shows absolutely that such an approach simply doesn't work. The result may be temporary peace, but the resentment in the defeated society never goes away and it will show itself in one way or another. After all, just look at what the role of the Mentors has always been – to remove militarism from the core of the society's DNA to allow full growth to maturity."

"Just as with religion," said Alana. "The two are inextricably linked and need to die away for continued growth."

"Exactly," said Ben. "We can't do it here. It contradicts the absolutely fundamental philosophies of what we are and what we do."

"So what's left?" asked Penny.

"There's an alternative we believe must be tried."

"Which is?"

"You," said Ben.

What? Penny sat back in her seat, her eyes wide.

"I think I may have some idea of what you mean," said Avram. "It's what began with Penny back in Lithuania when she tamed a mob of rioters, yes?"

"Hold it!" said Alana. "Penny managed to change the

mood of a bunch or rioters, maybe fifty of them. You're seriously suggesting that we can do the same with a whole *species?*"

"Let's examine this seriously," said Ben. "Penny was the first to discover this talent. Avram only developed his after Vilnius, but he's become a strong exponent. We've identified the same talent in some of our apprentices, which is what qualified them in the first place, but we have no idea if others ever did and if they did, if they used them. Maybe a few, maybe *lots* of people found the talent but didn't realise it and merely became successful diplomats, negotiators or even just cooled off family difficulties without having any idea of how they did it. But Penny is the first and so far, she has the talent stronger than anyone else."

"But I don't know if I can do it, or if anyone could handle some millions of people, especially an alien race." Penny's voice was harsh with tension.

"No, we don't know," said Ben. "And it's not a matter of affecting a whole civilisation, just an invading group. But the fact is that you and Avram have been involved with the original Blueprints company and then the Second Foundation from the very beginning. You were Garry's first hires. You've both demonstrated the telekinesis talent first seen in the beginning, and while your daughter was the first to show the ability to diagnose illnesses in people, you both developed it soon after, better than almost everybody. I suspect it's a fair bet that the mood-altering talent is also there at superior levels in both of you, particularly in you, Penny."

Penny and Avram looked at each other, partly in astonishment and partly in amusement.

"Well then, dear wife and mother of our child," said Avram. "Are you up for saving a civilisation?"

"We have to give it a fair go," said Penny. "Okay Ben, how do we go about this?"

* * *

"I don't think I will ever get over that experience," said Avram. He was still breathing heavily after the ship had returned from hyper-space into normal space and was rapidly approaching the small world now appearing in the depths of blackness ahead of them. "We covered nearly two thousand light years in that short time?"

"We did," said Ben. "And I assure you, nobody ever gets really accustomed to it, regardless of how cool they may seem."

"And you're sure the Mentors have acquired enough knowledge of the species' language for our translators to work?" asked Penny.

"Not entirely," said Ben. "Our people have been listening to many hours of the invaders' speech, watched their actions and we have a workable translation system, so there could still be some weakness. But we should able to do the job."

"Providing our talents work," replied Penny. She didn't seem confident.

"There's only one ship here," said Ben. "As far as we can tell, the crew is about two hundred strong, the officer class running it is just fifteen."

They fell silent as the ship drew closer to the planet ahead. Soon, they began to see oceans and continents. From their briefing, Avram and Penny knew that the population of the planet was just over a billion, scattered over three continents and a few islands. The species, known as Species Nine was only at about Earth's Middle Ages technology, no machinery and some ocean transport by sail. Numerous regional languages existed and none of the societies had yet established any form of national governments.

"There's the invader ship," said Ben as they hovered about three thousand metres above the surface of a flat plain. A few small villages could be seen and there were signs of agriculture in the square fields with various crops. Next to one of the village communities, in stark contrast to the primitive nature of the area stood a gleaming metallic shape, resembling an inverted pudding basin.

"The fact that they have landed their ship indicates that they have gravity control," said Ben. "That thing is a quite a bit larger than ours, but they should be sufficiently shocked when an obviously alien ship lands next to them. We'll also switch on that fear-inducing device that we normally use to keep people away from the cloaked ship, but at a low level so they don't get paralysed with terror, just unsettled. Let's head down, eh?"

Steadily, the scene below them grew larger as they descended and gently settled about fifty metres from the other vessel.

"Translators on?" said Ben and all three checked that the pendants on chains that Ben had handed out during the descent were hanging round their necks.

"I know we've visited several planets by the holodeck at home," said Avram, his voice a little hoarse from tension. "But actually being on an alien world two thousand light years away is just not the same."

"Agreed," said Ben. "But this one is easy. Gravity is about ten percent less than on Earth and the atmosphere is breathable."

Slowly, the door to the outside world opened like a camera lens and Penny and Avram took their first breaths of alien air.

"A bit strange," said Avram. "Some odd smells, a slight tingle in my nostrils."

"Probably the local vegetation," said Ben. He led the way outside and the three stood silently as Avram and Penny experienced standing on an alien planet.

"Where is everyone?" asked Penny looking around.

"Probably watching," said Ben. "The locals will be hiding, the invaders will be watching while they get over the shock."

Nothing moved for nearly ten minutes and then a small group of people emerged from the far side of the alien spaceship and began slowly advancing on the trio.

"Carrying weapons," murmured Ben. "Don't worry, remember what I told you before we left, the translators also generate a force-field around you. Nothing can get through, including insects and microbes."

"I'm relieved to hear it," said Penny.

Avram studied the newcomers. All were dressed alike, a uniform Avram decided, in a dark brown leathery substance with metal belts, helmets and they carried weapons that resembled ordinary assault rifles back on Earth. Their faces were humanoid, but very pale white and with huge dark eyes. Avram thought they have originated in a low-light world.

"Okay, you two," said Ben. "Can you do that emotion-changing thing?"

Penny began to reach out with her mind. For a while, nothing happened. But with a jolt, she found herself seeing waves of something coming from the advancing group. It had colours, vibrations and she sensed that Avram was seeing the same thing. The colours were raw, tainted with dark patches and the waves were jagged.

"They're frightened," she murmured, lost in the new experience.

"Can you do anything about it?" said Ben, softly.

Penny tried to visualise smoothing out the edges of the jagged waves, wanting to them change to a more normal wave. Nothing happened.

"I'm not having any luck," she replied.

But in front of them, something was happening with the armed aliens. The rigid, military line up wavered, body language went from disciplined control to tense, nervous movements. Some of the troops looked around in bewilderment and then back at the visitors with interest.

"But you've done something," Ben said.

"Nothing positive," Penny said. "Ben, I don't like this."

"Keep working on it," said Ben.

Penny concentrated hard. The waves of harsh, jagged emanations from the aliens remained ugly, hostile and filled with fear. Almost lifting herself from her body, Penny fought hard to minimise the anger and fear she was reading, but nothing changed. Breathing hard and with rising anxiety, she tried to relax and withdraw her mind from the danger she could see.

"Nothing, Ben," she said.

"It may be because the brains work in a different way from those of humans. Keep probing, you may find the pathway."

She nodded and resumed her concentration.

Avram made the first move and began to walk to the group ahead. He held his hands up in a universal sign of non-threatening greetings. The troops watched him carefully, some of them still displaying nervousness.

"Hello," he said. "Are you guys having a good day?"

From his chest, the pendant hanging on a chain emitted strange sounds. When it stopped, the troops looked astonished. One of them spoke and the sounds he made were incomprehensible to Avram but the pendant handled it.

"Greetings," it said. "Who are you and where are you from?"

Behind Avram, Ben and Penny moved up to stand with him.

"We are travellers from a distant world," said Ben. "Could we come inside and talk to your leader?"

There was no response from the troops.

"We mean no harm," said Avram. "But we would like to talk to you."

They didn't see a signal, but in one movement, the troops directed their weapons at them.

"Oops," murmured Ben. "That's not good."

It got worse. The troops opened fire. A white beam flickered from the weapons. Penny felt a wave of heat surround her and for a moment, she lost her vision. She heard a cry of pain and realised it was her own.

Vision returned and the heat faded. She looked ahead and saw the troops looking bewildered and frightened. She tried to read the brainwaves, but beyond a tiny tendril of fear, she saw nothing.

"The shields worked," said Ben. "Back to the ship. There's nothing to be gained here."

Slowly, the three of them moved back the short distance to the ship. When they were just a few metres from the entrance, the troops fired again. Once more, Penny felt the heat and a momentary loss of vision. She heard an outbreak of screams from the aliens and when the vision cleared, she saw them all lying motionless on the ground.

"Inside!" snapped Ben and pulled the other two into the ship and the door closed behind them.

"What happened?" asked Avram, his voice shaky.

"The ship is programmed for defence," said Ben. "The shields protected us, but after two attempts to kill us, the ship reacted. It fired back with a far stronger weapon than the others had."

"They're all dead?" asked Penny. "Did we really need to do that?"

"Actually, that puzzles me," said Ben. "It was a stronger reaction than I would have expected. Those troops should have been merely disabled, not killed. I don't know why the ship reacted that way."

"Can you find out?" asked Avram. "Does the ship's computer have the ability to answer such questions?"

"It does," replied Ben. "Sometimes, computer logic makes it hard to get the right answer, but we'll have a try when we've got clear and we have some time."

"Ben, the other ship has left!" called Penny standing by the viewer screen.

"To be expected," Ben replied. "They've been hit by something stronger than they are and inexplicable. They'll be heading home."

"Can we follow them?" asked Penny.

"We've already left," said Ben.

"We can do that?" said Avram. "We can follow them through hyperspace?"

"We can. It will take about half an hour, depending on the distance, and once we've reached their solar system, we'll take a lot more time to see just where they land. Then we'll go down and see what we can see. Meanwhile, I see chicken, salad, chips and a dessert of apple crumble. I suggest we rebuild our strength."

"I don't think I can eat," said Avram. "Being attacked by alien forces has killed my appetite."

Despite the levity of his words, his face was pale.

"Same here," said Penny, feeling her insides churning with the reaction of having a group of armed soldiers shoot at them.

Ben nodded. "I understand. I suggest you retire to your cabins for a while and try and recover."

* * *

"This is strange," said Ben. "This world is known to us, but it's been uninhabited for some decades."

"Can you explain?" asked Penny.

"There was once an intelligent species here," said Ben. "But they simply disappeared a few decades ago and the world has been empty ever since. It's one of the mysteries we've been unable to solve so far, though some people think it's the same process as happened to our previous Mentor race."

The three of them looked down the viewing screens as Ben commented. They were on the edge of the atmosphere above a large island that stretched from the planet's equator to most of the way up to the ice-covered polar regions. The city was about halfway along, on the eastern coast.

"Quite a small city, considering it's the world capital of a species that can travel through hyperspace."

"They didn't build it," said Ben. "The previous civilisation did. The present occupants must have simply taken it over."

"Won't they have spotted us?" asked Penny.

"They have," said Ben. "The ship's computer has sensed a form of radar bouncing off our hull."

"How do you know that?" asked Avram. "In fact, how do you control this ship? I've never seen you do anything to make us fly or take orbit. And now you know the people down there have seen us? How is this?"

"Easy," said Ben with a smile. "I've got a little control device buried in my shoulder. It gives me communication with the ship's controls. It's almost like reaching out with my hand, and I just tell the computer what I want and it tells me what it finds out."

"Incredible," said Penny. "Will we get fitted out that way?"

"Once you're in advanced stages of development," said Ben. "When and if it's determined that you are the next Mentors, it's one of the technologies we give you. Time for us to go down."

Twenty minutes later, they had landed in a park near what appeared to be a massive building complex.

"That other ship landed nearby," said Ben. "And the computers have been scanning the region. They heard conversations and speeches indicating this is a government centre."

Avram suddenly laughed. The others looked at him.

"How often have we seen this scene in sci-fi movies?" said Avram through his laughter. "Alien ship lands in the capital city, fear and terror grips the world, military takes defensive position and then alien emerges, saying, 'We come in peace. Take us to your leaders.' This is all a bit trite! I never thought we'd be the ones doing it!"

Penny laughed with him. "Enjoy it while you can, dear husband! But I think we have work to do."

The laughter faded quickly as reality set in.

"They tried to kill us before," said Penny. "Can the ship still protect us?"

"It can," said Ben. "It scanned the other ship automatically and we have weapons far more powerful and sophisticated than those the invaders have. Let's go," and he led the way out as the doorway opened.

They emerged into a warm, pleasant atmosphere and gravity that felt the same as on Earth. A smoky scent of some vegetation reached them together with a sweet smell of flowers something like frangipani.

"This is nice," said Penny. "Our second alien world in a few hours. I could get to like this."

"It's deserted," said Avram. "Not like the sci-fi scenario at all. No armed forces, no crowds of frightened people, it's not what I expected."

"Can you read any mental workings?" asked Ben.

"Nothing yet," Avram replied.

"The same," said Penny.

They reached the buildings and saw an impressive doorway that was open.

"Into the lion's den," said Penny and the three entered to find a huge lobby. In front of them, large glass doors revealed a scene that could have been the political meeting place of any parliament. Several hundred people sat in rows on both side of the hall while at the front, between the two was a small group of half a dozen individuals before a single man seated on a dais.

"What an incredibly familiar setting," murmured Avram. "This looks like they have a form of democracy already. And they're waiting for us."

"Let me do the talking," said Ben. "You two read the atmosphere and start doing that trick of yours if you can."

They walked through the empty space and stopped a few metres from the dais. Avram and Penny extended their senses out into the crowd.

"Very frightened," murmured Penny. "But intensely interested. It's almost as if they are pleased to see us, perhaps because they're distressed by something and see us as maybe helping them."

"Penny," said Avram. "I'm reading those minds far more clearly than before. It's as if there's a booster somewhere and it's helping me."

"You're right!" said Penny. "I just got the same. I wonder if..." She concentrated hard and saw the same jagged waves of fear and anger that she had seen in the minds of the troops earlier. She worked hard and this time, her efforts were rewarded. The sharp edges smoothed out, the dark patches mellowed into the same milder colours of the rest of the waves.

She looked at Avram and saw he was experiencing the same.

"Ben," she said softly. "Somehow it's working better. We're both having an effect this time. I don't know what's happening, but something is helping us."

"Interesting," said Ben and turned to the man in the chair. "I greet you all," he said and his translator boomed out incomprehensible noise. "We are not hostile, we will do you no harm, we merely wish to get to know you, since we did not know of your arrival in these worlds."

The man in the chair responded, the sounds were meaningless, but a voice spoke from all three of the translators.

"Who are you and why did you destroy the troops on my ship?"

"They fired twice at us. We had no recourse but to respond in kind."

"And why do you come here and threaten us now?"

"There is no threat," said Ben. "This region of the galaxy has only one intelligent species and that is the one you had conquered. So we were astonished when you suddenly appeared and we came to see who you were. But I must tell you, we do not allow one species to rule over another, so we suggested to your crew that they should return home."

"And who are you that can tell us what to do?" said the other.

"Watch it, Ben," said Penny. "He's frightened and getting angry."

"Can you do something?"

Penny concentrated her mind on the aura of the man on the dais. The jagged edges of fear and anger were very sharp and spiked and the dirty red patches in the aura showed the same emotions, occasionally concentrated. She focussed on those, but unlike the results with the larger audience, she achieved no relaxation in the fear.

"There are many intelligent species in this galaxy," said Ben. "Some are reaching high levels of technology such as you have, others are still at a level of farming and agriculture like those you ruled, while others are still very primitive. We are the mentors, guardians, protectors of all these species."

"And just how do you protect planets throughout the whole galaxy? Nobody can do such a thing."

"His anger level is rising," murmured Penny. "And so is that of the others on the platform."

"And the whole room is getting hostile," added Avram. "This is getting a bit fraught."

"You make such a claim without knowing who and what we are?" said Ben. "Isn't that a little rash?"

"There are just three of you," said the other. "What is to stop us killing you here and now?"

"Nothing at all," said Ben. "Except for the absolute certainty that a day later, this planet would be cauterised, leaving nothing, no trace of your occupation."

The alien seemed to shrink back in his seat.

"Good bluff, Ben. That terrified him," said Avram. "Classic reaction of a bully faced with a superior force. He's frightened. That makes him more dangerous."

"But there's no need for that conversation," continued Ben. "Our reason for being here is to welcome you into this family of races. We would like to get to know you and we are particularly interested in how you arrived here in this advanced stage of technology without our being aware of you before."

"They're still frightened," murmured Avram, his hand firmly over his translator. "But now they're interested and they badly want something."

"That is one problem," said the other. "We don't know where we are and we don't know how we got here."

"Can you explain how it happened?"

The other man waved at the few hundred people in the hall. "This is all of us," he said. "We were in a colonising ship, going from our home world to another one which we intended to colonise. When we made one of a series of jumps through hyper-space, we must have miscalculated because we ended up in totally unknown space. We have no idea where we are and we cannot identify a single star that is familiar to us."

"How long ago was that?" asked Ben.

"Some forty of this planet's years."

"So you have established a civilisation here," said Ben. "Why would you invade another world?"

The other looked around his group as if puzzled by the question.

"Why wouldn't we?" he said. "Why should we bother trying to develop a whole new agriculture to feed us when we can take it from those who already have it?"

"Is this what your people do?" asked Ben.

"It's how we have progressed for many years. We have grown rich by those means."

"It will no longer be your approach," said Ben. "As of now, your ships will be unable to leave the solar system. You may explore other planets within it, but there are no populated ones."

The other man rose to his feet in fury. "Then how are we supposed to survive?" he shouted. "You will kill us all!"

"Danger level," said Penny. "The whole room is winding up."

"What can you do?" said Ben.

Penny and Avram turned to face the few hundred others in the room.

Penny did as before, studied the aura emanating from the mob and concentrated. She sensed Avram doing the same. She fought had to go deeper and deeper into the sharp, jagged edges of the rage and the diseased colours of the patches of hatred. For a while, it seemed it would overwhelm her, she felt as if she was drowning in the emotions flooding the room and she began to panic.

"Ben, we've lost them. It's getting worse." Her own fear began to rise.

On the stage, armed men had appeared, weapons pointing at the three of them.

To Penny's right, an explosion rocked the building and the wall collapsed. Screams of the injured filled her ears and others tried running to the other side as a huge shape appeared in the space left by the wall.

"It's the ship!" shouted Ben. "Run for it."

As they struggled against the hordes of people trying to escape, a sharp beam appeared from the ship, aimed at the stage where the armed men and the leader were standing. All of them disappeared in a flash of fire.

The entrance to the ship opened up and all three flung themselves inside. The door closed, the ship moved away but through the viewing screens, they could see what happened. The building collapsed into ruins, almost completely flattened.

The ship soared skywards as Penny, Avram and Ben fell into the armchairs, gasping for breath. Silence reigned for some minutes.

Ben stood up and walked to the view screens.

"We're in orbit," he said. "I don't know why, I told the ship to take us home." As he finished, he let out a gasp of shock. "Oh my God!" he exclaimed. "Look at this."

The other two joined him and stared down at the planet's surface. Flames had erupted at the spot they had just left. As they watched, the flames exploded into a massive ball of fire that spread at an impossible rate across the entire land mass. Within minutes, there was nothing but charred, smoking ruins.

"What the hell caused that?" whispered Penny. "The ship's weapons didn't ignite anything."

"This is all wrong," said Avram. "Yes, I know they were going to try and kill us, but that reaction – it's insane. The building was razed to the ground, several hundred people were killed. And now much of the planet has been cauterised. The ship could have rescued us without that excess."

"Everything about this is weird," said Penny. "That over-reaction, the way we suddenly got a boost to our mental skill, none of this is natural. Something else got involved."

"Then it's time to talk to the computer," said Ben. He took a seat and indicated the others do the same.

A voice filled the room. No obvious loudspeaker could be identified. The words were incomprehensible.

"Command, use the language of English, planet Earth," said Ben.

The voice returned.

"Ready for evaluation," it said.

Ben smiled at the curious expressions directed at him from the other two.

"I initiated the session from my internal controls," he said. "The computer is now set for a debugging session." He looked down at his lap as if to concentrate.

"Command, provide reasons for killing the life forms outside the ship," he said.

"Unable to comply," said the computer.

"Command, explain inability to comply."

"No life forms were killed," said the computer.

"Interesting," Ben murmured. He thought for a few seconds. "Command, why were the weapons fired?"

"Compliance with program instruction C45, cauterisation of infection," said the computer

"Infection?" Ben was startled. "Command, you did not recognise an intelligent life form armed with weapons?"

"No intelligent life form was identified."

"Command, when the guns were fired again at structures on the ground, was that also cauterisation?"

"Affirmative."

"Command, did you identify the infection or were you instructed to apply cauterisation?"

"Instructions were received."

"From whom?"

"Unable to comply."

"Command, were the instructions from me?"

"Negative."

"Command, were they expressed in any language in your library?"

"Negative."

"Command, how were they expressed?"

"Unable to comply."

"Curiouser and curiouser," said Ben. "I think I'm beginning to understand. The computer would recognise any life form that has evolved in this galaxy. It didn't recognise those aliens, so it assumed they were an infection. When you get an infection of some sort, you apply antibiotics. The idea is to completely kill the infection, not just selected parts of it."

"Are you saying that they originated from outside the galaxy?" asked Avram.

Ben nodded. "Remember what they said? They didn't know where they were or how they got here. And remember that it has taken far longer than normal for my people, the mentors for this galaxy to realise a new, intelligent race had arrived and then we only discovered it by accident?"

Penny was silent, reviewing the comments.

"Are you saying those aliens were the infection?" said Avram. "How can that be?"

"It's possible if they were never part of the galaxy at all," said Ben.

"Ben how is this possible?" Avram's face had gone pale. "And who or what decided they were an infection?"

"That's the interesting part," said Ben. "The computer should have asked me for clarification and a decision. It didn't, but somehow got authorisation to wipe them out."

"From whom?" said Penny. Her face was twisted with the distress she was feeling at the large loss of life they had witnessed.

"I believe we must start to face up to a possibility that has never occurred to us before," said Ben. "Remember, I told you that somehow we learn about new species evolving in a way we have never understood? Many of our theorists have suggested that the galaxy is partially sentient, it may react to stimuli in ways only possible to a living creature."

"Ben, you don't mean..." Penny was staring at him, wide-eyed, her hands before her mouth almost as if in prayer.

"I do," said Ben. "I believe we must start to realise that the galaxy sensed a problem, it boosted your mental powers to help control the alien infection and when that didn't work, it ordered the ship to destroy the aliens with a full blast of antibiotics. It probably wasn't a coherent instruction, more a reflex to protect itself."

"That's... that's barely possible to believe," said Avram, his voice shaky.

"And there's more," said Ben. "We also have to consider that perhaps the aliens didn't just stumble on the way and get lost. It must be possible, even probable that they were sent here."

"Sent here? By whom?" Avram's voice was weak and trembling.

"By another galaxy," said Ben. "Another sentient galaxy. And maybe this was an act of war."

Chapter Fifteen – The Birth of Karen Petrova Askins
August 2037

"She is the absolute copy of Karen," said Mary, as she sat in the office with her colleagues, looking at the images of the new-born child.

"She is just perfect," said Galina, holding the child. "She has that beautiful pale skin, jet black hair and wide, lovely mouth. I can already see her putting bright scarlet lipstick on!"

"We're just thrilled to bits," said Bill's voice from behind the camera

"So are all of us," said Garry. "It's wonderful to have another Karen Petrova back with us."

"And I bet she has Karen's intelligence as well," said Alana. "It will be interesting to see what she turns it to as she grows up."

"Whatever it is, she's going to do what Karen did and change the world again," said Penny.

"Absolutely certain," said Avram. "How is William Junior reacting?"

"He's over the moon," said Galina with a laugh. "He's looking forward to holding her. He's going to be a doting, adoring Big Brother."

"Feeding time," said Bill. "But we'll bring her into the office in a few days so you can all drool over her!"

"Drooling is guaranteed," said Garry. "We can't wait to welcome Karen Petrova Askins back to her Foundation."

* * *

Two weeks later, Bill, Galina and Bill Junior made a ceremonial entrance to the Foundation offices, wheeling a pram in through the front doors to a massed reception of the entire staff. Garry likened the event to a coronation and it seemed much like one, given the air of celebration that filled the building.

The pram was placed in the centre of the dining room and everybody was able to come and get a close look at the little one.

"She's looking straight at me!" commented a young researcher. "I can see her evaluating me!"

"I got the same thing," exclaimed a security officer, and several others joined in with general agreement.

"It's certainly a very adult look," said Alana softly to Garry. "There's a rare intelligence in that tiny girl."

"Did anyone think otherwise?" said Garry with a smile. "The next few years are going to be interesting."

* * *

2039

By general agreement, Karen Petrova Askins was dropped off most mornings at the Foundation offices by her parents as they went to the University. Everybody automatically felt that she would be well looked after in the Foundation's childcare centre and would get the chance to meet other children. She was two years old on her first day at the centre and adjusted immediately. Later that day, Bill came to collect her after his last class at the University, while Galina was still running a workshop in Mandarin.

Avram and Penny joined him in the nursery as they took every opportunity they could to see the little girl.

The childcare centre manager was almost breathless.

"She spoke to me in French and English and later in German," she said to Bill as they watched the child sitting in the library with a book open before her.

"Not a surprise," said Bill with a smile. "Galina talks to her in all those languages and she's picking them up quite well. She'll start on Russian and Mandarin soon."

"I shouldn't be surprised," said the woman. "I heard that Galina was reading French at this age and she speaks multiple languages. Karen has obviously got the same abilities."

"What's she reading now?" asked Bill. "Can you see?"

"It's a book about the Solar System."

"Hah!" said Bill. "Apparently, the first day I was at pre-school, I was reading a similar book when my parents came for me. This kid is truly a chip off both blocks!"

"So she'll probably develop a new drug or two in the next few days?" said the manager, almost laughing at the extraordinary intellect she had seen that day.

"Either that, or a new proof of Fermat's Last Theorem," replied Bill with a straight face.

"Nothing will surprise me," said the woman. "I think we'll have some interesting times with this little girl."

"Count on it," said Bill. "In fact, here's a bomb blast for you all."

"What's that, Bill?" asked Avram. "You gave us enough bomb blasts in the past, what new thing can you give us?"

"A big one," said Bill, grinning widely. "This little photocopy of Karen Petrova is not the only child of Hector and Karen. When the embryo was implanted, we had already decided that one child was not enough. We had twins. Hector Forbes Askins is this little treasure's brother."

"You had twins!" Alana looked thrilled, as did the others in the room.

"Why have one when you can have two for the same price?" said Bill, suppressing a laugh.

"But you never told us!" exclaimed Mary.

"No, there was a reason for that," said Bill. "When they were born, Karen was a perfectly healthy baby, but Hector wasn't. He was very weak, underweight and had breathing difficulties. He went straight into an incubator and we really were not sure he'd survive."

"And how is he now?" asked Penny.

"Getting better and stronger, his breathing is fine but we've kept him at home with a nurse ever since getting him back from the hospital."

"And the prognosis?" asked Avram.

"Very positive," said Bill. "He's still a little frail, but the medics all say he'll grow up normally. Karen just adores him and stays with him all the time she's home, and Bill junior is the same. He gets a lot of love and attention."

"That's wonderful," said Mary. "And is he showing any genius traits like everybody else in the family?"

"Not sure," said Bill. "But one thing is interesting. We found that if we play classical music for him, he sits quite contented, obviously listening, because he cries when the music stops. So he gets a constant diet of Beethoven, Bach, Brahms and all the rest all night and he sleeps wonderfully well."

"When do we get to meet him?" asked Penny.

"Pretty soon," said Bill.

* * *

August, 2040

"Come on in," said Galina. "Welcome to the Askins hovel!"

"Hah!" said Avram. "Some hovel!"

"Well, it's only six bedrooms, four bathrooms, a huge garden with a pool and a complete nursery," said Bill. "I consider that to be slumming it!"

"We've obviously been paying you too much all those years," said Garry. "But I suppose you've sold a few licences for electrical goodies in your time?"

"Just a few," said Bill. "I followed the example of the first Karen – I design the stuff, other people pay me for a license to build them. The millions keep pouring in!"

The group entered the spacious house and moved to the luxurious lounge room with huge windows overlooking a beautiful lawn and a good-sized swimming pool.

"We're so glad you could make it," said Galina.

"What, miss the twins' third birthday?" said Garry. "Not a chance! Where are they, anyway?"

"With Bill Junior, as always," said Galina. "Those three are quite inseparable and they're happy with Angela, the nurse. We'll join them in a while after we've had a drink. We may surprise you."

"What, a Petrova/Askins/Forbes gathering surprise us?" said Mary with a smile. "Whatever could you mean?"

"You'll see," said Bill, suppressing a smug smile. "Anyway, drinks!"

Half an hour later, the adults moved to what Bill called the playroom. It was huge, filled with plush chairs, some fig trees in pots and the usual collection of children's toys. All three children were obviously delighted to see the arrivals, judging by the series of hugs and kisses that were exchanged with happy little ones.

They greeted the attractive young woman sitting in one chair.

"Quite a handful," said Avram.

"Total joy," said Angela.

"Notice the keyboard," said Galina, pointing to an electronic keyboard against the wall.

"Who plays that?" asked Mary.

"I do!" shouted Hector and dashed to the instrument, climbing with some difficulty and assistance from Angela onto the piano stool.

He placed his hands on the keyboard and all could see the total concentration that filled his face. He began to play and the rest of the room went silent.

The music was beautiful. Avram recognised the piece as a Beethoven sonata and was transfixed. He could not fault the technique. He glanced at the other two children. Karen was watching her brother with almost the same concentration that Hector was displaying and Bill Junior was watching with a smile of pride and delight.

The music stopped and the adults let out a collective sigh.

"Hector, that was simply wonderful," said Alana. "How long have you been playing?"

"Just a year," replied Galina. "One day, we walked past a music shop in town and Hector just demanded to go in. Once there, he stood by a baby grand, I lifted him to the seat and he went deadly silent as he picked at the keys. Within a minute or two, he was playing the C Major scale, all the white keys and was starting to touch the black keys. The sales people were stunned. We bought him a keyboard immediately and we brought in a music teacher who could hardly keep up with him."

"What else can you play, Hector?' asked Mary.

Without replying, the little boy began another piece but this time, Avram didn't recognise it. It had some characteristics of the Beethoven sonata and he thought he recognised a touch of Mozart, but couldn't be sure.

"That was fabulous," he said when it ended. "Who wrote that?"

"I did," said Hector.

Chapter Sixteen – First Mission, June, 2038

"You both proved yourselves on your first few alien body experiences," said William Kennedy in the holograph suite. "For many apprentices, inhabiting an alien body is a traumatic experience and as I said before, it's the time when many drop out of the program, as your compatriot did."

Olivia and Gernardy looked at him without expression.

"The first couple were certainly gut-wrenching experiences," said Gernardy. "But once we had adjusted, it became fascinating. You managed to avoid us encountering any others of those species at the time and I really don't know how I would have handled it."

"What I found really interesting was that each of us recognised the other as being of the opposite sex," said Olivia. She smiled at Gernardy. "I don't know whether that three-armed giant was a sexy charmer or as repellent as a rotting rabbit, but I could certainly tell you were male."

Gernardy laughed. "Same here," he said. "I recognised you as female immediately. I presume the body reacts automatically, regardless of the consciousness within it."

"Exactly," said Kennedy. "And what you proved was your readiness for a more complex mission."

"How complex?" asked Olivia.

"We want you to be part of a team that will do to an alien race what my people did to humans over seventy thousand years ago," said Kennedy.

"What, implement the DNA tracking and recording ability?" Olivia looked excited. "You mean we would be starting the entire process with a new species?"

"Exactly," said Kennedy. "We learned of this species a couple of hundred years ago and our analysts have recommended that they are ready to receive this characteristic. Humans were at the Neanderthal stage when this occurred. This species is at an equivalent stage."

"I assume we won't be alone for this?" said Gernardy. "This is a learning exercise under supervision?"

"Of course," said Kennedy. "You will be part of a team with three others, more experienced in the training. What you might call journeymen. All have spent some time on Earth among humans and they will be showing you how all this is done."

"Who is the subject of this?" asked Olivia.

"As already indicated, this is a primitive race about equivalent in development to the later stages of Neanderthals on Earth. A major advantage for us is that they are humanoid, similar to humans, just minor facial and internal body structural differences. They have no viable language yet, so there is no requirement for you to be machine-taught an alien language, but it means the bodies the team will inhabit will be able to speak human languages. The others are all competent English speakers and the physical characteristics of the species you will be inhabiting allow for human speech."

"And just how is this done?" asked Gernardy.

"The process is simple," said Kennedy. "Each of you will carry a brief-case sized back-pack and all that is required is to be within a kilometre or two of any group you see. It means travelling on foot quite often to find new areas."

"And this will implement the DNA changes all over the world?" Olivia sounded sceptical.

Kennedy shook his head. "There are several teams in place in specific locations. All of them were sent to local bodies in the last few days and a ship carried a number of these units to each team, landing at night and unloading."

"How long does this process last?" asked Gernardy. "And how long will we be there?"

"You will need to be there for seven days," said Kennedy. "The equipment releases micro-organisms and these spread for weeks after release. Once you have covered a wide-enough area, you no longer need to be there."

"Our team will know who we are?" asked Olivia.

"They're expecting you," said Kennedy. "Time you were transferred to a new body a thousand light years away."

Olivia opened her eyes and saw rock. As her mind cleared, she realised she was lying on her back on some sort of bed, staring at the ceiling of a cave.

"Just stay still, don't try to move or speak," said a voice outside of her vision. "Give it about ten minutes and you'll be ready."

The voice had tones and sounds that she had never before heard but she recalled Kennedy saying that the species she was now inhabiting was sufficiently humanoid that human speech sounds could be made.

"Your colleague, Gernardy has also arrived safely," said the voice. "When you are ready, we'll plan our first outing."

A short time later, Olivia felt able to sit up and look around. She saw four other people in the immediate area and it really was a cave, she saw. It was open to the outside but inside, the comfort level was quite high, with a number of camp chairs and some equipment that she could not identify.

"Well, hello, Olivia," said the voice she had heard before. The speaker looked very much like the images she had seen of Neanderthal humans and the effect was a shock. It was a man, she saw, wearing what looked like animal skins.

"My name is Hassan," said the voice. "How are you feeling?"

"I think…" she started to say but only a faint croak emerged.

"It takes a few tries to get the vocal cords working," said Hassan. He smiled, but Olivia thought the expression looked dreadful on the primitive features.

She tried again. "I think…" This time, the words were intelligible but still hoarse. "I think I'm fine," she said, feeling easier every second. "Where's Gernardy?"

Hassan pointed at a figure lying on another bed. "I suggest you sit by him and be the first voice he hears when he wakes up," he said. "It will be an easier return to consciousness."

"Sounds like a good idea," she said, this time feeling her voice to be more natural. She pulled one of the camp chairs over to Gernardy and watched as his eyelids flickered and then opened. Like Hassan, he resembled a Neanderthal human.

"Hey, Gernardy, it's Olivia," she said. "Don't try and move or speak for a few minutes. I woke up a little while ago and it takes some time to become fully functional."

She looked down at herself and then again at Gernardy and realised both were wearing similar animal skins to those worn by Hassan. He saw the look.

"Artificial," he said. "But nobody could tell the difference. However, it's a bit more tailored to your personal shape and size to ensure comfort, so we'll fit in with local standards perfectly okay."

Within a short while, Gernardy had recovered enough to stand up. He stared at Olivia.

"You look bloody awful," he said.

"Well, you're no fashion model yourself," she replied. "Please don't smile, it's horrible."

"If you two have stopped exchanging sweet nothings, we need to plan our week," said Hassan. "First, the other members of the team. That's Jack, that's Helen and that's Kwong."

All looked similar but with enough differences in facial features to be identifiable. Telling the woman apart from the men was less easy, but Olivia realised the same would apply to her.

"Now, the environment," continued Hassan. "This is a regular cave, but there's a force field across the front, nobody can get in except us. Notice that you have what appears to be a bone necklace round your necks, a standard feature in this era, but one of those bones lets you enter the cave, another one is a navigator that will direct you back here should you get lost. There are a couple of others with specific functions."

Olivia studied the necklace. There was nothing to indicate that any of the bones were not natural.

"We have cooking facilities here, powered by micro-nuclear power plants," Hassan continued. "Also medicines, antibiotics, bandages, everything we might need and an emergency communication device should we really get into trouble. If we activate that, a ship will be here within hours and we'll get lifted out. However, if required, your consciousness will be returned to your own body back on Earth. All okay?"

"When do we start work?" asked Gernardy.

"Almost immediately. Today, Olivia and I will go walkabout in an area we've marked out. Gernardy, you'll go with Jack. You'll each carry one of these backpacks and simply walk around the areas. If you meet any locals, stay calm, don't do anything threatening. If they do approach you, sit down, make gentle noises. You may find that one of them might start picking fleas from your hair and clothing! Offer the same courtesy, it's a common display of cooperation and friendship."

A short while later, the journeymen and their apprentices set out to start the distribution of the process to give a primitive race the power to see its own history.

The scenery looks primitive, thought Olivia. The country was rocky, little greenery and only a few stunted trees and bushes. But some of the bushes carried fruit.

"Something like apples," said Hassan. "Rather sour to our tastes, but edible in an emergency. The locals like them, though. Let's pick just a few each as possible peace offerings."

With a few of the fruit put into their packs, they resumed the walk

"Wildlife," said Hassan, pointing out movement amid the bushes.

To Olivia, they looked like small pigs, though much skinnier than any Earth-based pig.

"They eat the apples too," said Hassan, "and they're the main food source of the locals in this area."

Another hour passed without incident. The scenery had little to offer, mostly flat, rocky terrain and some distant mountains shrouded in cloud.

And then...

"Oh, oh," said Hassan. "Locals. Stand still."

Three individuals had appeared from amid some trees. As far as Olivia could tell, they were all male. They didn't seem threatening, but Olivia was aware that she knew nothing of the customs and habits of the people. She stood still as instructed.

The others approached slowly.

"Peaceful, I think," said Hassan. "Sit down, take your pack off and get those apples out."

Once seated, Hassan began making gently grunts and sounds like a happy baby and Olivia imitated him. The others approached until they were just a metre away. Hassan picked up an apple in each hand and held them out as an offering, Olivia followed. One of the men came forward, cautiously took an apple from Olivia and bit into it.

This seemed to be the signal for the others to do the same and within minutes, Olivia thought the scene was like that of a children's picnic. A few moments later, all apples consumed, the party broke up with what seemed mutual friendship.

Another two hours of steady walking passed before another interruption occurred. This time, it wasn't so friendly. Five men appeared walking towards Olivia and Hassan. This time, they seemed threatening, with growls of rage becoming audible as they got nearer. They each carried a spear of what looked like a straight branch with one end carved into a point and burned black

"Stand still," said Hassan. "This is a hunting party and we probably represent competition."

"What do we do?" asked Olivia, starting to feel some fear of the threat.

"See that bone on your necklace, the one with a black ring in the middle?"

She looked down and identified the bone.

"Got it."

"If they get any closer, press that bone. We've all got the same equipment, but you might as well get the practice if it's needed."

Olivia watched the group intently. They had stopped and were staring at the two of them. The growling became louder and the men began shaking their spears in an aggressive manner.

"Now, I think," said Hassan and Olivia pressed the bone.

An immense siren scream began. It hurt Olivia's ears and both she and Hassan put their hands up to protect their hearing. The effect on the others was immediate and profound. They turned and ran, emitting howls of terror and vanished into the trees.

The awful sound stopped.

"That'll provide some interesting stories over the camp fire," said Hassan. "Let's get home, time for a drink."

Chapter Seventeen – A Second Invasion, 2038

"Goddamn!" said Ben, irritation and worry showing in his face. "They're back again." He had been sitting quietly in the lounge of the Foundation office when he suddenly jerked in shock.

"Who's back?" said Avram. He and Penny stared at him from the coffee table where they were sitting in relaxed mode discussing the next apprenticeship training assignments.

"The extra-galactic invaders," said Ben. "The same species that invaded before and caused such damage before the ship cauterised them."

"And you just heard that?" asked Penny. "How?"

"The same technology that transfers a consciousness across space. They can send me a short message in the same way. Anything longer, I use the communicator."

"And what did you hear?" Avram looked fascinated.

"Another ship of the same species that we tackled before has landed on a lightly-populated world that we've had under observation for a few decades. They're behaving in the same way as the last mob did."

"Can we do anything about it?" asked Penny. "I didn't like the way the last episode turned out."

"But it might be our only available action," said Ben. "You two are still the most advanced in that emotional control ability, could you face trying it again?"

Both Penny and Avram were quiet for a few moments. Finally, Avram spoke.

"We must," he said. "But there's something we should try when we get in the area."

"I know what he's thinking," said Penny. "And he's right."

"Then let's go," said Ben.

* * *

"Similar sort of world to the last crisis," murmured Penny as they looked down on the small, green planet.

"But very pretty," said Ben. "It's a smaller world than Earth, but the potential for life is great. Greater core density means gravity is just a little higher than Earth's, but high oxygen content is resulting in quick intelligence growth. We have high hopes for the humanoid life form here to develop rapidly."

"Where are they now?" asked Avram.

"Proto-human," said Ben. "Maybe a hundred thousand years from becoming something like Neanderthal man, if that's the direction their development takes. Let's take the orbit lower and see if there are any signs of habitation."

He didn't speak, but the ship began a smooth descent until it was about ten kilometres above the surface. Physical features became more obvious from this altitude and they began to make out forests, lakes and mountains.

"What's that?" Penny interrupted the silence of the group inspection and pointed at a dark patch in the middle of greenery.

Without any obvious instruction from Ben, the ship stopped its horizontal movement and began to descend towards the area in question. A few minutes later, it landed at the edge and the external door opened, allowing in a light breeze of beautifully fresh air. The three occupants stood by the doorway and stared out.

"It's been burned," said Avram.

"I think I can see bodies," said Penny and pointed.

"We'd better check," said Ben and began walking down the ramp. "Your shields are operating," he said, looking back at the other two and they followed him until all three were on the ground.

"Gravity just a little higher than home," said Penny. "This grass is luxurious, those trees look healthy and the air is lovely. This would make a perfect colony for humans one day."

"Not a chance," said Ben. "It's occupied by intelligent life. That's why we're here, because somebody wants to colonise it."

They stopped at the awful sight of some tiny bodies, half burned amid the ashes of tree branches.

"Looks like they had developed enough to build some sort of shelter from branches," said Avram. "But that doesn't look like any form of bush fire or grass fire. It's too localised."

"It's weaponry," said Ben. "They've been slaughtered. Look, several other bodies in the area."

For a few moments, they examined the area and counted thirty tiny victims of a deliberate mass murder.

"Let's get out of here," said Penny, tears running down her face. "Avram and I need to put a plan into action."

* * *

The three sat in the lounge room of the ship, their faces pale from the evidence of the slaughter they had seen.

"The last time we tried to intervene, we failed," said Avram. "Then it seemed the ship took over and cauterised the world of the alien invaders. You may remember that we discussed the possible causes of that."

"And I said I'd experienced something nudging me, pushing that emotional control ability to a new level," said Penny. "Avram got it, too."

"And we thought maybe the galaxy had developed some form of sentience," said Ben. "I know what you're thinking, but surely, something as ancient, still primitive and as massive as a galactic intelligence would operate at speeds far too slow to communicate with us?"

"Almost certainly," said Penny. "But what if it's still too under-developed for conscious communication but can react to external stimuli without conscious thought?"

"I suspect that is what happened last time," said Avram. "We're never going to have intellectual chats with this thing in real time, if we ever can actually transmit a message, it could take centuries for it to receive, understand and respond, but if we can call for help loudly enough, something may happen."

Penny and Avram sat comfortably in armchairs in complete silence. Ben had left them and was working elsewhere.

Avram began by trying to send out receptive waves from his mind. He was in almost a hypnotic state as he expanded his consciousness out from the ship in orbit round the planet, to the blackness of the space outside, trying to grasp the enormous void, hundreds and thousands of lightyears in all directions. He developed a sense of great peacefulness, looking at the universe from almost a godlike point of view, sensing comets in orbits round different suns, the radiation flying from massive bodies of heat, the gravity waves from black holes.

With an almost audible click, he sensed Penny's presence within his own mind.

"Is this telepathy?" he asked silently and wordlessly, the question taking just a fraction of a second, more a concept than a sentence.

"I think so," she replied in the same way. "It's beautiful."

"We need to start asking for help," he said.

Avram kept trying to expand his awareness further out, further yet and suddenly...

His tank swerved under him in the loose sand, and he bumped his shoulders painfully against the rim. The multi-damned sons of syphilitic jackals had struck across the Suez on the holiest of holidays, and their cousins, the offspring of diseased bitches and pox-infested camels had followed the example on the Golan Heights. Israel had reeled, punch-drunk, and the enemy slime was flowing towards the borders like filth from an overrunning sewer. But the army and air force had gathered fast and were starting to hit back with fury. The Egyptian bastards were running back to Suez, leaving their boots behind them, their tanks were like ducks in a shooting gallery... Shamah Yisrael, Adonai Elahaynoo, Adonai Erhad...

"What the hell was that?" Penny's shocked, silent voice shook him from the astounding memory that had exploded into his mind.

"I don't know," he said, his body trembling like somebody who had just escaped violent death. "It was just something I saw, almost as if it was my own memory. I think there are more..."

Patience, only patience, that's all it takes, the child will learn, just be patient. For the tenth day in a row of many months of such rows, we start again, I show him the letters. Just one small child of seven years in a class of only six, in a school of only eighteen pupils in a small country town somewhere in outback Australia. The country is fighting bush fires everywhere, the long drought is impoverishing almost everybody in this and every other small town but all I can do here is try and get one small boy to see what joy there can be in words... Once more boy, this is an 'a,' this is a 'b'... if you see these letters together, they make a word, say it boy, try it, see the word, how it forms. Today he looks at me and smiles, looks back at the page and takes a deep breath. He's not staring without comprehension, he's... Dear God, he's reading! He sees it, he reads the whole line and a grin of pure triumph spreads across his small face. Napoleon may have conquered Europe, Anthony won Egypt, Alexander may have taken the world, but nothing compares to this moment of total, utter joy as my pupil takes his first, staggering step into the world of books...

"I saw that!" Penny's silent voice echoed in his mind. "I'm sure that was the memory of somebody else, somebody who has died and is now part of this galactic entity. Somehow we just got her memory. How is this happening?"

"I think we're getting somewhere," Avram said then lost himself as he (or was it Penny?) intercepted a new memory from some unknown person.

She wasn't nervous. There was no longer time to be nervous. For the first time the seat on her right was empty, she was on her own, the propeller was spinning and she had to get to the runway. There was nothing in her mind now, nothing but the fact of taking an aeroplane away from the flying club, to the runway and getting airborne.

"Belmont Tower, Quebec Juliet Quebec ready to taxi," she said, not even feeling proud that she showed no nerves, her voice was clear and confident, professional.

"QJQ, Belmont Tower, take Alpha, Charlie to Runway Two Four and hold," said the calm voice in her earphones.

Carefully, she released the brake, allowed the idling engine to pull her along the surface of the apron, to the turnoff indicated and soon after she stopped a few metres from the runway. It was only a few seconds later that the calm voice spoke again.

"QJQ, clear for takeoff, winds from 250, fifteen knots."

She opened the throttle a fraction, eased onto the runway, still not nervous, turned to look straight along the seemingly endless distance, opened the throttle accelerated, lifted into the air and climbed away.

"My God, I'm solo!" she sang loudly, laughed with delight and then resumed her intense concentration...

"Who got that one?" said Penny. "You or me?"

"No difference," said Avram. "Something else is happening."

He began to feel a presence. It was huge, warm, loving, almost how a baby must feel when held in its mother's arms.

He and Penny were the same mind now he knew, and they were both sensing the presence of this new entity.

Together, they began sending a signal that they were afraid, that they needed strength to combat an external danger, one that would kill without thought, they had to modify that anger and hatred, they needed help.

They felt the strength flow into their bodies, their minds changed as something affected them and exhilaration flooded into their bodies.

Slowly they separated, resumed their individual selves, opened their eyes and looked at each other.

"We can do it now," said Penny. "Let's get Ben."

Just like the first time, the ship landed a short distance

from the alien ship. Just like before, the three of them walked outside and stood quietly on the soft green grass and watched as an armed squad of soldiers left their ship and advanced on them.

Just as before, Avram and Penny reached out and read the emotions flooding from the alien minds, raw fear, murderous anger, bright red and jagged, like the teeth of a huge saw, crimson with blood.

Penny addressed the jagged fear, smoothed out the lethal teeth, turned the bright red edges of fear into gentle green waves of acceptance and within a few moments, the anger and murderous intensity on the faces of the troops had faded.

"Who are you and what are you doing here?" asked the troop leader. Even through the translation devices, the tones seemed friendly, just curious, not threatening.

"We come from a world far from here," said Ben. "We've come to visit and see if there is anything we can do to help you settle."

"We must inform our authorities about this," said the soldier.

"Of course," said Ben. "Where are they?"

"On the southern tip of this continent."

"Then we will visit them with you and talk about future developments," said Ben.

This time, there was no violent reaction from the military leaders of the invasion force. Penny and Avram smoothed the emotional stresses of the leadership even before they had entered the building and within minutes, Ben had extracted an agreement from the leaders that there would be no further conflicts. In return, the aliens would settle another continent and develop a technologically-advanced culture that would one day assist the indigenous life form to grow.

"We'll need to keep an eye on them," said Ben as they entered their own ship. "Maybe you'll need to return here, if not you, some of your equally-skilled colleagues as they develop in future years, but eventually, the culture of peaceful co-existence will become the standard. This is a whole new chapter in the mentorship story."

"I cannot believe that we talked to the galaxy," said Penny, the enormity of the events of the last few hours beginning to show in the faces of both young people.

"And that's another new development," said Ben. "I cannot begin to imagine the implications of all this."

Chapter Eighteen - The Galactic Mentor Council - June 2040

"You have progressed well," said Ben. "You two have only been in training for seven years now, and your development has been impressive."

"The last time Kennedy gave us any praise, he sent us off on a field trip," said Olivia. "Can we expect something similar from you this time?"

"Not exactly," said Ben. "This is a critical moment."

"Critical for whom?" asked Gernardy. "Us, or the whole programme?"

"Those and the entire future of Humanity's development as potential mentors."

Olivia and Gernardy looked briefly at each other.

"That sounds serious," said Olivia.

"It is. I am going to take you to meet the Council. You will represent the entire human race."

"Council?" Gernardy looked confused. "What Council?"

"This is where you get to learn something unexpected," said Ben. "As I told Garry and the other senior members of the Foundation some time ago, I report to a Council of very influential people of my home planet and that Council directs policies for all our mentors in the galaxy. We term it the Mentor Management Council. But here's the thing. We are just one of five galaxies with similar operations."

"Five!" Gernardy and Olivia let out the same gasp of shock together.

"You mean there are four other galaxies with Mentors doing the same stuff you do?" Gernardy said.

"There are," said Ben. "Each has its own Management Committee that dictates policy. But it meets very rarely, I get my instructions communicated to me and I may only meet them every decade of so. But the others also contain intelligent life sufficiently advanced to need their own mentors to guide the less developed species."

"And this is who we are going to meet?" asked Olivia. Her face reflected a mix of excitement and concern."

"No," said Ben. "There's another council, this time composed of the lead mentors of each galaxy. It's known as the Galactic Mentor Council."

"And this Council meets?" Gernardy seemed in between astonishment and amusement. "They travel between galaxies and sit around a conference table? How often do they do this?"

"Yes, no, no and every few years," said Ben, smiling at the reaction.

"Please explain."

"Yes, the Council meets, no they do not travel between galaxies, no, they don't sit around a conference table and they meet infrequently when something needs debate."

"That still needs explanation," said Olivia.

"Until we met that race of pirates that the Ship destroyed as an infestation, we believed that travel between galaxies was impossible," said Ben. "That will need investigation now. However, although physical transport still seems impossible, because the hyperspace technology we use to travel within the galaxy does not function between galaxies, the technology of transmitting consciousness to other bodies is not limited by physical distance. In the same application, we can transmit a holographic image infinite distance without a time lapse and that is how the Council has met the last few centuries."

"So what could they possibly talk about?" Olivia looked more amused than shocked or confused.

"Mainly to compare notes on progress, any problems encountered that might cause revisions in the various programs and anything else that might occur. But they also like to see the potential Mentors in the other galaxies and this will be the main point of your presentation to them."

"And you want us to represent Humanity to this extraordinary group? Ben, that's one hell of a responsibility. Don't you have anyone else more experienced and qualified? What if they reject us?"

"They can't. Each Galactic Mentor race has complete control of their process and the decision. Consider this a courtesy call merely for them to see progress and what sorts of species are being considered for the vital role. We could have called on Penny and Avram, but we decided you needed the experience and exposure to the Galactic bureaucracy arrangements. Anyway, they're busy having a second child!"

"And when is this meeting going to happen?" asked Gernardy.

"In about an hour. Just time for me to give you some idea of what it will be like.

* * *

Ben, Olivia and Gernardy sat comfortably in armchairs in the holodeck room.

While they did not appear to be at a conference table, eight other images were in front of them, each seated in a chair of some sort in a semi-circle. All looked like normal human beings, no alien appearance at all.

"There are two Mentors from each of the other galaxies. They are the most senior Mentors for their galaxy, they manage all the other Mentors on various planets. They have all used human appearance for this meeting," murmured Ben. "That's done by the transmission equipment, the image presented is an option. And all of them will appear to be speaking English, just as your words will be translated into each of the members' languages."

"Clever technology," said Gernardy.

"Members of the Mentor Council, I greet you," said Ben. "I am of the Mentor species for this galaxy, I can be addressed as Ben. The two people being presented to you are members of the human species, one of the three now being considered to replace mine sometime in the future. The female is called Olivia. Olivia, raise your hand."

He paused while Olivia did as asked.

"The male is called Gernardy."

Gernardy waved a tentative hand in the direction of the images before them.

"I invite your questions, Council members. Is one of you designated Chairman today?"

A middle-aged, balding man on the right side of the semi-circle raised his hand.

"That is my honour, Ben. And may I start by saying welcome to all of you. This is the first meeting in over four of my planet's years, some ten Earth years. And welcome to Olivia and Gernardy. Could one of you tell us how long you have been in training?"

Olivia and Gernardy looked at each other for a second and a silent agreement was reached.

"Personally, I have been in training for seven Earth years," she said. "Humans have been entering the program for that long and at present, there are some sixty of us at various stages of the apprenticeship."

"I would like to know just how this immature, conflicted species can possibly claim to be under consideration as Mentors," broke in a woman opposite the chairman. She was thin, dark, with long brown hair that went down below her shoulders. Her face was without expression.

"We have been sending you reports on this matter for the last hundred years," said Ben. "Have your people not been reading them?"

"Reports? What reports?" the woman said.

Ben exchanged looks with Olivia and Gernardy and then stared back at the woman.

"Every one of you here has your replacements in training," he said. "All of us agreed to send reports every few years about the progress and indications of the likely selection. I have read all the ones submitted by the council members here but there is one obvious omission and that is yours. No report has been received from your galaxy for many years. Why is that?"

"Why should we bother with the goings on of inferior species in remote galaxies?" The woman's face still showed no expression.

"Inferior species?" said Ben. "Is this how you see us?"

The woman said nothing.

"We have all noticed also that there have been two occurrences of a species travelling between galaxies, both involving an invasion from your galaxy of a solar system in mine," Ben continued. "We have all so far resisted attempts at inter-galactic travel, having found that hyperspace routes between galaxies are quite unpredictable and unsafe. So, were these invasions deliberate attempts aimed at a specific galaxy? If so, we would all like to be informed of the technology."

For the first time, the woman showed expression. Her smile was cold and contemptuous.

"We just sent a number of ships out to see where they would end up. We had no idea that any would reach your galaxy. What happened to them?"

"The first crew behaved like pirates, enslaving the population of an under-developed world. When we found them, my ship cauterised what it said was an infection."

"Your *ship* did?" the exclamation came from a young man in the middle of the group. "How did the ship make such a decision?"

"This confuses us still," replied Ben. "My interrogation of the computer indicated some unknown source of the order."

A stir of interest ran through the group.

"One more piece of supportive evidence for a developing theory," said the young man. "All of us have seen small but positive signs indicating a growth of some form of sentience within the galaxy. We don't know if this sentience is a presence of its own or possibly that of the galaxy itself."

Ben took a deep breath. "Either way, that would explain some of the events we have seen in recent years. It could certainly explain why the ship reacted as it did."

"You said there had been two such invasions," said the Chairman. "What happened with the second one?"

"We persuaded them to behave like good little children and become good citizens," said Ben.

"Don't be stupid," snapped the woman. "Nobody could do that."

"That's all I'm telling you," said Ben.

The woman looked furious but said nothing.

"I think this is a subject for later debate," said the Chairman. "We must remember that we are here to meet the two humans who represent the potential Mentors for your galaxy. So let me ask you, what do you believe makes your claim to be possible Mentors a valid one?"

Olivia looked at Ben who nodded.

"In our discussions with Ben and his predecessors, we believe there are two main factors," said Olivia. "The first is the fact of our high developments in the Arts. Three times, humans have developed all artistic forms to exceptionally high levels after long periods of relative darkness. Ben tells us that this is unique among the contender species and it is a vital requirement for mentorship."

She sat back and touched Gernardy's arm.

"But Humankind is now showing additional talents which are also unique and more dramatically so than the Arts developments," Gernardy said. "Quite early on in our development, once we discovered the ability to read our DNA and look back through time, many of us developed telekinesis skills. For some years, we used this for further developments in the arts and sciences, but we are thinking now that telekinesis is merely a side effect of an even more critical skill, so far shown in only a tiny number of people."

He realised he had the full attention of the Council.

"A few of us have found an ability to modify the emotions of other people," he continued. "We believe that, like telekinesis, more and more humans will discover this ability and develop it into a much stronger force. If this is true, I cannot think of a better talent for Mentors to have. This development has not been included in previous reports until we were certain that it was not just a temporary mutation."

The council seemed shaken.

"This is a terrible and dangerous talent," said the dark woman. "This is not something to be allowed to develop. I recommend that humans be declared a severe danger and be wiped out."

The Chairman rose to his feet.

"I see a worse danger," he said. "You, madam, represent a hostile, dangerous influence. Your galaxy is the only one to have ignored all the developments in the rest of us and it is your galaxy that has sent out invading, war-like forces. If there is sentience within our galaxies, it looks probable that yours is not a healthy one. We may just have to quarantine you."

The woman didn't reply, but simply vanished as she broke the holographic connection, as did her associate who had not spoken.

The Chairman resumed his seat.

"It worries me and baffles me," said Ben. "How could such a species become Mentors if they all display that level of intolerance and xenophobia?"

The Chairman looked down at his hands. "I believe we may have problems in that region," he said. "They could not have been appointed had they always displayed such characteristics. They have only become this way in the last two hundred years. However, let us resume learning about these humans and how they might perform, should they eventually become the Mentors for their galaxy."

Chapter Nineteen – A Change in Plans - 2041

Olivia still had not got used to being transferred to an alien body on a planet many light years from home. This was her fifth assignment as an apprentice and although she had watched many holographic images of the world to which she was travelling and the species she would join, nerves still caused her hands to sweat and her breathing to accelerate a little as she entered the transfer room. But she calmed herself by thinking of the warm welcome she would receive from the journeymen Mentors who would greet her as she awoke in the new body and the excitement of dealing with an alien race.

It was her first solo mission and she found she rather missed Gernardy.

"It only needs one," the controller had said back on Earth. "You and Gernardy have both shown exceptional abilities as apprentices, so we decided to give you a job with a couple of more experienced journeymen but without your partner. I'm sure you'll be just fine."

She opened her eyes and looked around her. She was in a comfortable-furnished room, there were flowers in vases at various points and two individuals were seated across from the bed on which she lay. As she knew to expect, they were immensely tall, nearly three metres by human measurements, as thin as broom handles and tiny faces set atop necks the length of her forearm.

Looking down at herself, she saw the same shape, a physical shape that had developed in this race living on a world where gravity was slightly less than on Earth's moon.

Slowly, she eased herself upright and sat on the edge of the bed.

"Careful," said one of the others. "Getting accustomed to such low gravity takes a while." No smile accompanied the words, unusual in this situation where the more senior journeymen were always friendly and supportive to the less-experienced humans.

Not thinking too much about the issue, Olivia concentrated on getting to her feet and balancing herself on the long, narrow feet. Standard apprentice practice was to move around within a safe space for a few hours before venturing outside, so she carefully moved to the window and looked out.

As she had expected, having seen the sights of this community on the holodeck back on Earth, there were few buildings, widely spaced apart and all of them about the height of a three or four floor building on Earth and no wider than a little over a metre. But she knew that no building on this planet exceeded two storeys to allow for the elongated, thin shapes of the inhabitants.

"It's never the same, seeing a new planet for real, compared to the holodeck views we get in training," she said, turning with a smile to her two colleagues. Astonished, she saw that one had left and the other was standing, looking as if he (and she somehow know it was a male) was also ready to leave.

"If you will excuse us," he said, "we have some personal matters from home to attend to. Will you be all right for a few hours?"

"Well... yes," she said in some doubt. "How long will you be?"

"Perhaps two hours," he said. "There is food and drink in that cabinet."

Without another word, he opened the door and left.

"Good grief!" muttered Olivia. "This has never happened before. What's got into those two? They seemed really uncomfortable with me."

"This is a small town," said the one who had spoken last to her. "The population is about 35,000 and we are here because there have been some disturbances over the last few years."

Olivia had learned that his name was Rang-hi Pak.

"Our advisors have asked us to see if we can detect the cause of these disturbances and identify any way of reducing the stress," said the second man. Again, Olivia had been able to sense that he was also male. Pak had given his name as Spen-ju Sem. This was the first time he had spoken and so far, as they walked around the town, he had kept further away from her than had Pak.

Almost as if they are shy of me for some reason, she thought to herself. *What's going on?*

"And have you found any causes yet?" she asked.

"Not yet," Pak replied.

They really are shy of me, thought Olivia. *This is weird, they're supposed to be my trainers and they're treating me as if I was their boss. I wonder if this new talent of mine can help.*

Two years earlier in her apprenticeship, Olivia had been visiting her family in Renmark and they had gone to the local school to pick up her sister's child, a six-year old called Robert Quinn. As they approached the school yard, a small disturbance broke out. A group of kids were shouting abuse at one little girl who looked terrified, huddled into a corner of the fence.

Before anyone else could get there, Olivia ran to the group. With a shock, she realised that she could sense anger and hatred in the bullies, directed at the little girl and her fear was quite palpable in Olivia's mind. Still not understanding what was going on, she concentrated on the bullies and saw their emotions as red and black, jagged shapes, vibrating like electric saws. She also saw some self-loathing in that jumble of emotions. Not at all sure of what she was doing or how she was doing it, she put all her mind into that ugly mess of rage, smoothed out the cutting edges, slowed down the vibrations, turned down the colours into a smoother, dark yellow shade.

Hardly noticing that the bullies had quietened down and were standing silently, looking confused and ashamed, Olivia turned her attention to the little girl. She saw in her mind some similar shapes displaying anger, but also much fear and shame. Again, she concentrated on the mass of painful shapes and colours, smoothed them out and saw the girl stand up confidently, stare back at the bullies and laugh at them.

"What the hell..." said Allison, Olivia's sister, just as a teacher ran out of the school building.

"What's going on?" demanded the woman.

"Whatever it was, it seems to have settled down," said Olivia. She watched as the bullies all moved away and headed out of the school yard.

The teacher advanced on the little girl. "Are you okay, Sophie?"

"Yes, miss," was the answer. Sophie looked up at the teacher's worried face and smiled. "They won't do that again."

She smiled at Olivia and then ran out of the yard.

"That's curious," said the teacher. "Sophie has always been a shy child, very under-confident because of her family's poverty, the worn clothes she wears and the basic food she brings for lunch. Some of the kids are real brutes and they bully her badly."

"Somehow, I doubt they'll do it again," said Olivia, highly confused by what had happened yet aware that she had made something powerful occur.

"Okay, where's young Robert Quinn?" said Olivia. "Ah, there! Let's go home!"

Olivia sent her mind out to the two aliens with her. Without surprise, she found herself seeing their emotions.

I was right, they are shy, she thought. But it's more than that. They feel inferior, junior and there's a touch of resentment. It really is as if they see me as their teacher, their boss, somehow superior, our roles have been reversed. What the hell is going on?

Unable to solve this problem, she concentrated on the task of becoming familiar with the alien environment and its people. She had been given the standard forced education in the language before leaving Earth, so had no difficulty in listening to conversations, reading signs and generally observing.

But something was not quite right. Several times, she and her two colleagues were in conversation with some of the local people, usually just simple social discussions on the weather or the price of food, even occasionally on local politics. Normal practice for an apprentice was to stay away from major involvement, let the journeymen handle the conversation and so minimise the risk of appearing ignorant or strange. But several times, she found the other two standing back, almost trying to force Olivia into the leadership of the discussion.

As evening descended and they returned to their residence, Olivia finally found the courage to question the other two.

"Pak, Sem," she said as they laid out the food from the refrigerator. "You are supposed to be training me, you're the far more experienced residents on this planet, my role is to follow you and learn from you. And yet, today you seem shy, uncertain, you have forced me to take the lead in some of the contacts we have had. Can you explain this, because it has confused me?"

She watched as the two went quiet and appeared uncomfortable. Again, she reached out and touched their minds and once again saw stress, shyness, a sense of inferiority.

"It is difficult," Pak finally said. "We understand our respective roles, we know that we have been here for some years and you are here only for the first time. And yet something, we don't know what, is telling us that you are the leader, you have abilities we don't have and that perhaps the role of apprentice is not why you are here."

Shocked, Olivia pulled her mind back.

"*Something* is telling you? And you have no idea who or what?"

"That is correct," said Pak.

Baffled, Olivia had nothing to say. In silence, they finished their meal and retired to sleep.

The next day brought on a crisis.

Walking through the town in the morning, they saw a group of the local residents, perhaps twenty of them conducting a meeting. Looking at them, Olivia saw that they were physically a little different from the others she had seen so far. They were significantly shorter and had a considerable growth of hair atop their small heads, unlike the others.

"These are Dunkarsi," said Pak. He seemed to have taken over all communications with Olivia. Sem had retreated into silence in her presence. "They are the residents of the continent almost on the opposite side of the planet. Sometimes, there are racial tensions between the two forms and the Dunkarsi are regarded as inferior by many of the others."

"Racial issues?" asked Olivia. She had found very little information on this problem in her briefings on the planet.

"There are no racial differences," said Pak. "Just physical, but these do seem to have caused some bigotry and conflict."

"How sad," said Olivia. "We're starting to grow out of such nonsense on my world."

"Ours too," said Pak. "But this is still a primitive society. Such issues are common on less developed worlds."

They resumed their walk around the town, occasionally talking to locals, buying some foodstuffs and observing a peaceful community.

It didn't last. A roar of many people erupted from a block or two away and people began running toward the sound, followed by Olivia and her colleagues.

The sight they saw was appalling. A mob had attacked the small Dunkarsi group and were beating them with sticks. Horrified, Olivia knew she had to try the skill she had discovered so recently. She extended her mind, saw the red, angry, raw knives of the rage in the mob, like raging forest fire and began trying to influence it. Losing all sense of self, she enveloped the entire mass of hatred, began to smooth out the sharp edges, dull down the raw anger and slowly began to take control.

The beatings stopped, the attackers retreated from the victims, dropped their weapons and started to look around, expressions of bewilderment on the faces.

"What were we doing?" Olivia heard several people say. Some of them began to touch the Dunkarsi people, some tenderness being shown, other appeared with medical equipment and began cleaning up the wounds. In a short while, the crowd had dispersed and Olivia concentrated on the Dunkarsi. She sensed the fear and bewilderment in their minds and slowly eased the emotions until full calm had returned.

"That was your doing," said Pak, a statement not a question.

Olivia began to withdraw her mind from the others. She was exhausted but also elated. She knew Pak was right, she had caused this massive emotional shift in the mob and averted a tragedy. This was a far more dangerous crisis than the one she had experienced with the schoolchildren two years ago and she was aware that she had developed an extraordinary talent, one that had been demonstrated by a few others in the past but not to the extent she had just shown.

Five days later, she returned to Earth.

"This is curious," said Ben. "Just what is influencing the more advanced journeymen to stand back and give you the leadership is utterly without comprehension. But even more curious, is that two other apprentices have reported similar experiences."

"Did they need to modify some sort of violent behaviour?" asked Olivia.

"They did," said Ben. "And both of them had previously shown the same ability that you have, very much stronger than anyone before."

"It's baffling and a bit scary," said Olivia. "The idea that something is influencing other species is disturbing."

"Indeed it is. I suspect the entire program of apprenticeship development might be changing, but how or why is incomprehensible."

"And my next assignment?"

"Not yet decided," said Ben. "But let me say, you and Gernardy have shown the best performances so far. We'll keep you together for as long as seems necessary and you should be prepared, we'll give you the toughest assignments. You both tested very strongly with that mental ability to modify emotions and we'll watch you with great interest."

"Interesting," said Olivia. "But a bit scary."

"The whole job is that way," said Ben. "Interesting and scary."

Chapter Twenty – New Holidays – March, 2041

"Damn, blast and hell!"

"Granddad, what the hell happened?"

"I bashed my knee on the door post!"

"Granddad, you have to be more careful! You're not a young man anymore and you're not steady on your legs." The young man moved across to the old grandfather, took his elbow to help him across to the armchair but the hand was shaken off with an irritable shrug.

"I may be eighty and I know I've got arthritis in my knees, but I tell you Ken, I'm sick to bloody death of being an invalid! Sod it, I played professional rugby in my earlier years and I bloody well hate being an invalid."

"I've no doubt, but maybe you should be grateful you've reached this age and as rich as bloody Rockefeller. Lots of people don't get either."

The old man looked up at the other, with an angry expression.

"So what's the point of being worth a few billion dollars if I can't enjoy it, eh? I'm stuck in this bloody mansion, my legs hurt, my arms hurt, my hips hurt, *everything* bloody hurts, I can't eat a decent meal anymore. Fuck me dead, I wish I could be young again."

"Granddad, you know that's not possible. Stay there, I'll pour you a scotch and then I have to go out, meeting some friends."

The old man grunted and reached for the entertainment system controller.

"Yeah, I suppose. Pour that scotch and then go ahead. I'll be fine."

Ken looked uncertain but took the car keys from the hook in the hall and left.

"Sometimes, the old bastard is a pain in the arse."

Ken took a gulp from his glass of beer, put it down and stared hard at the bubbles..

"But you can't walk out because you have to make sure you get something in your inheritance." The elegant, almost-beautiful woman across the table from him smiled in understanding. "What's he worth, five billion?"

"Rather more," said Ken. "But I reckon it'll be a few more years before he shuffles off the mortal wotsit and I'll get my reward for being his carer all this time."

"More than five billion, eh?" said the second man sitting next to the woman. "What the hell does he do with all that loot?"

"He's pretty good actually," said Ken. "Lots of money to various charities, arts groups, universities and all that sort of stuff, and I'm certainly never short of cash, but I reckon he'd spend it all to be a young man again if that was possible."

"You think?" The other man looked thoughtful. "Ken, can you set me up to meet the old bastard? I may have something of interest for him."

"I suppose so. But what the hell could you give him that he doesn't have already? He's housebound, in a lot of pain and crabby as hell."

"We might surprise him. Set up the meeting, will you?"

*   *   *

"So what do you think you can sell me that I don't have already?"

"The one thing you so desperately want and nobody else can give you, Mr Symonds."

"You know what, over the years I've seen more smooth salespeople offering me something unique and impossible to get any other way and always at a massive price. The only reason you're here is because Ken asked me to see you. So, alright, tell me what your miracle product is and then get the hell out of my house."

"Your youth, Mr Symonds."

"Hah! My youth? Yeah, right! What is it? Some miracle lotion or potion or pills or something? Fuck me dead, can't you be more original than that?"

"Oh, it's a lot more original than that."

The other man leaned back in his armchair. He was in his thirties, rust-red hair descending into sideburns down to his jaw line and immaculately dressed in a suit with a waistcoat, beautifully polished black shoes, all in a style dating back to the late twentieth century that was making a major comeback in wealthy circles.

"Mr Symonds, let me first tell you that what I will offer you is quite illegal. Should you decide to call the police in at this point, I'll face lengthy interrogation, deep suspicion and probably a long period of police surveillance. If they decide to take a sample of my DNA, it'll reveal an appalling crime and I'll spend the rest of my life in prison."

Symonds stared at him.

"Now you have my interest," he said. "Go on."

"You will no doubt be aware that this world of ours is now in fairly constant communication with intelligent species on other planet, even to the point of visits to other worlds. Some trade routes have opened up and a lot of new and amazing things are being sold."

The old man nodded, his eyes fixed firmly on the speaker.

"What is not well known is that the human race is being trained to be mentors and guides to many of the other species. It is planned that we will take over from a more advanced race that has been playing that role for us for about a hundred thousand years."

"I didn't know that. How come you do?"

"I have a close relative who is in that program. He has not always been discrete."

"Go on."

"At the more advanced stages of training, the apprentices actually spend time working on the world that will come into their care. As most of these species don't look all that much like humans, their appearances have to change."

"This doesn't make sense. First of all, how do our people visit these worlds? There's not a liveable planet within hundreds of light years of here, so there's no way of actually going to one. Second, if I still believe you, how much surgery can be done to a person to make them look like an alien? I think you're bullshitting me."

"Let's take both questions together. There are two ways of visiting other planets. First, the race that is currently our mentors and guides has long had the technology to travel throughout the galaxy in very little time. I understand from my relative that the ships take a couple of hours to get far enough away from the solar system so that the effects of the speed won't be obvious and then the trip to another solar system takes just seconds, regardless of the distance involved. I don't pretend to understand this, but it uses something called hyperspace."

Symonds stared at him. His eyes were bright and seemed to cut through the other man's face to his brain.

"And second," he said.

"Second, is that one doesn't need a spaceship for some purposes. There is also a technology that can transfer a person's consciousness to another body. So for each apprentice, a body is grown from a vat rather than through normal reproductive systems, the consciousness is transferred to that body, with language and culture knowledge also implemented. No surgery required."

"I don't want to become an alien on some far planet. The idea is totally repellent."

"And many apprentices have found that. They have panicked, gone quite mad, totally unable to cope and their training is cancelled immediately."

"So they can be brought back?"

"They can."

"But again, I have no intention of doing anything like that."

"The point, Mr Symonds is that if one can grow an alien body in a vat, one can also grow a human body. That is how our mentors have visited Earth and stayed here for many years."

The silence rang in the room like a gong for over a minute.

"And you can do that?"

"We have spent years obtaining the technology. It's quite illegal but we can do this. We have several bodies growing in vats, some already stored. I could select one of a young man of about twenty years of age, transfer your conscience to it and you would rediscover the joys of your youth again."

"And what happens to the original body? Does it die?"

The other man shook his head.

"No. We will provide the technology to keep the body alive until it dies of natural causes."

"And what happens to the man I have become? Can I keep living a full life in that body?"

"No, Mr Symonds, you cannot attain immortality that way. That was certainly a dream once, but it's impossible. Your consciousness will die when your body dies and the host body will also die."

"This sounds a lot like all those fables of the devil offering eternal youth in exchange for the soul. It all sounds too extreme and not at all safe."

"I'm not Satan, Mr Symonds, our offices are in Sydney, not Hell, there are no flaming swords or eternal fires, no damnation and we can't use your soul, even if you have one. We're just a group that has gained access to some astounding technology and we're able to sell an incredible service."

"And assuming I believe all this, and I'm not certain that I do, how much do you charge for this service?"

"Can you put a price on regaining your youth, Mr Symonds?"

"Try me."

"Fifty million dollars. That's loose change to you."

Symonds stared thoughtfully at the carpet.

"What if I want to try this thing out and prove it to myself? Say, just a short period?"

"The initial set up is expensive, but if you want to try just one day, that will cost you five million."

"Let's do it," said Symonds.

The nameless young man opened his eyes and stared at the ceiling. After a minute or two, he looked around him and saw a nurse sitting against the wall.

"How do you feel?" she asked.

He sat up, feeling energy in his body that he had not experienced for decades. He looked down at his body dressed in shorts and a tee-shirt and saw a flat stomach and muscular legs.

"This is real, then?" he said in wonderment.

"It's real," the nurse said. "You are twenty years old again and perfectly fit and healthy."

He stood up without effort. There was no pain in his joints, no stiffness. He started to walk and almost fell over. The nurse rose rapidly from her seat and steadied him.

"It takes a little while to get accustomed to a new body," she said. "Your dimensions are different, the weight distribution is different, muscles you've forgotten about are back in play. Let's do some exercises."

For fifteen minutes, she led him through simple physical movements, sit-ups, knee bends, toe-touching and others and gradually, he felt more and more sureness in his movements.

"Okay, that will do," the nurse said. "Now, you have until tomorrow morning. There are clothes that fit you in that wardrobe. Here's a wallet, it has a thousand dollars in it, but no credit cards, driver's licence or any other form of identity because you have no identity. It does have this address, however. This body is one we use for a short-term transfer as you have requested. Bring it back in one piece."

"I can go out?"

"Yes, you're free all day so long as you return before dawn. Have fun."

She walked out of the room and the young man opened the wardrobe door.

* * *

For two hours he just walked. He moved briskly through the streets and buildings that surrounded the secret structure where he had woken up, revelling in the deep breathing, the energy and the absence of pain.

He came to a park and accelerated his pace, striding effortlessly along the paths and down to the river. At one point he came across a dog, a beautiful Border Collie and bent down to try and stroke it. He had always related well to both cats and dogs and he expected the friendly reception that had been his normal experience.

But the Collie backed away from him, not in fear but in seeming confusion.

"That's odd," said a woman walking up to him. "She's usually a very friendly old girl."

"And dogs always like me," he replied, looking round at her. She was young, not much older than he was, he thought and felt a surge of longing he had not experienced in years.

"Dogs are psychic," she said and stepped nearer to the Collie, placing her hand on the animal's head as if to calm it down. "Maybe there's something different about you today."

He almost laughed. "Yes, there is," he said. "I'm not quite myself today."

She looked hard at him as if trying to see through his eyes the person inside. "So it seems," she said. "Try and get better." She moved on and the dog followed close at her heels as if needing comfort.

The young man's eyes followed her until she vanished round a bend, remembering the surge of physical longing that had almost engulfed him when he first saw her.

He resumed his brisk walk, thinking about the odd encounter with the dog and then his sudden reaction to the young woman.

"This is bloody amazing," he said aloud. "I think the main thing to do is use these muscles and lungs today."

As he walked along the river, he came up to a boat jetty and saw to his surprise, several ancient old rowing boats lined up. As he looked around, he saw that there was a definite demand, entirely among young couples, several of whom were on the water, all being rowed by the man and the woman sitting in the back enjoying the experience. He turned to the man sitting in a chair with a bag by his side.

"How much for the boats?" he asked.

The man looked up, shaded his eyes from the sun.

"On your own, are you?"

"I just want some exercise. I used to row at college."

"These ain't no racing eights, no sliding seat," the man said with a laugh and stood up. "Ten bucks for half an hour."

A few minutes later, the young man was on the river, thoroughly enjoying the power he was putting into the oars, feeling stomach muscles he hadn't felt in decades and pouring strength into his shoulders and arms. He felt almost like shouting his exhilaration to the world.

After returning to shore, he found a restaurant.

"It's been a bloody boring diet for years," he muttered to himself. "Let's see what I can cope with now." He studied the menu and deliberately selected a meal of sausages, fried potatoes, continental sauerkraut and a dessert of apple crumble. "I couldn't have got through a quarter of this without acid reflux," he said to himself and studied the people around him for a while until the meal came.

He found that he enjoyed it immensely, experiencing tastes that he'd forgotten about in the last couple of decades. He paid cash and left.

The rest of the day he spent simply enjoying the physical health of this new body. He rented a bike and rode round the park several times, driving himself to greater and greater speed, aware of lung power that he'd forgotten.

Some of the other time, he spent sitting on a park bench, watching young women pass, some walking dogs, some running in shorts, others dressed in the style of the day, dresses in materials that had come from the newly-opened trade routes with other civilisations. They reflected the wearer's moods and were immensely popular with the young people especially females. Some of the women made his breath shorten and his heart beat a little faster.

"Now, what about those girls?" he thought as dusk fell. "There's still probably the regular after-work drinks thing. Let's find a bar."

He walked along the streets looking for the commercial district and soon found it. Some of the buildings were disgorging lines of workers and he followed one group of girls to a bar, took a seat at the counter and watched the social gatherings.

"On your own?" said a female voice behind him.

He turned and saw a beautiful young woman with deep red-brown hair down her back and her body nicely displayed in a figure-hugging dress that glowed with a light blue tint and shifted between that and a yellow gleam.

He swallowed, staring at her, unable to speak, feeling a shyness he had not felt since childhood.

"Er..." he said and tried to swallow. He had no idea how to respond, the beautiful image before him had almost wiped out his mind.

"Oh dear," she said with a look of irritation and walked away.

"Christ alive," he muttered and drank some of the scotch he had ordered when he had sat down. "That's going to need work."

An hour later, he returned to the building he had left that morning, annoyed at his social weakness but the decision made to return on a more permanent basis.

* * *

The next few weeks were busy in the Symonds household. The word was put out that the patriarch, Jeffrey William Symonds, internationally known financier and philanthropist had suffered a stroke and would be confined to his home. A series of nurses were hired to take care of the comatose and unconscious man in a specially prepared and equipped hospital ward in the Symonds Mansion.

Paperwork was prepared that gave the grandson, Kenneth William Symonds full authority over the finances and privately, Ken was forcefully advised that he should provide a home, financial support and anything else required by a twenty-one year old man named Jeffrey Allenby. Much secretive work was done by people skilled in such matters to create the persona of Jeffrey Allenby, a birth certificate being the critical one and a record of education at schools in Sydney and Melbourne.

And then one day, the old man was laid out on his bed, some equipment was attached to his head and a few minutes later, a young man called Jeffrey Allenby came to full consciousness in a secret building in the western suburbs of Sydney, given various files, a wallet with generous amounts of cash, full identification documents and credit cards and allowed to leave.

Jeffrey ran the five kilometres to the railway station.

Chapter Twenty-One – The End and The Beginning - November, 2042

"Has anyone seen Ben?" asked Penny.

"Not for a week," said Garry, reclining at ease in an armchair in the Foundation lounge.

"He didn't say anything to you before leaving?"

"Not a peep, but he almost never does. I think when he gets the call home by the Mentor Council, he snaps over there immediately."

"Hmm," said Penny. "And when he gets back, there's usually some significant news."

"Indeed," said Garry. He got to his feet with a sudden burst of nervous energy and began strolling round the walls of the lounge that were covered with pictures of past individuals who had played parts in the growth of the Petrova Foundation over the last few decades. He paused before the portrait of Karen Petrova. "I wonder if she could ever have dreamed of just how much she and Hector would change the world," he said.

"I doubt even that genius could have foreseen it," said Avram. "And not just our world but the others where our apprentices have been working for the last few years."

Garry kept walking.

"This one of Ben is interesting," he said. "This was done soon after the Foundation was set up here about twenty-five years ago and he looks exactly like he does now."

"Not surprising," said Mary. "Effectively he is the same man. The Mentor sent to Earth over the last couple of centuries has always used the same name and the body grown in the vat for him. It's provided good continuity for us."

"He's never told us anything about life on his home world and he's never said anything about who the various entities have been who have worked with us."

"If we get nominated to be the Mentor race, I hope we decide to follow the same path," said Garry. "It's made a hugely difficult task a lot easier."

There was a tap on the door and a young man walked in carrying a sheet of paper.

"Good morning, everyone," he said and placed the sheet on the coffee table before Penny. "Latest figures on the apprenticeship program."

"Thanks, John," she said and picked up the paper. "Interesting," she murmured after a few moments."

"Tell me," said Garry and resumed his seat.

"We have thirty-five apprentices on other worlds," said Penny. "They bring the total of apprentices who have passed through our program or are still in it to fifty-three. Of those, two have graduated to Journeyman standard and seven have died in accidents, mostly on alien planets since they first started."

"The deaths were tragic," said Garry. "Sometimes I miss the days when this Foundation was leading the world in inter-planetary communications and advising nations on how to handle the changes. Now we're a school for apprentices, almost like a military academy where going into harm's way is an expected part of the job."

"I agree," said Penny. "But this is interesting. All those out on training assignments have reported the same experience that Olivia was the first to have a few years ago. The journeymen who were supposed to be guiding and training them have in every case taken a back seat to them as if they were the boss and the journeymen were the juniors."

"This is getting weird," said Garry and was about to ask more but the door opened.

"Ben!" exclaimed Penny. "Welcome home."

"Thank you," replied Ben. He walked to the coffee machine, poured a mug and joined the others at the coffee table.

"Ben, what's wrong," asked Avram. "You look worried. Has it been a difficult trip home?"

"I'm glad you're both here," said Ben. "What I have to tell you must be told straight to the Foundation directors."

"That's us," said Garry. "This sounds worrisome."

Ben sipped at his coffee and looked hard at the tabletop. The fatigue showed in his features and his face was thinner than the others remembered it.

"There has not been a child born on my world for thirty years," he said abruptly.

"Good grief," said Penny. "This is dreadful. Have you been able to find a reason for this?"

"We have, but it's not a medical one."

"Then what?" asked Penny. "How does a whole population of billions suddenly stop having children?"

"It's part of something bigger," said Ben.

"Ben, what could possibly be bigger than this?" said Garry.

"Several connected factors have given us the answer," said Ben. "Remember when I first went out with Avram and Penny to find the rogue planet inhabitants who had taken over another world?"

"How could we forget," said Avram. "That was scary as hell."

"Remember how the ship seemed to make a decision to cauterise the planet, but later we realised it had received an instruction from some unknown source?"

"Which we finally decided must be some sentient entity within the galaxy," said Penny.

"Exactly. And it appears that the same force is preventing further births at home."

"But... why?" exclaimed Penny. "What possible reason could any intelligent entity do such a terrible thing?"

"It isn't actually a terrible thing," said Ben with a small smile. "Our records show that this is what happened to the race that was the Mentor species for the galaxy before us. When they died out finally, some records were found indicating that many of them knew what was happening. The entire race was ascending to some new spiritual level."

"And this new spiritual level is joining the galactic intelligence that we have found," said Mary, suddenly understanding. "This is what is happening with you."

"Another factor," continued Ben without answering. "When I came in, you were talking about how your apprentices on other planets seem to be regarded more as supervisors than the journeymen from other species who were supposed to be guiding them."

"How is that related?" asked Garry.

"I'll come back to that," said Ben. "One of the most extraordinary things we have discovered about the human race as we worked with you was the telekinesis capability. No other species in any of the galaxies with which we and the other mentor races have dealt over the millenia has demonstrated any capability remotely like that. But then we discovered that telekinesis was only a side-effect of the real power in humans, that ability to modify emotions."

"Not many of us have that," said Penny.

"No, but a number of you have demonstrated that, especially Olivia and Gernardy who are almost as strong as you, Penny and Avram and we need to investigate how it develops and whether we can help develop it further."

"Of course," said Garry. "By how does this relate to the tragedy affecting your planet?"

"A moment," said Ben, rose to his feet and went back to the coffee machine.

The others looked at each other and understood that Ben needed a few moments to gather himself. They said nothing. A few moments later, Ben returned, sat down and looked at them.

"In my species, we have individuals with a degree of empathic connection with other minds far greater than anything found here. We gathered a few of them together and left them alone to try and establish any form of contact with the galactic intelligence that we think exists."

"And did they?" asked Penny.

"They did. This intelligence is not yet self-aware or coherent, it mostly resembles a baby human who can cry when it needs food or is afraid, chuckle when it is happy and somehow makes its needs known. That is what this massive sentient being at the heart of our galaxy is. Our empaths were able to work out what those needs and wants are."

He paused.

"It is afraid of the rogue galaxy that sent out invader ships to other galaxies. It fears the mental sickness displayed by the dominant species who became the Mentors in that galaxy. It has recognised that the human ability to modify emotions is the single most powerful weapon against that danger, it perceives Humanity as the antidote or even antibiotic against a disease. It needs you to become the force that is one above the mentor role for which we once considered you."

The others stared at him, too shocked to speak.

"This Karen Petrova Foundation must continue its role of training apprentices to go out and assist teams help other species to grow. But now you have a more important and critical role. Now you must work to develop this ability to affect emotions to a far greater level than any human before has shown. And you don't have a lot of time."

"How long?" asked Garry, his face white with shock from what he had heard.

"My race will be gone within a century," said Ben. "You must be ready to take over the leadership by then."

The others again exchanged looks. The shock was still strong in all their faces, but Garry suddenly smiled.

"Then we'd better get started," he said.

Chapter Twenty-Two – A New Mission - 2046

"This is your first serious mission in mentoring and the facilitation of long-term change in a society," said the group leader.

Olivia didn't reply immediately. This was her tenth transfer to an alien body on a remote planet and the experience was still traumatic enough to need some time to recover, though her confidence in becoming fully functional after a transfer increased each time. She looked over at the other bed to see her partner, Gernardy and somehow recognised him, despite the body form. She looked down at herself and saw the same body. Slender, alabaster-white skin, long arms that reached down almost to her knees, but otherwise humanoid. Her hands had six digits and included an opposing thumb, not unlike a human hand.

Carefully, she sat up just as Gernardy did the same and they gave each other a slight wave of acknowledgement.

Despite the intensive cultural and language training they had been given through direct transmission of data to their brains, adjustment was still a major issue. Finally, she looked around the room and saw the other members of the mentor group with which she and Gernardy would share the next few months.

"Think you can stand up now?" The group leader was looking at them both, obviously aware of the requirement for adjustment.

"I think so," said Gernardy and carefully got to his feet, followed by Olivia. Gravity was lower than on Earth, but some of the lightness he felt was probably also due to the slender body shape.

"Tell us what you know," said the leader. "We're not fully aware of what your briefing covered before you left home."

"I know that we are going to work on facilitating some meetings between individuals that have been identified as critical to the growth of maturity," said Olivia.

"We are one of several such groups on the planet with similar missions," said Gernardy. "We're operating in a group of nations in the southern hemisphere that all speak the same language, the one we have been given."

"Good," said the leader. "We have been developing this mission for over a hundred local years, mostly in data gathering."

"We've been told that," said Gernardy. "But can you give us more details?"

"We have learned that several key developments on your own planet occurred because of intervention by groups like ours," said the leader.

"You mean like the many contacts between Petrov and Forbes family members?" said Gernardy.

"Exactly. It was forecast by our systems that eventually this would lead to the DNA discoveries that were essential for Humanity's growth."

"The systems sound fascinating," said Olivia. "We were amused to discover that one of your people gave some ideas about it to one of our greatest scientists and writers and it was developed into a hugely successful fictional series. It was called "Psycho-History.""

"And that's what we have," replied the leader. "We have been building a data base for over a hundred years and now we have a detailed chart of all the cultures, the histories, the languages and everything that makes a civilisation. We can analyse those and identify what is needed for the next step in this planet's growth."

"And how then do you make them happen?" asked Olivia.

"Then we get into much finer detail. We can identify groups of people who could influence other groups and then a further level, individuals who would influence other individuals to act in desired ways."

"And this is something you have done for the mission for which we have been sent?" Olivia seemed amused and intrigued.

"It is. As you have been briefed, this is a society just on the edge of scientific learning and research. A major step would be when they discover the nature of germs, microbes, disinfection and all the other factors that improve health. They have experienced some serious plagues in the last few centuries and now our systems tell us that if they can reach this stage of medical discovery, the population can grow much more successfully."

"And where are you with this project?" asked Gernardy.

"We have identified two individuals, a man and a woman who have both shown high intelligence and curiosity in the topic," said the leader. "All their interests coincide, but they don't know about each other yet. We need to have them meet. It is a bonus that everything suggests they will find each other sexually attractive when they do meet and are likely to work together."

"Sounds like a useful project," said Gernardy. "How do we start?"

* * *

Over the next six months, Gernardy and Olivia fully immersed themselves in the alien society and worked with the rest of the team in setting up connections, influencing organisations to arrange a conference on scientific matters and finally became involved with meeting the two main subjects and nudging them to attend the conference.

Finally, Olivia took on the step of introducing the two people, posing as a teacher at a school in the region.

'We have a problem," said the leader. "Those two should really have got on well, been mutually attracted and enhanced the entire scientific movement into research in the process of germs, infections and then cures. But they were both as hostile as they could be."

"Interesting," said Olivia. "Your predictive software went off the mark a bit there."

"Disappointing and worrying," said the leader. "It's critical that those two ignite the scientific community."

"Then I have an idea," said Olivia. "I'm pretty good at this strange ability we humans seem to have and nobody else does but my friend and colleague here, Gernardy is one of the best. Let's put him to work."

"So they tell me," said Gernardy. "Let me see if I can do something about this."

Gernardy stood quietly in the conference room where the conference attendees had gathered for the final lecture. He identified the two people he would try and bring together and they were standing in opposite corners of the room as if creating the greatest distance between them that they could.

He watched as four of the team, two to each of the subjects gradually manoeuvred them towards the centre of the floor, by engaging them in conversation, introducing them to another attendee until they were no more than three metres apart and could not avoid realising the proximity of the other.

Gernardy pushed out his senses and identified the brain waves of the couple. Both showed jagged edges of anger and resentment levelled at the other.

"So that's the problem," Gernardy said to himself. *"They're both jealous of the reputations and accomplishments of the other!"*

He concentrated first on the young woman. He smoothed out the jagged edges radiating from her mind, eased the harsh red colours to deeper, smoother blues and yellows and saw her anger reduce.

Then he turned his attention to the male, saw the same pattern of angry, sharp-edged waves directed at the woman and again, smoothed them out and changed the colours to milder, more gentle hues. He had no idea how he was doing this, but he had demonstrated superior skills at the process and somehow it worked.

He returned to the woman and concentrated on directing her senses at the man, slipping in waves of affection and understanding. He did the same to the man and then nodded at his colleagues who again gently moved the two together, one of them introducing them to each other as if not knowing that they had already met.

"We met earlier," said the woman.

The man smiled. "And somehow, we got off on the wrong foot," he said.

"We did, I don't know how, but let's start again, shall we," said the woman. "Tell me about the work you've been doing, it sounds a lot like mine."

"And I've heard about your research," said the man. "We should see if we can be more effective together."

* * *

"You were right, those two have really hit it off!" said the leader. "How you two achieved that is beyond me, but it's a massive breakthrough."

Gernardy had re-joined the rest of the team and they were watching the effects of the two proto-scientists as they became increasingly excited by the work they were both on, mixed with the obvious physical chemistry between them.

"Well done, all of you," said the leader. "And special thanks to the human members on their first major mission."

"Thanks," said Gernardy and Olivia nodded.

The process had been fascinating and she had noted what other apprentices had noted, that the more experienced journeymen mentors had frequently deferred to Gernardy and her.

She looked forward to getting home.

Chapter Twenty-Three – New Bodies for Old - November 2046

The doctor sat up, put away her stethoscope and looked at her patient.

"Your heart is still strong, about right for a man of forty-five. But the lungs are failing as a result of inhaling the gas when you were trapped. But the worst part is that your legs will never regain function again. Too much nerve damage. I'm truly sorry, Peter, but you won't walk again and your life expectancy is limited."

"How long?"

"Maybe five years. Perhaps a few months more or less."

The man sat silently as tears welled up and ran down his cheeks.

"So no chance of playing Rugby for England, then?"

The doctor smiled.

"No loss of courage I see."

"It's going to take all I have," the man said.

The doctor sat back and looked thoughtful.

"Peter, there may be an option. It won't extend your life but it could make the remaining years most liveable."

"How's that?"

"Some amazing technology has been developed over the last decade. It's been a state secret all over the world for reasons I can't tell you, but just a few days ago, the United Nations voted to release it for general use."

"What, some form of stem cell recovery? I've heard that people can now regrow some body parts and organs. Is this what you have in mind?"

"I did consider that at first, but now that we've had the complete examination, the damage is so extensive, it would take years of being in an induced coma and I'm not sure even that could fix it."

"So not stem cell regrowth?"

"Rather more dramatic than that. You can have a completely new body."

"What? That's insane, surely?"

"Not any more. Peter, over the last few years, science has been given a technology to grow an actual human body. It functions perfectly well when power is fed into it, but otherwise it has no independent life."

"Good grief, I had no idea."

"It's been well hidden. The real use of this technology is still highly secret, but we can use it for cases such as yours."

"But you said it needs power to be considered alive?"

"That's the other amazing technology. We can transfer your actual consciousness into the new body and that provides the energy for the body to be fully alive."

"Holy shit! Doc, this sounds more like science fiction than medicine."

"Peter, all technological advances have sounded like science fiction when they were first introduced. This is now possible, but there are two caveats."

"Which is?"

"First, your own body has to be kept alive artificially somewhere. The government has been building specialised storage facilities for this because it will need significant infrastructure."

"Sounds bloody expensive."

"It is, but the economic analysis has been interesting. These buildings don't need to be in major cities, nor do they need to be like a hospital. They will be built in remote areas and will not need advanced technologies – just some power to keep the body alive and monitoring through advanced technology. The required room is very little, bodies can be stacked in small spaces."

"Doc, it sounds brutal, but if the consciousness is away in a healthy body, why not let the damaged one die?"

"That's the second caveat. If the original body dies, so does the consciousness in the host body."

"Oh."

"Oh, indeed. The host body can be used again if a new consciousness is transferred to it, but it we have found that the consciousness dies with the original body."

"That's certainly a drawback."

"Actually, I'm grateful that it works this way. If a consciousness could be transferred again and again, we will have some people, those with money or power, able to live pretty well for ever. The rest of us would not be so lucky. I think this fair. You will get your time, but no longer than you would have done. At least this, way, you can live normally."

"I suppose I can see the other side of the economics," said Peter. "If a useless body is stored away somewhere, then the new host can still work, still create, still be a useful member of society without the massive expense they would incur under normal condition."

"That was part of the debate," said the doctor.

"So how do we go about it?"

"New bodies are being grown in increasing numbers and stored until needed. I can enter a specification for a body much like the one you have now."

Peter grinned, the most lively his face had been. "Can you get me one that's a bit taller?"

The doctor laughed. "Can I assume you want be a man again?"

"Good god, is that an option? To be a woman?"

"It is. And there have been quite a few gender changes already."

"No, I think I'll stay as I am, thanks. Just a bit taller."

"I'll see what I can do," she said.

* * *

"We're finally going to have a holiday after all these years," the old man said.

"We've been planning it for some time, but we think we need some advice," said his wife.

The travel agent smiled at them.

"You seem a very nice couple," he said. "Let's see what we can do. My name is Graham."

"Keith and Eva," said the old man.

"So what sort of thing do you have in mind?"

"That's where we need advice. We haven't travelled much in our lives and we don't really know where would be suitable."

"Do you want to go overseas? There are some beautiful places in this world."

"Not sure about that," said Eva. "The only time we left England was a one-day trip to Paris because Keith had always wanted to take the train under the Channel. That was twenty years ago."

"And how was that?"

Keith pulled a face. "I didn't like it. The food was weird and we couldn't speak French. It was fun going up the Eiffel Tower and Eva like seeing the Mona Lisa in the museum, but there was too much walking around."

"And you're a bit older now, so nothing too strenuous, I suppose?"

"Quite right. Eva's got wonky knees and hips from arthritis and I've put on a bit too much weight. Are we making this difficult for you?"

"Oh no, plenty of choices! How about a cruise in the Mediterranean? Lots of sun, warm weather, great food and entertainment and a lot of the people on the ship are your sort of age group."

"That sounds nice," said Keith.

"Ooh, no! Keith dear, I've heard so many stories about people behaving badly on cruise ships, some riots, quite violent and even a couple of cases where disease has broken out. You're not getting me on a cruise ship, no way!"

"Okay, then how some beautiful places like the Australian Barrier Reef? Some people think it's the most beautiful place on Earth and you can just take boat rides around it, on boats with glass bottoms so you can see all the beautiful corals and fish."

"That sounds lovely! What do you think, Keith?"

"It does, but Australia? Graham, how do we get there? It's a hell of a long way."

"You fly of course. There are several routes but normally, you fly over Europe to maybe Hong Kong, or Singapore, or even Dubai and then onto Sydney or Brisbane."

"And how long does that take?"

"About twenty hours of flying time and you could take an overnight break in whichever city you go by."

"Twenty hours in an aeroplane? There's no bloody way we could handle that! Think of all the diseases being blown around. I've heard these planes carry about four hundred people in them."

"Oh dear, I have to agree with my husband! Twenty hours with four hundred people in an enclosed space! We'd never handle that."

The travel agent sat back and looked at them. "I have another option you could think of. It's all very new and quite expensive, though."

"Money's not a problem," said Eva. "We've got nobody to leave our money to and we're quite well off. So what are you thinking about?"

"How would you like to visit another planet?"

"What? How could we visit another planet? And which one?"

"So no doubt you've heard that we have at last found other planets with intelligent beings on them?"

"Oh yes! We've been reading about this for a couple of years."

"Good! Well, we have ways of actually taking you to one of them."

"Good god! But how? Doesn't it take years to travel to another planet? And even then, is the air okay to breathe? Can we eat the local food?"

"That's the great part. You don't go in your own body."

"How do you mean?"

"The technology we've been given lets us put your mind in the body of a being from that planet. You'd actually be one of them, breathe their air, eat their food."

The old people stared at him.

"That sounds incredible! Eva, do you believe this? We could actually go and visit another planet?"

"Keith, I really don't like that at all. That scares me. How do we talk to anybody? And how long does it take?"

"You'd be given the language before you leave. And the transfer is immediate, less than a few seconds."

"I'm really not sure. How about you, Eva."

"Not for me. Sorry, no, that's just too scary for me."

The travel agent nodded in understanding.

"I think you're right. Even young, healthy people have found the experience very stressful. So I've got a better idea."

"What's that?" Sensing something interesting, the old couple leaned forward.

"When you do these transfers to another body, the body has actually been specially grown for that purpose. It's not alive unless there's a mind occupying it. The science was given to us to do that and the governments all over Earth have agreed that there's no ethical or legal reason why we can't do it. The body isn't an actual person, you see. And we've grown them already for visitors from those other planets. So if we can transfer a mind to another planet a few thousand light years away, we can also transfer them to a human body here on Earth."

"Oh my God! I think I see where this going! You could put us into the bodies of younger people? Keith, did you get that?"

"I certainly did. I think that's very exciting! To be young again! How incredible!"

"Like I said, this is expensive. The process is simple enough, though we don't actually understand how it works, but the main issue is keeping your own bodies safe and well. We have specialist facilities for that now, but it means constant care by medical staff in a hospital-like building."

"Eva, this sound perfect!"

"Yes, dear, let's do it. How long can we do this for, Graham?"

"A month is recommended. Can you take that long?'

"Heavens, yes!"

"One more question then. Do you want to go as the man and woman you are now or would you like to exchange sexes?"

They stared at him.

"You mean... you mean I could go as a woman and Eva could be a man?"

"That's exactly what I mean. It's a popular option for couples."

The two old people stared at each other. A tiny smile appeared on Eva's lips.

"I've always wondered..." she said.

"Me too! Let's do it!"

The travel agent reached for the documents he would need.

Chapter Twenty-Four – A Gathering of Earth's Mentors - 2042

"We don't do this very often, but this meeting is indicated now," said Ben.

"I think we are all curious," said the holographic image of a young woman.

Six other holographic images in front of Ben made various sounds of agreement. Physically, these mentors were on six different planets located around the galaxy and the same technology that allowed instantaneous communication across infinite distances for the rare meetings between inter-Galactic Mentor meetings was being used.

"The situation is changing rapidly," said Ben. "It has become critical that we review the developments as they concern the human species here on Earth."

"They do appear to be unique," said a man who appeared to be sitting on Ben's immediate right but was actually fifteen thousand light years away. "My teams haven't met one yet, but I hear occasional comments from other teams elsewhere."

"So far, human apprentices have only been assigned to three different planets," said Ben. "There's no doubt that they have unique abilities. Let me review what has happened since they qualified for the apprenticeship programs about ten Earth years ago. As many of you may know, one extraordinary development soon after humans began studying their DNA and looking back through time, was the appearance of telekinetic abilities in many of them. It was never all that strong, no more than an ability to move small objects very short distances, but the electronics genius who has been involved with this operation from the start developed an enhancer that permitted some significant changes in medicine and the arts."

"But I gather that you developed the same ability, Ben," said a man a few places away.

"It was a shock," agreed Ben, "and I have never been able to understand how I did that. No other individuals of any species among the journeymen on Earth or anywhere else has been able to do the same so far. However, while fascinating and puzzling, it proved to be the relatively unimportant side effect of another, far more powerful ability that a number of humans have developed, that of being able to modify the emotional state of other people."

A stir of interest rippled around the group.

"How effective is it?" asked one of them.

"Extraordinary," said Ben. "One of the humans was able to calm down a mob in one country. She was also able to avert a severe attack on my group when we confronted the invading force from the hostile galaxy of which you have all heard. Another young woman was able to calm down a mob while on assignment on another planet."

"That was my team," said a man on Ben's left. "It was a case of racial intolerance on the planet, a small group of a minority race being attacked. She calmed everything down. It was impressive and bewildering."

"And that's what we need to discuss," said Ben. "But humans are still very new to this business and few of them have so far been assigned to work with your teams among alien races. But what is so obvious is that many of them have special abilities already and we must assume that more of them will develop those talents. In recent years, we have discovered two more of our apprentices a young man and a woman have it already, almost as strong as the original exponent. It would be useful to give them the chance to use them. It doesn't mean only in cases of violence, but when you're working on nudging one or more people into a course of action that has been identified as helping the people move along the path to maturity, I recommend that you give the human apprentices an opportunity to use that unique talent."

"So that's what it is," said another woman in the group. "One of my teams had a couple of human apprentices join them and the others on the team all reported that they felt safe in deferring to them, despite the limited experience they had in working with alien species and in an alien body."

"I'm sure you'll all find the same as more and more humans join your teams," said Ben. "But don't go too far with this. Remember, they are still very inexperienced in working in an alien body in an alien society and not all of them have this mental ability yet. You still have a duty of care, a responsibility to train them. But if the opportunity arises and your apprentice can demonstrate this ability, give them the opportunity."

Nods and sounds of agreement ran around the group.

"And now something else," said Ben. "This is even more astonishing."

The group studied him with interest.

"In some ways, this may also be connected to the human species," continued Ben. "I'll explain how, later. But in recent years we have confirmed what has been suspected for some time, that there appears to be some sort of living entity at the core of the galaxy, relatively close to the black hole which we now know is present in every one of the other four galaxies which are represented in our Mentor Council."

"An entity? What form of entity?" asked one of the group.

"We're not yet sure," said Ben. "We think it may be a form of intelligence, but we really don't know."

"Is any form of communication possible?"

"Not so far," said Ben. "Not in any way we can imagine, but it's possible that if it really is a life form, it could live such a long time that any communication might be simply incompatible. It could be that a single thought could take years to complete and it could not detect thoughts from us at all."

"And how will we study this further?"

"At this point, we have no idea. The only clue we have seen so far is that it is possible that the entity reacted in some way when the alien forces arrived in the galaxy. This might just have been some form of frightened reaction, without conscious thought, but we do not know."

"So it's not likely that we'll learn much more for a long time, possibly centuries," said the man on Ben's right.

"You are most likely correct," said Ben. "Let's leave the topic for now and conduct our review of each other's activities on their planets, what projects you are running, what successes, what failures you have had and what problems you have encountered."

Chapter Twenty-Five – The Lives of the Children - 2047

"The kid has graduated high school," announced Bill Askins. He sat back in the armchair of Garry's office, radiating smiles and pride.

Garry and Alana showed no surprise.

"She's ten, right?" said Alana. "She's definitely following in her mother's footsteps."

"One nice thing about that," said Bill. "She knows that Karen is her biological mother and she's seriously proud about that. But there's no way she thinks of us as anything but her real parents. She's has been a total joy ever since she arrived. And the same with Hector."

"The great thing is that they both get the intellectual stimulation from you both that they would have got from Karen and Hector," said Garry. "How many languages does Karen speak now?"

"French, German, Russian, Mandarin, Italian and Spanish," said Bill. And it's not just that she can speak them better than any translation device can do, she reads them, studies in them, she can even do maths in all of them."

"At ten," added Garry, smiling. "So now, what about University? What will she study and where?"

"We've suggested that she take a couple of years before that," said Bill. "This is all happening even faster than with Karen and we're worried that she could burn out early if she's pushed too hard. You can imagine the pressure on her already, with this high school graduation. Let's give her a childhood for a time."

"A good idea," said Alana.

"But we've already heard from Cambridge," said Bill. "They agree she should wait two or three years, but a place will always be open for her."

"Could you and she cope with the separation?" Garry looked concerned.

"Won't have to," replied Bill, looking smug. "They've invited both Galina and me to take up lectureships for that time."

"No surprise at all," said Alana. "And Hector? We're all going to his debut at the Sydney Opera House next week and that's no surprise, either. You'll take him to England as well?"

"Of course. The London School of Music has pleaded with us to send him there, so that's a guarantee."

"What's he playing in Sydney?" asked Garry.

"Tchaikovsky's Piano Concerto Number One," said Bill. "And if he gets called for an encore, he'll play a sonata of his own composition. Not bad for a ten-year old!"

"Those two might yet overshadow their parents," said Alana.

"I'm taking bets on it," said Bill.

* * *

2051

(The Sydney Morning Herald, July)

"The Tchaikovsky International Piano Competition for this year in Moscow was won by fifteen-year-old Hector

Forbes Askins. Hector was granted dispensation to compete, being just a month below the normal lower limit of sixteen. His performance of the Rachmaninoff Fourth Piano Concerto received the unanimous award of the judges' panel. One of them stated his view that the performance was equal to the acclaimed performance and recording by Vladimir Ashkenazy with the London Symphony Orchestra in 1995, considered by many to be the finest interpretation of all. Hector, who lives in Newcastle, NSW has been playing since he was three years old and made his debut at the age of ten at the Sydney Opera House, playing the Tchaikovsky First Piano Concerto with the Sydney Symphony Orchestra."

2052

(The Sydney Morning Herald, July)

"The Sydney International Piano Competition for this year was won by sixteen-year-old Hector Forbes Askins. It caps a remarkable year for this young resident of Newcastle, having won the Tchaikovsky Competition in Moscow last year and the Chopin International Competition earlier this year. Hector's performance of the Prokofiev Piano Concerto Number Three received international acclaim and has been recorded for commercial distribution."

2053

"This Institute is accustomed to academic excellence," said the Chancellor of Cambridge University. "We have seen remarkable names pass through these walls. Stephen Hawking, Isaac Newton, Charles Darwin and Alan Turing to name but four. One extraordinary graduate was Karen Petrova who gained her Honours Degree and then

Doctorate in Pharmacology here in 1972 and later went on to change the world in ways all of you will know. So it is a particular pleasure to award simultaneous First Class Honours degrees in Quantum Chemistry and Astrophysics to Karen Petrova Askins and with it, the Chancellor's Award for Academic Excellence. Congratulations, Miss Askins!"

2054

(The Sydney Morning Herald, July)

"The scintillating career of Hector Forbes Askins continues with his acclaimed performance of the Mozart Piano Concerto Number Nine in E flat Major (K271) for the Van Clyburn International Piano Concerto held this year in Dallas, Texas. One of the judges commented later that she had not heard anything like this since Van Clyburn himself, Vladimir Ashkenazy and Daniel Barenboim in their heydays. "Simply dazzling," said Kristen Vasilieva, herself a past winner of the Chopin and Van Clyburn competitions."

2056

"The Doctorate in Astrophysics is awarded to Karen Petrova Askins. Congratulations, Doctor Askins!"

"Dear Doctor Askins, the Faculty of Science welcomes you to your Post-Doctorate Fellowship at Harvard. All of us are very excited at the prospect of working with you...."

2060

(The Sydney Morning Herald, July)

"Hector Forbes Askins of Newcastle, NSW, who has

achieved significant international fame as perhaps the finest concert pianist of the day is about to embark on a world tour, giving concerts in over thirty countries over the next twelve months. There is considerable excitement at the news that Askins will debut his newly composed four piano concertos on the tour, beginning in Heidelberg. The first, which he played in Sydney with the SSO two years ago was received with delight, many experts rating it as equivalent to similar works by Mozart, Grieg and Prokofiev and there is massive interest in the new works..."

2060

"Dear Doctor Askins, all of us, Faculty and staff at Oxford University are delighted that you will join us for the new university year. We are aware of the number of offers you have received from Universities around the world and your decision to join us is most welcome...."

Chapter Twenty-Six – Just What is Life?
July, 2061

William Gareth Askins sat back in his armchair and accepted a mug of coffee from Garry.

"Thanks," he said with a smile and looked around the room.

"We're so sorry to hear about your father," said Penny. "Bill was the very first employee of Blueprints, he started even before Garry took up his position."

"And without his genius, we might never have got started on this wild ride," added Garry as he resumed his seat with his own mug of coffee.

"You have no idea how proud I am that my father is considered one of the greatest electronic engineers of all time, my mother is a renowned linguistics professor and my great-uncle is Isaac Asimov," said William.

"With good reason," said Ben. "But from what I read about you, it's possible that at the tender age of twenty-nine, you are at least the equal of your father in his field. William, you called us saying you had some extraordinary discoveries about Bill Askins Senior."

"Correct," said William. "When Dad died a couple of weeks ago, he left me a cabinet full of papers. No instructions, no explanations, but the solicitor who handled it said Bill had instructed him that these documents could be explosive, cause massive social unrest and I must be told to guard them with my life."

"So where are they now?" asked Penny.

"In the bank's safety deposit vaults. But that's why I'm here. This must be one of the safest places on the planet and I would like to transfer them here where I can go through them in complete safety."

"Absolutely," said Ben. "We'll organise an armoured vehicle and armed guards for the transfer. I have no doubt the military will be happy to provide additional security."

"Sounds perfect," said William. "And you can give me an office?"

"Of course."

"Great. I'm due my sabbatical year from University. I plan to take it here."

* * *

Askins looked weary.

"We've hardly seen you the last three months," said Penny. "And from the look of you, you haven't been spending your time on a rest cure."

"You're right," said Askins. Even his voice sounded weak. "I've been going through Dad's papers. I don't even know how to start telling you about what they cover."

"Start any way you can," said Garry. "One thing about working in this Second Foundation is that the astounding becomes quite ordinary, the mind-blowing is merely a surprise. What have you got?"

"You know how we always remember how Karen Petrova said that she would change the world?"

"Of course," said Ben. "It's become almost a biblical truth."

"I think my Dad is going one better," said William.

"You'd better start," said Penny.

August, 2035

"I'm grateful for the opportunity to see my device at work," said Bill Askins.

"Professor Askins, your work has changed the nature of surgery," said the heart surgeon. "We're honoured that you should come here and see what we do now."

"What's the situation?"

"It's a dangerous one," said the surgeon. "The patient is a sixty-year old male with a seriously damaged heart. Two days ago, he suffered a bad fall at home, broke three ribs, one of which has punctured a lung. We're going to try and move the damaged rib away from the lung and repair the organ, all with telekinetic forces enhanced by your device. But the risk is high. Conventional techniques are not possible and would prove fatal."

"Thank you, doctor. What I want to do is measure the forces coming from your head and the extent to which the amplifier increases the forces. I have some ideas for improving the technology but I need to see it in use."

"No problems. We're going to operate in about thirty minutes. Let's get you scrubbed up."

Two hours later, the surgeon looked up at Bill and around the operating table.

"Sorry people, we couldn't save him. Time of death is three twenty-two. Thank you, everybody. Professor Askins, did you get what you wanted?"

Bill didn't reply. When the surgeon walked over to him, he was staring in fascination at the instrument panel monitoring the telekinetic enhancing device.

"Professor?" the surgeon asked gently.

"Something happens when we die," said Askins in a whisper. "And I just saw it."

July, 2046

"What Dad's notes described was a tiny burst of energy emitted by the body as it died," said William. "It was not any form of energy that had been detected before, it was something quite new and it was the unique technology of the telekinetic enhancement device that reacted to it. Somehow, the design Dad had built tracked energy waves that had never been seen before. It looks like he was severely distressed to find that all his work in developing the telekinesis enhancement device was in the wrong direction. Purely accidentally, it led to the discovery of this body energy."

The others in the room were silent.

"Dad then decided to follow up with further research," said William.

September, 2035

"There's a question of privacy of our patients at their most vulnerable point," said the Hospice Director. She had shown no reaction to Bill Askins' request but now she voiced some concerns.

"I can't deny it," said Bill. "But there is no question of observing them in person, no question of recording their voices or any sounds they may make as death approaches. The device is now the size of a briefcase and can be placed in a drawer or the foot of a cupboard and will be totally unobtrusive."

"And you say it might record some form of radiation at the point of death?" The director looked doubtful. "I've never heard of anything like that before."

"There's never been anything like it before," said Bill. "It's something I saw recently when a patient died on the operating table, I'm not sure what it might be, but I really do need to verify the finding. It might be one of the most critical medical discoveries of all time."

"Well, all right, Professor Askins, your reputation makes it difficult to refuse. We have thirty-two patients here, all of them could die at any time. You want to put a device in every room?"

"Not every room, no, just one somewhere secure. The device will record the energy burst as a person dies, if that is what I saw before and also the time. I can check that time against your own records."

"I'm still not sure I like this, professor, but all right, please proceed. When can you have the device here?"

"By the afternoon," said Bill.

July, 2046

"Three weeks later, Dad had a recording of that same burst of energy with seventeen of the patients," said William. "The time of the burst and the time of death were the same in all cases."

The listeners in the room let out a collective small gasp.

"There have been many theories of what constitutes consciousness," William continued. "People have weighed bodies before and after death to see if there was anything that was actually life, and never found anything. But I think Dad has actually found the answer."

"The human soul," whispered Penny.

"That's what Dad believed," said William.

The silence in the room lasted several minutes as each of them absorbed the information and its implications.

"There's more, isn't there?" said Ben. "Knowing Bill, he must have put everything into finding the rest of the story."

"Quite right," said William. "Now that he knew the format and nature of this tiny energy form, he set to work to design a detector for it and find the source or repository.

He took one of the basic principles of science as his guideline."

"Energy can only change, it cannot be destroyed," said Garry.

"Correct," said William. "So Dad set out to find out where that energy went, if it had changed at all, if so, to what? He spent the next six years working on that and if Bill Askins spent six years working on a problem, you can be damned certain it was one hell of a big one."

"And?" asked Penny.

"It's Bill Askins. Of *course* he found it," said William. "He found that the energy left the human body when it died. That's every human body. He wasn't able to track them beyond the solar system, somehow they vanished, but he found traces of the energy all over the galaxy, all tracking to something close to the black hole at the centre of our galaxy."

The shock in the faces of the others in the room was clearly visible.

"So there is a life after death?" said Garry.

"That's what Dad concluded. It's not in any form that the religious teachings have proposed. It doesn't mean that we retain our sense of self, we don't meet others and chat about our lives while sitting on a white cloud playing a harp. But the central body of that energy is there, it grows with each and every human death and by any standard you care to apply, it's alive."

"Does that energy contain any self of sense, any memories of its human life?" Garry asked.

"I haven't found anything in Dad's notes so far that might indicate that," said William. "But I can't imagine how one could examine these little bolts and analyse them in any way. They are travelling at light speed, possibly greater."

"I thought the speed of light was the absolute," said Garry. "How can these things break that?"

"Quantum science suggests it may be possible," said William. "But Dad wasn't a quantum physicist, he said that stuff was all too spooky for him."

"You said the main source of energy was close to the black hole at the centre of the galaxy," said Ben. "Does that mean they are somehow linked?"

"I saw a note in the files that Dad had raised the same question but I have yet to find anything further."

"But it does mean that the human bolts can take some thousands of years to reach the centre," said Ben. "If that thing is an individual entity of some sort, it must have a massively different sense of time. It could have been there since the galaxy first formed, a few billion years ago."

"It's an interesting possibility," said William. "But Dad thinks it's more likely that it began forming with the first humanoids on Earth and probably also with other intelligent life forms in the galaxy. That puts it maybe a couple of million years old."

"Older," said Ben. "My people have been around for two million years and there was a mentor race before us. I think five million years is more likely."

"And it leads to another, related question," said Penny. "Where does this energy in the body come from? Is it passed to the embryo at the time of procreation, just like the DNA is?"

"Dad asked the same question and he had problems with it." Suddenly he gave a wide, expansive smile that showed perfect teeth. "I think I should play you a recording. I found this in Dad's DNA record. He discussed these issues a lot with Galina, my mother and I found several records in his DNA. This one starts when they were discussing how to get more recordings of the death emission of energy."

He took a tiny device from his short pocket, touched a switch and laid it on the coffee table. Both voices were clear and easily identifiable and the listeners smiled at the voices of the deeply-admired founder member of the foundation and the immensely popular Galina.

"So how can I get a number of people's death experiences to prove what I saw in the hospital?"

"Easy, dear Village Idiot. Come out with me and I'll kill a few people and you'll have the recordings."

"Galina, my dear murderous wife, I don't think that will work. The cops would just take a DNA sample from the corpses and see you doing your professional thing."

"Hmm, a pity. I haven't killed anyone in years now, I need the exercise."

"Not this way, lass! Think of something else."

"Still simple, beloved Village Idiot. Go and talk to a Hospice. Somebody dies there almost every day. See if they'll let you leave a device there."

"Ah! Good thinking."

William stopped the recording as the listeners all laughed loudly.

"Village Idiot! That's what Karen called Bill the first time she met him," said Garry. "I remember Greg in England telling me and that always amused him."

"And it looks like Galina adopted it," said Penny. "And she still has that thing about killing people. Was there ever any evidence that she could or had done?"

"Another example of her deadpan humour," said Garry. "When she first came to my office to give me a whole batch of Karen's notes and computer files, she said her two skills were languages and killing people. It took a while to recover from that."

"And had she ever done so?" asked Penny curiously. "Sometimes I wondered just what Galina's history was."

"So nobody has ever told you about that episode where Galina proved the point?" said William.

"You mean she actually killed somebody?" said Garry. "She certainly never mentioned it to me."

Looking round the curious faces in the room, William paused for a moment. "I was very young, about one year old. I found this in Dad's DNA track also, so it's how he saw it."

May, 2033

"Amazing events with the Foundation, eh?" said Bill.

"Not anything we could have seen just a couple of years ago," said Galina.

"Careful with that stroller," said Bill as they reached the crossroads. A high kerb had to be negotiated and Bill moved to the front wheels of the stroller containing their first-born, William Gareth, all of a year old and lifted it down to the roadway.

"Do you miss the life?" asked Bill as they strolled across the intersection.

"Sometimes," said Galina. "I've enjoyed all that travel to various countries as part of the advisory teams to governments, but it was getting exhausting. How about you?"

"The job hasn't really changed," said Bill. "An academic role at the university is calmer and less frantic, but I still have problems to solve, new electronics stuff to design and helping doctoral students, though I'm glad I don't have a teaching role."

Galina laughed. "Me too! You'd be a lousy lecturer!"

He didn't reply but stared ahead. Three young men were approaching and their faces didn't reflect a warm welcome. They stopped in a line across the pavement, blocking progress by Galina and Bill.

"Well, what have we got here?" one of them men said. All three were dressed alike, jeans, tee-shirts and base-ball caps and were about the same size and build. They looked fit and muscular.

"Looks like one chubby old geezer, one skinny woman and..." a second one advanced and peered down at the stroller. "A tiny little sprog."

"Do you think they'll have any money?" said the first. "They look like posh bastards."

"Okay, children," said Galina. "Here's your choice. You can walk away or I can kill you. What's it to be?"

All three men laughed.

"What, you think you can kill all three of us, do you? What a hoot!" said the first man. "You some sort of Special Air Service commando, are you?"

"Oh, she's far worse than that," said Bill. "I advise you to take the first option."

"Hey, old chubby speaks!" said the first one. "And will you kill us also?"

All three laughed at the jest.

"No, I'll just watch," said Bill. "I haven't seen her kill anyone for a couple of years now, so this will refresh my memory."

The three men looked at each other a little uncertainly then turned back to Bill and Galina.

"Give us all your money and we might let you go," said one of them.

Galina smiled. "Take the stroller, will you, Bill?" she said and stepped away from it. "Now then, children, I can see you're stupid, so I'll go easy on you. I'll just kill one of you, one of you can have two broken legs and the other one, two broken arms. You have twenty seconds to make up your minds or I'll make them up for you."

"You fucking bitch!" shouted the first man. "I've had enough of that crap. Let's get 'em, guys."

They launched themselves at Galina while Bill stepped backwards with the stroller.

Galina dropped to one knee and ducked her head as the first man reached her. As his knees met her shoulder, she stood up fast, one hand behind his knees and he went flying into the brick wall of the building next to them. His head met brick with a crack and he dropped, motionless. But even before that collision, Galina kicked out so fast that Bill couldn't follow the motion. Her foot made contact with one of the men's legs and the crack was quite audible, immediately followed by a scream of pain just as her right hand slammed into the third man's arm with similar results.

"Well, that's one dead, a broken arm and a broken leg," said Galina, not breathing hard. "I did promise two of each, so are you ready, children?"

They were interrupted by the arrival of a police patrol car, siren blaring. Two officers got out and stared at the scene.

"Somebody called us a few moments ago that three thugs were threatening a couple with a pram," one said. His sergeant's stripes looked newly sewn on. His colleague bent over the fallen man.

"This one's dead, Sarge," he said. He looked at the two others who were weeping in pain and reached for his radio. "Two-Three to base, we need an ambulance to the corner of Richards and Meldrum, one dead, two broken limbs. Need backup for the ambulance. Better send a detective and camera crew as well."

"What the hell happened?" asked the Sergeant.

"As you heard, three thugs attacked us, my wife dealt with them," said Bill.

"YOU did, Madam?"

"I did," said Galina.

He stared at her. "Holy shit!" he said.

A siren sounded a few blocks away and an ambulance arrived. The Sergeant turned to his colleague.

"John, once the scene of crime officer has arrived and cleared it, go with those three, I'll head back to the station with these two. Sir, madam, a homicide detective and camera crew will be here shortly, that's standard when a fatality is involved. But now, will you take the little one and fold the trolley and we'll head back to the station?"

An hour later, Bill and Galina were sitting in the waiting room of the police station, little William sitting on his father's knee when the Sergeant returned.

"Your DNA samples confirm the story," he said. "We read through the same incident from both your viewpoints and we saw them attack you without provocation. A coroner's report will be prepared. But Madam, I have never seen anything like it before. Where did you learn unarmed combat like that?"

"I had some excellent teachers."

"And you, sir, can you do that stuff as well?"

"Hell no," said Bill. "I'm just an elderly physics professor at the university."

Finally, the sergeant lost his deadly serious expression and laughed.

"Then you and the kid are safer than anyone in the world," he said. "And the kid needs to get to bed. There's a car waiting outside to run you home. And thank you, this has been an educational experience. There's no need to take statements from you, the DNA recording is all we need."

"Good night, officer," said Galina.

July, 2061

"Good grief!" said Garry. "What happened?"

"The cops took DNA samples of all them, saw the entire episode and reported justifiable self-defence to the coroner. Nothing was ever done. Apparently, the cops were most impressed and a bit scared of Mum!"

"Not surprising," said Penny. "I don't think any of us had ever heard that story."

"I did often wonder just what training Karen organised for her, or whether she'd had military experience before coming to work for Karen," said Garry. "But I watched her a few times in the gym and she was quite fearsome in the various unarmed combat skills she showed. I had no doubts that she could do what she said if needed."

"It would be interesting to look at Galina's DNA," said Penny. "Nobody ever has, to my knowledge, so it's something you might want to do some day, William. I'd love to know where she got that rather frightening talent from."

"Maybe, but let's get back to the main story," said William and restarted the recorder. "And now the second question."

"I'm pretty sure that energy gets given to the embryo at conception, just like the DNA."

"Absolutely certainly."

"So how can I get to observe it? I can't ask a lot of married couples to have this device in their bedrooms."

"No, I agree, they'd start to have curious ideas about this famous electronics genius. It wouldn't do your reputation at the University much good."

"Damn right. Any ideas, other than killing people?"

"Sometimes, beloved Village Idiot, you live up to Karen's name for you! Where do you think most procreation takes place, apart from the bedrooms of young married couples?"

"Ah! Good thinking again!"

"Sometimes I think Galina was just as bright as Bill," said Avram.

"Professor Emeritus of Linguistics? Yes, I think so," said William. "I do have remarkable parents. Anyway, he followed Galina's suggestion, went to a fertility clinic and got consent to leave a device in the laboratories when fertilisation took place."

"And the results?" All of them waited with barely suppressed impatience as William put the recorder away.

"Initially, he found that the device didn't detect anything but an almost impossibly small energy between sperm and egg, not enough to examine. So he took a couple of months, enhanced it further and tried again."

"And this time?"

"A month later, he had over a hundred recordings. He had been correct, a tiny amount of energy was passed to the embryo at conception. That energy grows as the child grows. We've never been able to detect it before, but now we can."

"Good grief," said Penny. The others were silent as they tried to absorb this information.

"Dad had another idea about all this," said William. "Dad began to think that the whole telekinesis thing and the emotional control that we first saw in Penny but is appearing in a few others now, these things may not be a result of studying DNA and the human history records as we thought. They may be coming from the energy source. He thought it was trying to teach humans something or prepare us for something."

"Could this energy force be what communicated somehow with me when we first encountered the aliens on that world and ordered the ship to cauterise the planet?" Penny's voice was weak from tension.

William nodded. "Dad believed that we were right when we suggested there might be some form of sentience in the galaxy and it's growing."

Garry drew in his breath sharply. "Is this God?"

"I don't know," said William.

There was a moment of silence in the room.

"Of course, what it needs," continued William, "is a top flight astrophysicist to study this phenomenon."

"And who…" Penny stopped and laughed. "Surely not?"

"We've been talking about this," said William. "She decided there was no way she could avoid working on our father's discovery. She should be here any moment."

Penny, Alana, William and Garry stood at the large picture window overlooking the parking lot of the Foundation building.

"I used to get worried sick watching Karen arrive," said Garry. "She was a terrible driver and she always owned a Ferrari, a Lamborghini or a Maserati which she changed every year and yet she never had an accident. Her insurance premiums were probably horrific but they were buried in the corporate policy for both Life Technologies and Blueprints and all their buildings and equipment and everything else with them."

"That's about right," said William with a laugh. "Mother told me she was always worried when Karen set off in one of her exotic high-performance cars. Mother said she used to try and persuade her to go in the Rolls so Mother could drive her."

"Oh lordy, I think she's inherited Karen's taste in cars," said Garry. As he spoke, a bright red Ferrari swung into the gates and approached the building. It stopped exactly equally between the two lines of the parking spot.

"But not her lack of driving skills," said Alana.

The car door opened and a woman climbed out. She was dressed in a flowing blue dress and she carried a white handbag to match her white shoes.

"But she has adopted her dress sense," said William, grinning broadly.

"Dammit, I can almost feel the tension rise in the building," said Garry.

"That's something else you've described, Garry," said Alana. "The air almost crackled with electricity when Karen arrived."

"We haven't seen her since she was thirteen and left for England," said Garry. "But she looks the absolute image of the first Karen."

"We should go down and meet her," said Alana. "I think I'm quite nervous."

In the lobby, the scene was extraordinary. Almost the entire staff of the Foundation had gathered and in the middle was a finely detailed copy of Karen Petrova. She stood motionless, almost a statue until Alana, Garry, Penny and William arrived, then the alabaster-perfect features broke into a smile, the bright scarlet lipstick enhancing the beautiful face under black hair with a ponytail hanging down her back.

"Hello, Big Brother," she said and walked up to William, giving him a hug. Then she turned to the others.

"Yes, I am," she said.

"Exactly like the first Karen?" said Garry. "You most certainly are, but I suppose everybody says that at first meeting."

"Exactly. So I get in first!"

All of them burst out laughing then Alana took her hand and waved at the crowd. "Ladies and gentlemen, this is a huge delight to welcome Doctor Karen Petrova Askins to the Karen Petrova Foundation."

The crowd broke into a huge cheer and wide smiles were everywhere.

"I'll come round and meet as many people as I can a little later," said Karen. "But I have some immediate things to work out with my brother, so please excuse me for now."

As they climbed the stairs to the office, Penny looked back.

"Can you sense the happiness in the building?" she said.

Karen smiled.

They took seats in the office and relaxed.

"I still have some confusion in my mind," said Karen. "I know intellectually that Karen was my biological mother, even though she died many years before I was born and I know that I look exactly like her in every way. But I was born to Galina and Bill and they are my real parents and this new Village Idiot is my brother, even though we have no familial relationship at all."

William grinned cheerfully. "I do look like Bill, I agree and that village idiot face protects me!"

"We're just so delighted you decided to come and work with us," said Olivia.

"How could I not? That discovery of Bill's is just too incredible to ignore. I want to spend all the time I can investigating this galactic entity, measure it, evaluate it, learn everything I can about it. I can't imagine a better object of study for an astrophysicist and quantum chemist."

"We have an office for you," said Garry. "List every piece of equipment you want, we'll set up a laboratory and observatory if you need it."

Karen nodded. "I will. But I think what I'd like to do is wander round, meet everybody and see how the place has changed since I was last here as a toddler." She rose to her feet, waved and walked out.

"Wow!" said Alana into the silence.

"She does have that effect," said William.

Chapter Twenty-Seven – The Great Expansion - 2062

"One of the greatest problems that has affected us all, every species on all five galaxies in our group is the inability to travel between galaxies," said Ben. "We have always found it impossible."

"And yet we discovered two rogue ships that invaded our galaxy and we know they came from another galaxy and which one," said Avram.

"That is what has worked up a number of great minds at home," said Ben. "But now we actually have a ship from that galaxy, and we are going to examine it and probably tear it to pieces to see if we can find out how it got here. We should have done this years ago but we didn't think the threat of another invasion was all that great. We've assembled a team of our best programmers and they are heading to the ship now. Would you like to come along and see what we can do?"

"Damn right!" said Penny. "I'd love to see how your people work."

"What she said," said Avram. "You're the only person of your species we have met so far, so it would be nice to meet a few more."

"On which point," said Penny, "are you physically different from us?"

"Not that you would notice," said Ben. "It's one reason why we sent mentors from my people to Earth. However, many of our apprentices and journeymen that came here were physically very different and it took them some time to adjust to human bodies."

"So when are we going?" said Penny.

"Pack a bag, and will be off in about an hour. My ship is already on its way here."

* * *

The alien ship stood alone on the empty plain. A second ship which had brought the programming team from Ben's planet was at least a kilometre away. The ship which had brought Ben, Penny and Avram stood next to the programmers' ship.

"The programmers want to make sure that no instruments on their ship will affect the alien ship," said Ben. "Let's go and join them and see what they are up to."

Penny and Avram looked with interest at the five people in the lounge of the alien ship. Three were men and none of them looked in any way different from any person on Earth. One of the women looked up at the new arrivals and gave a small wave to Ben, while the rest concentrated on several metallic boxes on the floor. A large monitor stood against one wall and several lines of data were displayed. Avram and Penny studied the screen but could make nothing of it.

"Your language?" asked Avram.

"One of many," Ben replied. "Although my world has been united under a single government for some centuries, there are still a few dozen languages spoken. But that display is mathematical, the universal language of science. The team is trying to find the location of the ship's computer. But remember that you have the translation system in your pendants and you will understand when the team members speak."

Silence fell on the room and the visitors took seats in the armchairs distributed in the area.

"That looks like the control centre!" One of the team looked up and smiled at Ben. The monitor was now filled with lines of incomprehensible symbols. "Now we have to identify the access codes," she continued.

Silence fell again as every member of the programming team stared at the monitor as the data scrolled slowly down.

"There! That looks promising," said the woman. "We'll concentrate on this section. Each of the team will download it to their own computers and see if they can identify the instruction that allows somebody to access the control."

Ben nodded. "You may remember when I tried to find out how our ship got the orders to cauterise that first planet, I spoke the word 'Command' and that identified me and gave me access to further orders."

"Yes," replied Penny. "I was most impressed."

"That's what they are looking for now," said Ben

The silence resumed.

It was over thirty minutes before one of the team raised his hand.

"Here!" he said. "That's it! I have no idea what the word means, so pronunciation may be a problem."

"Can you change it?" asked the woman who appeared to be the team leader.

"Yes," said the programmer. "Everybody, silence. I'm going to speak a new command order."

The room went deadly quiet as the man stared at his own computer.

"Command," he said clearly and watched the screen change. "I think that did it," he said.

Let's check," said the team leader. "Quiet everybody. "Command!" she said.

The large monitor against the wall flickered and the display changed to new lines of data.

"Acknowledge new controls," said the woman.

"Acknowledged," said the ship's computer. The woman grinned cheerfully at the three visitors. "I told Ben we're the best," she said and turned back to the monitor.

"Command!" she said. "Identify the planet on which we are now."

"Unable to comply,'" was the answer.

"Command, give reasons for that response."

"There is no record of any name assigned to this planet."

"Command, do you have the galactic coordinates of this planet?"

"Affirmative."

"Command, display those coordinates."

"Complying."

Several lines of symbols appeared on the monitor. All the programming team studied them intently for some minutes.

"That's correct," one of the men said.

"Command, how did you acquire those coordinates?"

"They were calculated when the Ship's Captain ordered the landing here."

"Command, so you did not receive an order to fly to these specific coordinates?"

"Affirmative."

"Command, what were the last coordinates that were in your flight plan?"

"Displaying."

Silence fell again as the programmers examined the lines of data on the screen. It lasted almost five minutes.

"That's a position in inter-galactic space, not inside the galaxy boundaries," one of them said.

"Can you be more specific?"

"Stand by," said the programmer and consulted his own computer. "Five light minutes from the nearest star in the north-west quadrant of the galaxy," he said.

"Command, what were the previous coordinates?"

"Displaying."

A new set of lines of data appeared. Again, silence fell as the team examined the data.

"That's insane," said of them after a few minutes. "It's just a position thirty thousand light years into intergalactic space. There's nothing there."

"I think I'm starting to understand what this is all about," the team leader said to Ben. "Command, display the last three programmed coordinates you were given."

"Displaying."

Again, a short period of silence as the team studied the data on the monitor. All of them let out exclamations of astonishment at the same moment.

"This is even more insane," said the team leader. "That looks like a series of random jumps all over inter-galactic space." She looked over at the three visitors. "It's hard for me to explain just how illogical all this is. Let's see if the ship can explain itself. Command, were those tracks through known hyperspace coordinates?"

" Affirmative.."

"Command, display the paths relative to this galaxy."

On the screen, the image changed. The faint outline of the galaxy appeared in the bottom right hand corner and in the centre were three lines shown in orange. They were straight, and the end of the first was just a short distance separated from the beginning of the second, which then almost joined up to the third. But the directions were not constant, though overall, they led to the galaxy.

"Now I think we know what this is all about," said the leader. She came over to where Ben and the other two were sitting. "We know that the rogue galaxy was sending out dozens, maybe hundreds of ships, all at random. It looks like they were just taking random jumps through hyperspace. Each jump would have been recorded back at base, with the end coordinates stored in the main computers. Some of these ships just vanished. But I'm now sure that the tracks were all recorded and those that led to this galaxy, even if they zig-zagged all over the place were fed into the computer of this ship. The same was probably done for ships that eventually reached other galaxies."

"Sound likely," said Ben. "How long would this have taken?"

"Could be years. But now that we have a documented path, we could send the ship back to its base in its own galaxy in just hours."

"But what happened when it got here?" asked Avram. "The crew did not know which planets could be invaded safely."

"True," said the team leader. She turned back to her team. "Ladies and gentlemen, will you now interrogate the ship and get the records of every path taken to get here? But I'll ask a question first. Command, how did you find this planet.

"Unable to comply."

"Ah, I think I see. Command, did the ship conduct searches through this quadrant of the galaxy using very short hyperspace jumps to each solar system?"

"Affirmative."

"Command, how long did that take? Give time in standard months of home planet."

"Thirty-seven months."

"That's about four Earth years," said Ben. "The crew just kept looking until they found a planet suitable for them."

"But does this mean that once you have the complete track from the rogue galaxy to here, we could follow it back?" asked Penny.

"That's exactly what it means," said Ben. "And not just to the galaxy, but to the home planet of the mentors as well. It's time to call another meeting of the Galactic Mentor Coordinating Council."

"What the hell is that?" asked Avram.

"You'll see," said Ben.

Chapter Twenty-Eight – The Galactic Mentor Council Meets - 2062.

"This is the second meeting you will have with the Galactic Mentor Council of lead Mentors from each of the five galaxies," said Ben. "It's been a long time since the last meeting."

"I still can't get over the fact that there are five galaxies, all talking to each other," said Gernardy. "I know when Penny and Avram told us when you first brought it up with them, but *five?* How did such a group form when communications would be so difficult at these distances?"

"By accident," said Ben. "As you know, our technology is such that we have instantaneous communication around the galaxy using quantum concepts. What we didn't know was that civilisations in four other galaxies were developing similar technologies at about the same time and over a period of a century or so, signals from those were detected here. It proved that the same technology worked over inter-galactic distances as well as within the galaxy."

"So you started talking to each other?" said Olivia.

"Exactly. And the more we talked, the more we discovered that all of us had similar problems, civilisations killing themselves off when they reached a certain level of technology, from wars, pollution, all the same as we had experienced. The whole mentoring process was created by mutual discussion."

"It's astonishing that all five of you appeared to develop at about the same pace," said Olivia.

"It may not be as much a coincidence as first seems," said Ben. "This central core entity we have all discovered within our galaxies may have something to do with it. But we'll talk about that as we learn more. Meanwhile, I must admit, this meeting scares me a bit. Every other time, we've met to discuss developments, clear up any misconceptions, nothing really conflicting. This time, we're going to present a battle plan."

"How do you think they'll take it?" asked Olivia.

"Probably fairly well, though there could be... okay people, showtime."

As he spoke, the images of the other council members began appearing in the holodeck room.

"Only six," murmured Ben. "Normally we get two from each galaxy. The rogue mentors have declined the invitation, it seems." He stood up and spoke clearly. "Thank you for appearing at this short notice, ladies and gentlemen. But we have important news for you."

A middle-aged man smiled and nodded.

"I'm the Chairman for today," he said. "I see the same two faces with you as before. Would you introduce them again to remind us?"

"Of course," said Ben. "These people are two of the very first members of the organisation that has been the leading force guiding Earth's development in reaching a state of consideration for future mentorship. Their names are Gernardy and Olivia. Would you identify yourselves, please?"

Gernardy cleared his throat nervously. "I'm Gernardy," he said. "I'm honoured to meet you all."

Olivia waved her hand. "I'm Olivia and I echo my colleague's words."

"Thank you and welcome," said the Chairman. "Ben, we cannot ignore such a request for a meeting, but I see our difficult member has failed to respond. Is this related to your call to us?"

"It is," said Ben. "As you know, for the first time we have been able to get hold of one of the ships from that galaxy. It was intact and my technical experts spent many hours examining it. The primary findings were critical. We have tracked the path the ship took between galaxies, something we have all believed to be impossible until now. We have learned the route the ship took and traced it back to the world on which it originated. We believe that is the home world of the Mentor race for that galaxy."

The other Council members reacted with astonishment.

"Was the route pre-programmed? Did they have a definite navigation plan to reach your galaxy?" asked a young man seated next to the Chairman.

"Quite the opposite," said Ben. "It looks like the ships they sent out performed random leaps through hyperspace. The coordinates were recorded back on home planet and if the ship vanished, as many did, they were just written off. But if they appeared somewhere heading to our galaxy, the end coordinates were recorded. Eventually, after losing many ships, they did have a flight plan that would take a ship to our galaxy, though not an efficient one."

"But you can send a ship back along that same route and finally reach the Mentor world?"

"We can."

The Council members stirred with interest.

"And what do you plan to do with this new ability?" asked one. "And does this mean that we can now set up regular travel between galaxies?"

"Sir, we cannot yet plan regular services," said Ben. "The path this ship found was pure random chance, and it is likely that many ships were lost before this one found a route. But as I said, the route is highly inefficient, sometimes doubling back upon itself. We could spend some years using unmanned probes to discover an efficient route between these two galaxies and then a similar period of time for other routes."

"I think we understand," said the Chairman. "But the first question – what do you plan to do with this information?"

"We believe that the unique talent some humans have developed to effect changes in attitude could be used against the Mentors," said Ben.

The Chairman nodded. "That sounds logical, though risky. Do you believe there are humans with this ability strong enough to make such a fundamental change in the Mentor leaders?"

Ben indicated Gernardy and Olivia. "These two people have shown a remarkable ability, Chairman. While we have been breeding the talent for some years now, my friends here are the most powerful humans we have yet found. We have concentrated their training on developing this talent to a level even greater that that held by the two previous people who helped us before. They would like the opportunity to use their talents."

"Do we know what physical form the Mentors take on their home planet?" asked the Chairman.

"We don't," said Ben. "The two invading forces we have so far encountered were humanoid, similar to humans. But they may have been subject races sent out to explore extra-galactic life and perhaps deemed expendable."

"Then there is some risk," said the Chairman. "The mental state of the Mentors is quite sociopathic, even psychopathic. They know what humans look like, so the sudden appearance of two of them could cause immediate violence."

"We are aware of that," said Gernardy, speaking for the first time. "But Olivia and I have agreed to take this risk. We have already found that the ship's protective systems will shield us against a weapon when we are in the vicinity of the ship and Ben's technicians have developed a personal shield that is portable and small enough to carry on our persons. These were tested when we accosted the crew of the first invading ship and found to be effective."

"There is a further defence," said Ben. "Once they have left the ship, it will lift off and hover a few thousand metres above them, always observing them and sensing their position if they are inside a building. Any attempt at violence will result in immediate rescue and retaliation."

The Chairman sat back. "I'm still very hesitant about this, but I see no alternative if we are ever to counter this threat."

Ben nodded. "Then I think we will proceed."

*　*　*

"A bit smoky and a couple of odd aromas, but the ship says the air is breathable," said Olivia.

Gernardy nodded and set off down the ramp. "Lots of people," he said as a small crowd gathered.

"Very humanoid," said Olivia. "And very frightened. Have a look at those minds."

Gernardy extended his senses out to the people. They were indeed quite humanoid, perhaps on average shorter than him, but that was nothing unusual on Earth. But as he touched the minds of the nearest individuals, the overwhelming reading was of fear.

"But I don't think they're frightened by us," said Olivia. "This feels like a general fear of life, of authority, of punishment, it's really weird. I've never experienced anything like it before."

"Can we do anything about it? Let's try soothing a few minds, see what happens."

Together, they reached out and sensed the minds of several of the crowd. As Olivia had said, Gernardy experienced a turmoil of emotions. There was an immediate fear of the alien newcomers, there was a general sense of fear, resentment, some anger, but these were not directed at Gernardy and Olivia, but were like a base current in a river, always there if not seen.

Gernardy tried his powers of changing the emotions. His first reaction was of being overloaded, the force of the fear and other negative emotions was too great to combat. He concentrated on just one mind and still felt the power of the fear was too great to overcome.

"That was not good," he said softly.

"You couldn't get through either?" Olivia sounded exhausted.

"It was like fighting a cyclone."

"About right."

"And I think we have set something off," said Gernardy, pointing down the road.

Advancing on them was a dozen-strong squad of troops, all carrying dangerous looking weapons.

"The Mentors here keep a close eye on what's going on," said Olivia. "Still, if these soldiers are taking us to the Mentors, that's what we wanted. Let's be friendly and non-threatening."

"Judging by those weapons, somebody is certainly frightened of us." As he spoke, Gernardy looked at the minds of the troops. Together with the general fear he had found in the minds of others, was a specific fear of the new arrivals.

"You're right," said Olivia. "Let's not give them any cause to lose control. I'm pretty sure our defence shields are operating but I don't want to test them."

Smiling at the troops, the two walked down to meet them and stood quietly as the men surrounded them and began walking back the way they had come. As they walked, the visitors examined the scene.

"Dull architecture," remarked Gernardy. "Almost that heavy block style that Stalin liked so much."

"I bet their art forms are just as boring. This bears all the signs of a repressed society."

It took only ten minutes to reach another undistinguished building. The guards stopped at the base of the steps but Gernardy and Olivia continued walking up the steps and into the vast hall past the doorway. They sensed the confusion in the guards and two of them raced forward to stand by the human visitors. Gernardy and Olivia hid their smiles as they sensed the confusion and anxiety in the troops.

"So where to?" asked Olivia. Her translator emitted strange sounds but the guard clearly understood. He gave her a worried look but began walking to a series of doorways along one wall. He opened one and gestured at them to enter. Inside, they found a spacious room. Two plain, wooden chairs were placed against one wall and facing them was a line of four chairs of far greater luxury and comfort.

The two guards left and closed the door behind them. The click of the lock being set was clearly audible.

"Looks like they were ready for us," murmured Olivia and took one of the wooden chairs.

"And it's an interrogation," agreed Gernardy. He took the second chair but turned it around and straddled it, leaning his elbows on the seat back. "They'll probably leave us here for quite a while to try and make us nervous."

"Probably," agreed Olivia. "But when they come, how about I do the talking and you study their minds?"

"Good plan."

Gernardy was correct. Thirty-five minutes passed before the door was unlocked and swung open. Four individuals entered and the human visitors studied them intently. Three of them were men, all dressed in imposing ceremonial robes. The fourth, equally adorned in coloured finery also wore a tall headpiece of what looked like a gold frame with a number of sparkling gems. Her face was heavily made up in a garish mixture of red and white streaks.

"You will stand for the Mentor Council," the woman said loudly.

"I don't think so," said Olivia and remained seated.

Under the heavy make-up, the woman's face reflected nothing, but Gernardy read fury in her. Similar rage ran through the minds of the three men.

The four Mentors took their seats, clearly deciding that argument was worthless.

One of the men spoke. "You are illegal invaders of our world. Why should we not have you executed at once as spies?"

"We're not spies," said Olivia. "We were in the area, thought we'd drop by and say hello. The visit is approved by the Inter-Galactic Mentor Council of which you are members."

"We were not present at such a meeting," replied the man. "We did not approve such an invasion. We can execute you at any time."

Olivia shrugged "You can try but you will fail."

While she was speaking, Gernardy was examining each of the Mentor's minds. They were all frightened and baffled by the arrival of the two visitors.

"Fail?" snapped the woman. "You have no weapons, we have guards outside the door."

"We may have no weapons on our persons," said Olivia, "but we have defences. And I should point out, we have examined your ship that you sent to our galaxy and found that your weapons are quite backward compared to ours. Our ship is above this building and any threatening move by you will result in a catastrophic response. I suggest you behave."

Gernardy read increased panic in all four minds before him.

"We know why you have come," said the women after a few moments restoring her self control. "Presumably you are exponents of that human trick of changing mental states? Do not try those silly games with us. We cannot be affected that way."

"Quite possibly," replied Olivia. "We have already looked at your minds and it is true, they are strongly disciplined by fear."

The woman smiled. "Fear is the best way to control populations."

"And suppress them," said Olivia.

"That too," said the woman in a satisfied tone.

"One thing history has shown in our galaxy is that despotic rulers always collapse at some point," said Olivia. "Your rule will collapse under its own weight at some future time, that is assured."

"We will not collapse, you are being foolish. Are you the best that your world could send? You are obviously inadequate."

"Maybe," said Olivia. "But there is another thing to consider. When despotic rulers collapse, the people tend to take their revenge in sometimes very brutal and bloody fashion."

"That will never happen here," said the woman. Her tones were angry and Gernardy read considerable panic in her mind.

"So why are you so frightened by the thought?" asked Olivia. "And you are seriously frightened, we both read that in your mind."

Gernardy went further into the woman's mind. He detected considerable strength, an ability to withstand interference and he doubted that he could affect her enough to change the rigid mindset. But there was something curious in the way the emotions were arranged, something almost... artificial. He switched his attention to the three men and found similar patterns. But then he saw a tiny gateway, an opening that could be used. He kept examining them.

"We are not frightened," snapped the woman. "But enough of that. How did you get here? It took us years to send out enough ships so that some might reach planets in other galaxies. How were you able to bring your ship here?"

"As I said, we had your ship torn apart by experts," said Olivia. "We tracked the path taken and we merely reversed it. It was easy."

Gernardy read anxiety in all four Mentors. He concentrated on the tiny opening he had seen and made a minute change in attitude, adding a capacity for empathy that was not there before.

"You mean you could send fleets here at any time?" asked one of the men.

"At any time," agreed Olivia. "With weapons far in advance of yours. We could bring about your defeat in weeks if we wished."

The four Mentors were silent. Gernardy read an almost catatonic state in all of them.

"But we won't," continued Olivia. "We have a much better way of ending this tyranny. Remember, when we took over your invading ship, we also controlled a number of your people. Now we can create new bodies in those forms and over the next few years, we will send hundreds of agents here in bodies that you will never recognise and slowly they will change the minds of you and your awful Mentors Council. It might take centuries, but the Universe is very young and time is not the issue."

"Enough!" shouted the woman. The door opened and two guards walked in. "Kill them!" she ordered.

The guards unslung their weapons and pointed them at Olivia and Gernardy. They felt a wave of fear, their hearts lurched and the soldiers fired.

But something stopped the beams reaching Gernardy and Olivia. At the same moment, the wall on one side collapsed to reveal the outdoors and hovering just metres away was the ship.

Gernardy took a deep breath and reached for Olivia's hand. Both of them had rapid heartbeats and increased blood pressure. "Time to go," he croaked through a dry throat and they walked through the wreckage of the wall to the ship which descended to the ground and opened the door.

Ten minutes later, they were in open space.

"I suppose that didn't go quite to plan," said Olivia.

"Not entirely," agreed Gernardy. "But we learnt a lot about them."

"They're humanoid, intelligent, but definitely paranoid."

"And they rule their worlds with fear. At least, that's what we saw on the home planet."

"Gernardy, did you get a chance to examine any of the Mentor's minds?"

"Yes, I did and there's something curious. I saw signs of some emotional manipulation."

"So did I!" Olivia looked relieved. "I peered into three of them and I saw the same thing! Do you think they've got some of the same talents we've developed?"

"It could be, but it looked like a fairly clunky job, not neat at all."

"I got the same feeling. But I did manage to slip a suggestion into three of their minds, that they needed to rethink what they were doing."

Gernardy laughed. "Great thinking, kid! I did the same."

"So I think the next approach is to wait until we have a few hundred trained people with even more of the ability than we have, put them on the planet and just work on the Mentors' minds. It might take a century or two, but eventually they'll change." Olivia looked pleased with the plan.

"That'll be our recommendation to the Council, then."

"I think," said Olivia. "That's worth having a drink."

Chapter Twenty-Nine – Karen Petrova at Work

The laboratory and observatory built specially for Karen and William to work on the new discoveries of the galaxy were silent for three months, just the odd few words of surprise, astonishment and delight punctuating the silence.

"This is truly weird," said Karen one morning.

"Tell me," said William across the room where he was working on a tracking device.

"You may have some changes to make in that thing."

"Explain, tiny sister."

"So Dad's device for recognising the little energy bolts when they leave the body has worked well," she said, sitting back in her seat away from the computer monitor. "And your little thingy for tracking them has done okay…"

"Thank you, Ma'am," said William with a straight face. "I'll try not to be hurt by that."

A tiny smile threatened to erupt across Karen's bright scarlet lips. "I've tracked several hundred of them now and they are certainly heading in the direction of the Galactic core. They leave at quite astonishing speeds, about thirty percent of the speed of light and that has proved the quantum theory that Einstein and others came up with, their mass increased as they accelerated. But then they reached the outer realms of the solar system and that's where the weirdness came in."

"You *are* going to get around to explaining that to me at some point?" William was smiling, knowing full well that his astonishing sister had come up with something astounding.

"Only if you're good."

"I will be, I promise."

"Better believe it. Now, what happens as they reach the edge of the solar system, somewhere around the orbit of Pluto is that they accelerate even more. At around fifty percent of lightspeed, they vanish."

"Ah! And that suggests they reach or even exceed the speed of light because they are beyond the capability of the trackers to see them?" William was concentrating hard. Something fundamental in modern science was developing, he understood and a current of excitement ran through him.

"And the Theory of Relativity, according to Einstein and almost everybody else except for those whacky quantum people like Bohr and von Neuman and Dirac say that nothing can exceed the speed of light." Karen's face was immobile but somehow radiated the same excitement that William was experiencing.

"So what's happening?" William knew what the answer had to be and his hands were almost shaking.

"Those bolts are changing into something else," said Karen.

"And that something else has so far been strictly in the realm of theory, right?"

"Absolutely no proof at all," said Karen, her smile starting to widen.

"Until now, right?"

"Indeed, big brother. I think we have evidence that these theoretical mysteries actually exist. Those bolts are converting to Tachyons and they really do travel faster than light."

"That'll make a lot of cosmologists and physicists wet their pants!" said William, his tone completely calm.

"Exactly," said Karen.

"So how do we get out and prove it?"

"I have an idea," said Karen. "But you'll need to modify that tracker thingy of yours first."

*　*　*

"Have you any idea of how mind-blowing it is for an astrophysicist to be sitting in a spaceship far beyond the limits of the Solar System?"

Karen seemed calm, but William could see the bubbling excitement within her.

"About the same as for a top electrical engineer," he said. "Ben, you're sure of this position?"

"We're five light years from Earth and on the estimated track of the energy bolts as they left. If they continue on track towards the galactic core, they'll pass us at something in excess of the speed of light." Ben seemed calm also, but he was clearly fascinated by the experiment being conducted. "What's the science behind this new toy?"

"Seriously strange science," said William. "Tachyons are theoretical, nobody has ever proven they exist or even what they are! In quantum theory, they're not particles, maybe waves, or maybe both, depending on the observer. But whatever is approaching at more than light speed will possibly be indicated by blue shift, I've based the new box on an ability to identify Cherenkov radiation and when the tachyons have passed, they'll leave a trace of red shift, but the line of the Cherenkov radiation will only appear at the moment the things pass us. Hopefully, I'll use the red shift to develop the likely direction."

"So all based on theoretical quantum science, none of which has yet been proven?" said Ben, looking doubtful.

"All I can do with this new box will be to detect such a passage," said William. "I wish we could catch one and examine it, but that's beyond any theoretical science we can imagine."

"No need," said Karen. "Just identifying something moving faster than light will give all the theoretical astrophysicists and cosmologists a major shock. Time you switched it on, William."

William nodded and touched a switch. Almost immediately a beep sounded and a line appeared on the large monitor. More beeps sounded and rapidly the monitor was almost filled with lines.

"Good grief," said William. "The damn thing works. Is every one of those lines an energy bolt heading to the Galactic core?"

"And composed of tachyons," said Karen. "A theoretical item that nobody has been able to prove exists. We've changed physics and turned it upside down!"

"So now we need to know where those little things are going," said Ben. "We've had our ideas, this will prove it."

"There's definitely something there near the core," said Karen. "Now we have to find out what it is and why those little beasties are heading there. William can you tell how many of them went past us?"

"Several hundred in the last few minutes," said William. "To be exact, ninety-eight a minute. And that's interesting."

"Why's that, big brother?"

"Because Dad's experiments showed that these bolts left the human body at the point of death. I just checked — there are on average a hundred and five human deaths a minute. So it looks like they immediately set off for the core."

"We've stumbled on something interesting," said Karen. "Ben, take us home! I need to work on this."

* * *

"The next step is to find out just what is the entity that is absorbing these energies," said Karen.

"There's some interesting data we've just received from the other Galactic mentors," said Ben. "It will influence what you're planning." He looked at the other two and they were watching him carefully. "Two of them have been able to construct the device that William designed and they got the same results. There is a minute energy bolt that leaves the bodies of all the intelligent species in the galaxy and heads off in the direction of the galactic core."

"And almost certainly will behave as we have found, converting to tachyons once they have left the solar system and travelling at faster than light," said William.

"Almost certainly," said Ben.

"Which makes it critical to examine the entities that are receiving these energies," said Karen.

"Just thinking about this," said William. "If this entity is receiving only the energies from intelligent species, that is humans as far as Earth is concerned, then it hasn't been going on for all that long. Even if we add your species, Ben, and the mentors that preceded you, that's maybe only three or four million years. Compare that to the age of the Universe, some fourteen point seven billion years, that's very little time indeed. If there is some form of sentient being at the core of the galaxy, it's barely a newborn."

"And just as likely to be the story with the other galactic entities," said Ben with a nod of agreement.

"Which gives me an idea," said Karen. "But that's for some future time. For now, the critical thing is to work out just what manner of critter we've got there by the black hole in the middle of the galaxy."

Chapter Thirty – Report to the Council - 2062

"It seems to be the human race that is calling these more frequent Council Meetings in the last few years," said the Chairman of the Galactic Mentor Council. "I regret that our problem members have failed to appear. But again, welcome to Olivia and Gernardy."

The six Mentors appeared to be seated in a semi-circle around the conference room, though the reality was a series of holograph images in the holodeck suite in the Foundation building.

"I believe that is a characteristic of a species that is taking significant leadership in inter-Galactic affairs," replied Ben.

"I believe that to be the case," said the Chairman. "So does this mean you have something critical to tell us?"

"Maybe the most critical development so far," said Ben. He watched as the other council members stirred with interest.

"In the very first years of the operation that became known as "Blueprints" in a country on the human planet Earth, there was a man called Bill Askins," said Ben. "He was a scientist in the subject of genetics but even more critical was his astonishing genius in electronics. It was Bill who developed the scanners that first detected the visual and aural records of an individual's life in their DNA and then the same records of the individual's direct ancestors.

"Every one of you has had a similar story of the same discovery in your species by a uniquely talented scientist and that is what has led to this Council and the mission we all have to develop the maturity of our races.

"However, the human Bill Askins has discovered something else and that is why I have called this meeting. All of us have had the same questions about ourselves – is there a life of some form after physical death? Almost as a sideline, an accidental discovery while researching the uniquely human telekinesis ability, Bill detected a minute energy leaving the body at the point of death."

All the council members reacted to varying degrees.

"You mean he discovered a soul?" demanded a man in the middle of the semi-circle. Ben couldn't see whether this was shock, outrage or simple denial.

'We don't know what it is," he said. "But what we did find was that the tiny bolt of energy set off on a track towards the black hole at the centre of our galaxy. Now, we have all so far realised that there appears to be some form of energy near to the black holes that exist in all our galaxies and findings to date indicate that it may be a form of intelligence. We have tracked the paths of these energy bolts and they appear to be heading for the entity."

"And you think that these entities might be some form of self-aware, intelligent creature?" The Chairman looked calm.

"We have had some experiences in recent years that suggest some influence on our actions," said Ben. "You will remember how our ship encountered the invasion force from the rogue galaxy and somehow accepted an order to cauterise that force. It is possible that the order came from this entity which was fearful of the infection it detected and it reacted like a living body, sub-consciously activating an antibody to an infection.”

“And where did the energy in the humans originate?” asked one of the Council members, a middle-aged woman.

“Again, Bill used his technology and found that a very tiny amount of energy was passed to the embryo at the time of conception. This energy grew as the child grew.”

“So what you are saying is that there is an intelligent entity living close to the central galaxy Black Hole and this entity is growing as the energy from dying humans reaches it? And does this also mean that when a species reached what you have described as “Ascension” and disappears, the remaining energy from every member of the race also joins the central entity?”

The Chairman was looking more composed and his face showed fascination rather than shock.

“This is our theory, Chairman,” said Ben.

‘But does this only apply to humans?” asked the woman council member. “What of the other intelligent species in your galaxy? And does it apply to all of us, also?”

“We think it likely Councillor and we are about to start testing with other intelligent species in the galaxy once we have built enough units to take around the several planets in question. But that is why I called this meeting. I hope you will all agree to conduct the same tests in your world.”

“But how do we do that?” asked the Chairman. “How can we get these units here?”

“Physically, we can’t transport objects between galaxies, we know that, but as we have seen, there may be ways of doing so in the future. But what we have prepared are the blueprints for the devices. We will transmit them to you immediately. Your technicians should be able to construct your own.”

“An excellent idea,” said the chairman.

After a few moments, Ben spoke again. "Do you all have them and are you confident your technicians can work with them?" he asked.

All the councillors signified agreement, and Ben signed off. "It will be interesting to see the results," he murmured to himself.

"I still can't over the idea that we've been talking to people from three other galaxies, all at the same time," said Gernardy.

"Damn right," said Olivia. "This is bigger than any sci-fi novel I've ever read. I was having trouble breathing all that time."

"Better get used to it," said Ben. "You may have to be members of that group one day."

Chapter Thirty-One – Analysing the Entity - 2062

"It is certainly alive, it's not really self-aware and communication is quite impossible," said Karen.

Thirty thousand light years away, in the offices of the Foundation, William Askins smiled cheerfully.

"You've been sitting in Ben's spaceship for eight months, getting as near to the Black Hole as you dare, studying that entity and that's all you've been able to find? Baby sister, is that all you've got?"

"Seeing as I was in the area, I took the opportunity to study the Black Hole as well as the core entity, so apart from a few thousand terabytes of data, some actual brain wave patterns of the entity, a good estimate of its size and age, its rate of growth and probably birth date, that's about it, Son of Village Idiot. You couldn't do any better."

William's smile became a laugh. "Well done, little sister. Are you coming home now?"

"Any day, now. We'd better brief Ben and then develop an idea I've been working on while I've been out here."

"I'll put the champagne on ice for you."

"Make that two bottles, big brother. We'll need it. Oh, and while you're there, will you pick up my new Ferrari? I got a yellow one this time, all electric and after all this time cooped up here, I need that driving with the top down to restore my perfect complexion."

"No problems, kid. Can I have your old one? My Subaru is getting a bit elderly."

* * *

"I measured the rate of new arrivals of energy bolts from all over the galaxy and related that to its rate of growth," said Karen. "Then, in the same way as we calculated the time of the Big Bang, I worked backward, allowing for population growth statistics that each of our galactic species provided and calculated that this entity is about three point seven two million years old."

"So, as you said, just a newborn baby relative to the age of the universe and that of our galaxy," said Ben.

"Exactly," said Karen. "So any form of dialogue is quite impossible, first, because it has no form of speech, vocabulary or conceptual thinking, just as any child of a few weeks old would lack and second, because its thinking process would be in centuries instead of seconds."

"So there's nothing we can ask it or tell it?" said William.

"Not in under a time span of centuries," replied Karen. "But I did detect something we can think of as brain waves, just as in a sentient species like humanity."

"And what did they tell you?" asked Ben.

"That this is a sentient, intelligent form of life and in time it will grow to be a self-aware entity."

"But it means that for a long time to come, we can do nothing with this discovery," said Ben.

"I disagree," said Karen. "But I need to work a lot on one of the major problems all of us in the galaxies that we know so far have and perhaps work out a solution."

"How long?" asked Ben.

"Probably two years. Big Brother Village Idiot, I'll need your help."

"I thought you'd never ask," said William.

* * *

"So you were right," said William. "They're at their slowest and most vulnerable immediately they leave the body."

They stood in the ward of the hospice where an old woman had just died. Between them was a box the size of a suitcase, grey, metallic sides all round and a monitor sitting on top. The screen showed a tiny spark flashing around the interior, bouncing off the walls in what looked like panic.

"Of course I was right," said Karen, her face expressionless. "This Karen Petrova is always right. And they would also be open to capture by an enclosed, powerful, electro-magnetic field. It took you a few months, but your design seems to have worked."

"Okay, so we've captured one, but it's looking very panicky. It needs to be on its way."

Karen nodded. "Let it go home to Mummy."

William switched off the power to the box and the monitor went dark. He looked at the other device in the room. "It's on its way," he said softly.

He turned to the body on the bed. "Thank you so much, Olga," he said. "You have helped us solve one of the biggest problems in the universe. We'll always be grateful." He turned to the nurse at the doorway and nodded. She immediately went to the bed, detached a number of electrodes from the body of the old woman and began preparing her for removal.

"Now the next step," said Karen.

* * *

"I'm a scientist," said Karen Petrova, "so I should not be shaken to the core by this, but I am."

"Come on, baby sister, it's not every day you find yourself in a different galaxy. Even an astrophysicist is allowed to be shaken up a bit by this." Only a faint tremble in William's voice betrayed his own reaction to having followed the path of the alien ships that had invaded their own galaxy back to their source.

"I know," said Karen. "But it still makes me quiver at the thought."

"Quiver all you want, little sister, but we have to go down there and do what we set out to do."

"You're right, Big Brother. Let's get on with it."

"The man is right," said Ben. "That's why we navigated our way to this point, remote enough to be safe from the local black hole and near enough to detect anything travelling to the entity and any waves coming out."

Karen nodded and seemed to take control of herself.

"William, will you switch on that equipment?"

A moment later, the cabin of the spaceship echoed to the same sounds that had been detected in the home galaxy.

"Much the same as before," said William with a satisfied smile. "Between a hundred and two hundred energy bolts in tachyon form peddling fast at super light speed heading for a space down near the black hole."

"Can you pinpoint the location?"

"Within six light hours of a central point," said William.

"Excellent, Village Idiot Brother. Alright, I have focused on that point, let's see if anything is radiating outward from there."

The cabin went silent for over an hour while Karen studied the monitor on her computer and made minute adjustments. At one point, she looked up at Ben and smiled.

"It's the same equipment I used to study the other entity," she said. "But as I expected, the frequencies of what I think are some form of brain waves are different from before and I'm still trying to find them." She turned back to her monitor and silence fell back on the cabin.

Over three hours passed before Karen moved again and she looked up at the two men.

"Got it," she said. "Now I can record the waves for twenty-four hours and see what we've got. What's for dinner?"

* * *

"It's been six months and I've run so many comparison analyses between the brain waves of the two entities, I've almost lost my mind," said Karen.

"Most unlikely," said William. "You've been doing work that no astrophysicist or quantum scientist has ever done before. You might be exhausted, tiny sister, but I suspect you are as happy as a kid left alone in a chocolate shop."

"You may be right, Big Brother. But I'm a bit stiff from sitting at that monitor for so long."

"And just what have you found? You gave me some thoughts a few months ago, but nobody has seen you since. Has it been worthwhile?"

"You know how everybody knows the story of how my biological mother, the first Karen Petrova said that she and Hector 'would change world' as she put it?"

"It's one of those global stories," said William. "She certainly fulfilled that promise."

"Well, dear Big Brother, you and I are changing the galaxies."

"Okay, that's pretty dramatic. Tell me how."

"What all these months have shown me is that the galactic entities are similar to each other. The brain waves are very much alike, they seem to be about the same age, both very much infants, they react to stimuli but not in any conscious manner."

"But there's something else, isn't there?"

"Yes, there is. The brain waves of our home galactic entity seem smooth, even, harmonious. Those of the rogue galaxy are a little bit jagged, uneven, a bit like a musical instrument that occasionally plays the wrong note."

"And is that what has affected the residents of the galaxy, particularly the mentors?"

"I'm sure of it. We were able to get a few agents down on some of the planets who recorded the brainwaves of several different species and all of them show some similar patterns to the central entity."

"Well, this is certainly stunning information, but what can we do with it? How does one go about treating an infantile intelligence on a galactic scale?"

"To be honest, William, I haven't the faintest idea."

"It's a pity we can't take some of our best people who have that ability to change emotions and grow them to galactic scale and let them loose on the thing.

Karen stared hard at him.

"What?" she said.

"Hey, it's a joke. There's no way in the universe anyone could give psychiatric treatment to a four million year old infant."

She continued to stare. "William," she finally said. "Your life to date has been astonishing for its total lack of value and achievement, but you may have just had the most brilliant idea of all time."

He looked back at her with a straight face.

"You'd better explain, because if you are thinking what I'm thinking, I have some more brilliant design work to do."

"I am and you do," she said.

Chapter Thirty-Two - Report to the Galactic Mentor Council - 2063

"Looks like the rogue mentors have failed to show up again," murmured Ben.

"Just as well," replied Karen. "Better they don't know what we're about to propose.

"Probably right," said Ben. "Okay, Showtime! Everybody's here now."

The same set of individuals who had attended previous meetings of the Galactic Mentor Council were now present as holographs in the holodeck room of the Foundation.

"Welcome to another Council Meeting," said the Chairman. "We seem to be having these with far greater frequency than in previous times and I regret the absence yet again of the one member who has shown hostility to us."

"I think it is better than she continues to be absent," said Ben. "This meeting will hear remarkable information and a plan to combat our major problem."

"That is interesting," said the Chairman. The other members all leaned forward in their seats.

"Let me introduce two more of my colleagues," continued Ben. "These are the children of two of the most influential members of our group on Earth. William Askins is the son of the extraordinarily brilliant electronics engineer who designed the equipment that first detected the characteristics of DNA that set off the whole development of Humanity as potential future mentors. Karen Petrova is the biological daughter of the founder of that group and both of them have been working with us for the last few years."

"Welcome to both of you," said the Chairman. "What is the information you wish to give us?"

"As you know," began Karen, "at the last meeting, Ben gave you the equipment to check if your intelligent species in your own galaxies displayed the same features as ours. That is, a small bolt of energy leaving the body as the point of death and leaving rapidly until your detectors lost contact with them."

"It was an amazing find," said the Chairman. "But we could not track these energy bolts beyond the limits of our solar systems when they simply vanished."

"That is the first part of what we wish to tell you today," said Karen. "But first, a question. Have your scientists theorised about the existence of an energy form, either a particle or a wave that travels faster than the speed of light?"

"Please wait,' said the Chairman and looked down at his desk and appeared to be studying a source of information. "No," he said after a few minutes. "Such concepts have never been more than speculation, not based on any solid science or observation."

"Ours have," said Karen. "While the concept has been strictly theoretical, a great deal of research has been conducted by some of our finest minds. We call these theoretical particles "Tachyons," but they may be waves rather than particles and their entire nature is all still a mystery."

"Are you about to tell us you have identified such particles or waves?" The Chairman looked excited, as did the other Council Members.

"We have," said Karen. "Again, it was strictly theoretical. Once we had tracked the original energy forms leaving the dead bodies and noting that they appeared to be heading to the galactic core and then vanishing as they passed the outer planets of our solar system, we theorised that they converted to tachyons, exceeded the speed of light and so were undetectable from where we were watching."

"Did you test if the same happened with other species in your galaxy?" asked the Chairman.

"We did and we found the same behaviour."

"This is fascinating," said the Chairman. "Were you able to investigate further?"

"Of course," said Karen, her bright red lips parting in a smile. "We took Ben's ship and positioned ourselves several lightyears from our solar system towards the middle of the galaxy and used William's enhanced tracking equipment. We were able to confirm that energy bolts passed us at faster than light speeds heading for the black hole region. We were able to count these as they passed and found that the numbers were roughly equivalent to the rate at which humans died on Earth."

The Council Members looked stunned. Briefly, Karen thought about just what they looked like in their normal shapes and how astonishment would have appeared. She was impressed by the technology of the holograph transmitters that converted the actual reactions to human-like expressions.

"Then we took the ship to another of the populated planets and did the same, again finding that energy bolts flew outward at roughly the same rate as deaths on that planet. We concluded the same would be true of all intelligent species, everywhere."

"This seems to confirm that there is a form of life near the black hole of each galaxy that may be displaying some form of sentience," said the Chairman.

"Exactly our conclusions," said Karen.

"Is it possible, do you think, to communicate with this entity?" The Chairman looked excited but also a little frightened.

"I will come back to that in a moment," said Karen. "But obviously, once had made these findings, the next step was to try and identify the nature of this entity and we have spent many months working on that question."

"And your presence here indicates that you have learned the answer." It was a flat statement rather than a question and indicated that the Chairman had reached his capacity for shock.

"The first question we tackled was the possible age of the entity," said Karen. "I was able to obtain the statistics for all the intelligent races that now inhabit our galaxy or have done in the past, their total numbers from their first emergence as intelligent beings to their end, their death rates from then and through to the latest figures for the populations, allowing for growth. Working on those data, I tentatively concluded this entity has been receiving energy for something over three million Earth years."

"So it should be well grown and mature by now, surely?" said the Chairman.

Karen shook her head, again briefly wondering how that image was translated to her holographic image being seen on their home planets by the Council members.

"Quite the reverse," she said. "We must remember that our scientists' best estimates are that the age of the Universe is fourteen point seven billion Earth years. Our own solar system is approximately five billion years old and the precursor to human life only developed less than a million years ago. So far, the indications are that the known solar systems may be six or seven billion years old but we have yet to discover an intelligent species that is more than three million years old and that includes the Mentor race that assisted Ben's species to develop as the next Mentors. Given the massive ages of the Universe relative to the ages of intelligent species, we think this entity is barely a newborn child. And that brings us to the question you asked, can we communicate with it? I have to think that we cannot, any more than we can communicate successfully with a child of just a few weeks old."

"But how then do you explain the episode when your ship appeared to receive instructions to destroy the invasion fleet and then cauterise the planet?" The Chairman seemed confused.

"An instinctive reaction when the entity is frightened by something unknown," said Karen. "Just as a child will flinch and cry out if frightened by something. A fully aware, mature entity would not have ordered the multiple deaths of cauterisation. But this entity, while not mature, is immensely powerful and it did not know what it was doing, only knowing that it was protecting itself."

"This is quite stunning," said the Chairman. "Have you any further ideas on where you will go next?"

"I have," said Karen. "Next step is to examine the entity as much as possible, try and identify its nature in far greater detail, if possible, gauge its size and anything else we can find. And that suggests a further course of action."

"Which is?"

"As you know," said Ben. "Once we had identified the route, inefficient as it was, to the Rogue galaxy, two of our best apprentices with the strongest ability to modify emotional states in other people actually went there and tried to meet the Mentor Council of that galaxy. It was less than successful, the mental disturbance everywhere is dangerously high."

"Yes, it was perhaps a foolhardy exercise," said the Chairman.

"I can't disagree," said Ben. "However, William and Karen here repeated the trip, but this time only to the fringes of the galaxy and examined the mental waves from the core entity. They concluded there was strong pathological damage but also major similarities in mental structures. I believe that if we can find significant differences between a healthy entity and one that appears to be less healthy, maybe we can find some way of effecting a cure."

The Council Members were silent.

"I think you've stunned them," whispered Ben. "Time to close this meeting."

Chapter Thirty-Three – A Meeting of Chief Mentors - 2064

Ben sat in his regular chair in the holodeck room. Karen and William sat next to him. This meeting had been arranged through the Mentor Councils of the other galaxies, excluding the Rogue galaxy which had refused to meet with him.

"As I explained earlier," said Ben, "these are the Chief Mentors, the individuals who manage the teams of mentors, journeymen and apprentices on the planets within their own galaxies. These are my direct managers."

A brief flicker occurred to his right, followed by three more and the holographic images of four individuals seated in various chairs appeared in front of him. For a few moments each of the mentors looked around and studied the others.

Taking a deep breath, Ben opened the proceedings.

"This is the first time we have ever met," he said. "I am deeply honoured to meet you all and I thank you for coming. May I introduce two highly influential members of the organisation on Earth that has played such a significant role in Humanity's growth and maturity? Their names are Karen and William."

What looked like a middle-aged man in the group spoke. His expression seemed pleasant and he waved politely.

"Welcome to both of you. I think we all sense the importance of this meeting," he said. "I know I feel the same honour to meet such extraordinary people as you are. But Ben, as you said, this is the first time the Chief Mentors of the galaxies have ever met because there has never been any need for such meetings. We are always fully briefed on developments by our own Councils and your mentor teams meet in a lower council to compare progress. I must therefore ask you, why have you called this gathering?"

Ben waved a hand in acknowledgement of the question.

"You have every right to be curious," he said. "But I needed to compare notes with all of you about some developments in our galaxy and the one that we have named the Rogue galaxy. I know that your Mentor Councils are aware of the difficulties caused by that galaxy, but I don't know to what extent the problems have affected you and how much you know about this and a few other matters."

"We know about that rogue council," said a young woman. "But events in other galaxies really cannot affect us, given the impossibility of travel between them."

"Then I have some disturbing news for you," said Ben. "As you know, nearly thirty years ago, we learned of an invading force on one of our planets. When we went to investigate, we found that the invaders, a few hundred armed troops had colonised the primitive people of that world. What we didn't tell you, as we wanted to be quite certain of this first, was that we found that they had come from the Rogue galaxy. They had found a way of crossing inter-Galactic space."

"What?"

The gasp of astonishment came simultaneously from the others.

"How did that happen?" asked the young woman who had spoken before. Her eyes were wide with shock and as he always did, Ben wondered if that was her normal expression of astonishment or was it just how the holographic system had interpreted some other form of surprise into this human image.

"We had to consider that the Mentor Council there had simply ordered a large number of suicide missions by ships who took random leaps into hyper-space, losing most of them in the process, but a few managed to find tracks to our galaxy," Ben said.

"Good God!" exclaimed an elderly man. Once more, Ben wondered what he had really said the thought crossed his mind that he would one day like to research just what forms of religions had ever existed in the civilisations in other galaxies.

"It was astounding," Ben said. "But now I have to tell you about two more developments and ask if anything similar has occurred in your experience."

The others leaned forward in their seats.

"One unique talent has developed in a small number of the latest species to enter our apprentice program," said Ben. "This is the human species, one that has had a complex history, not always a happy one and only received the DNA recording modification in the last few thousand of their years. They only discovered the ability to read those records a few decades ago and soon after, a few of them found a talent for telekinesis."

"We did read some reports on that from some mentor teams," said a young man. "But details were sparse. How strong was it?"

"Very weak," said Ben. "They did develop an electronic way of enhancing it and used it intelligently in various forms of arts and science. Let me ask, have any of you found such a talent in any of your races?"

He was greeted by shakes of the head from the others.

"I thought not. But then we discovered that telekinesis was just a side effect of a far more critical talent. A very small number of our colleagues in the group that led the developments in DNA studies on Earth found they had the talent to modify the emotional state of other people."

"Now that is interesting," said the middle-aged man. "How powerful is it?"

"A handful of them that we know so far have been able to calm a mob of a few dozen rioters."

"And does it only work on their own species or have you tried it with non-humans?"

"That's the critical point," said Ben. "When we three confronted the invaders, the initial response of the soldiers that met us was hostile, but our best practitioner of this ability was able to calm them down. However, when we travelled to their headquarters and again received a hostile reception, she was unable to get that result. The alien force tried to kill us. And that's where the next surprise occurred."

He looked around the group.

"My ship rescued us from the hall where this event was taking place. That was programmed and expected. We were able to get back to the ship which took us into orbit. However, without any instruction from me, the ship broke all normal procedures and cauterised the planet, destroying the entire invading force."

The shock in the room was palpable.

"When I tried to interrogate the ship's computer, it was unable to explain why it had done this. It insisted it had only cauterised an infestation and was unable to understand that it had destroyed an intelligent life form, something it is categorically programmed to prevent.

That's when we realised first, that the invaders had come from another galaxy and the ship could not recognise them, but even then, such drastic action without authority was outside the ship's programming."

"So something else ordered the action?" The young man looked shattered.

"Exactly," said Ben. "The ship did say it had received orders but was unable to say where those orders had originated."

"Have you since found out?"

"We have. We now know that there is a form of sentient, intelligent life near the core of the galaxy, not far from the Black Hole that is in the centre of every galaxy. But it is far too young in galactic terms for communication, in fact it is just a new-born infant. But it can react to stimuli and the order to destroy the invaders was merely a cry of pain and fear from an infection."

The others sat back in deep thought for a while, absorbing the information.

"Having completed similar research recently, it seems that there is such a core entity in every galaxy," said the young man.

"There is certainly one in ours," said Ben. "There appears to be one in the Rogue. We pretty sure that every galaxy has such a presence."

"And is the one in the Rogue somehow unbalanced and causing the behaviour of the Mentors there?"

"We think so."

"Can anyone do anything about it?" The middle-aged man looked concerned.

"We're working on it," said Ben.

The man looked at his colleagues. "Is any of this story familiar to any of us?" he asked and received silent shakes of their heads. He looked back at Ben. "I thought that mentoring a few dozen planets around our galaxy was complicated enough, but you have just cranked up the problem."

"It's all astounding for all of us," Ben said.

"And this new species, the humans, are they part of the solution?"

"They appear to be unique," said Ben. "Whether they will display further unique qualities in the future is unknown, but there is no doubt, their impact on the entire mentorship program has been extraordinary."

"So what next?" said the young woman.

"We don't know," said Ben.

"But we're working on it," said Karen.

"And I'm sure we'll find out," said William.

The council members seemed to have no response.

Chapter Thirty-Four – Galactic Psychotherapy - 2064

"As we all know now, Dad's original design of a device to suppress the human telekinetic ability failed miserably," said William to the small audience of Foundation members. "But like a lot of work by geniuses, it instead resulted in a device to enhance the ability and gave rise to some massive advances in the arts and in medicine. Call it serious serendipity."

A small laugh ran around the room.

"And as we have since learned, in trying to do further developments in that talent, Dad discovered the astounding fact that a minute bolt of energy leaves the body at the point of death and heads off into deep space and towards the central core of the galaxy. So call that Serendipity Two, reducing the whole telekinesis thing to merely a by-product of far more critical discoveries."

"That's the trouble with geniuses," said Ben. "Everything they do, even by accident turns out to be useful and critical."

"Exactly," said Karen, taking up the narrative. "And that discovery led to the discovery of an entity at the galactic core that appears to be self-aware, massive, growing but as yet, far too immature to deal with."

"And that may be the most astonishing discovery in all human history," said Mary. "Your work was amazing, Karen."

"Thank you. But it led to the conclusion that each galaxy has a similar entity. So far, we have only identified and analysed the one in our own galaxy and the one in what we have called the Rogue galaxy which sent out invading forces and in the process, gave us a way of travelling to that specific galaxy."

"And as you know," broke in William, "Ben facilitated our visit to that galaxy, using the sole hyperspace path that we know to exist letting us cross inter-galactic space and examine that entity. We found definite signs of psychopathy."

"Do you plan to use all this new knowledge in some way?" asked Mary.

"Indeed we do. But we have to find a way of placing some form of secret agency in the Rogue galaxy in what used to be called a "Fifth Column" to subvert the power that is causing this problem. For humans to try and live and work on a planet in that galaxy is too risky. The Mentors there would soon discover them. It has to be done by local species."

"Easy," said Ben. "And when we do that, just what are you proposing?"

"First thing we do," said Karen, "is examine exactly what happens during the process of this form of psychotherapy."

* * *

"Dammit," said William. "Prisons are a miserable place."

"Hard to avoid that," said Ben. "Everybody there is miserable, frightened, angry or all of the above. Not exactly a likely source of calm and loving kindness."

"I suppose so. But we've been here six times, so far and it depresses the hell in me each time."

"It's essential research," said Ben. "But this should be the last time. Got your gear? Let's go."

They left the car, walked to the entrance and were recognised by the guards. Step by step, they were passed through different parts of the prison until they reached the Metropolitan Remand and Reception Centre, the maximum-security section for men. William's electronic equipment had been thoroughly examined each previous visit but it got the same treatment this time as well from two harsh-faced guards before they were passed through. Another guard led them to a small meeting room where a middle-aged man was seated at the table. He stood up and smiled as the two visitors entered. Perfect white teeth shone in a deep black face and huge dark eyes studied the arrivals.

"Good morning," said William. "I'm William Askins."

"Johnathon Okoh."

"And I'm Ben Fulton."

"So I gather you're going to watch as I work on the subject?" said Johnathon.

"Yes, and I'm trying to find out what mental process is going on while you do," said William.

"With that electronic stuff?"

"Exactly. It's an amazing talent you have and I'm trying to work out just how you do it."

"Okay, but you won't interrupt the process at all?"

"Promise. We'll be watching from next door through the video monitor but we'll leave the monitoring equipment here. Who's the first subject?"

"A difficult case," said Johnathon. "He killed three children in a wild fit of rage two years ago. There seemed no reason for the anger, but his history showed similar outbursts in his past. Nobody killed, but some serious damage to bystanders. This is my first session with him as I try and change that mental state."

"We'll just sit still and read your brainwaves," said William. He and Ben left the room and entered another. A large monitor stood in one corner, already showing the office they had just left.

The door opened and two men entered. One was in uniform and he led in a young man in standard prison clothing, his hands cuffed together. The prisoner was taken to the table and seated across from Johnathon, his cuffs placed in a lock. He seemed in his thirties, his face thin, large eyes were dark and his demeanour was crumpled, as if all life had been beaten out of him.

The guard positioned himself in the corner and stood silently.

"Jackson, my name is Johnathon Okoh, I'm a psychologist. I'd like to talk to you about your history."

"Why is there a camera in here? Who's watching?"

The prisoner's voice was harsh, tense.

"Just two other psychologists, Jackson. They're observing me for professional standards. Okay?"

Jackson nodded.

Johnathon began asking simple questions about the prisoner's life and experiences, not touching on the murders or previous violence, but William knew he was really tuning into Jackson's emotional state. He concentrated on his own equipment and saw that something was being generated and recorded.

Gradually, the questions began to address the violence in Jackson's history and then the murders of the children and the prisoner was obviously becoming more and more agitated and angry, his voice rising, spit falling from his mouth. And then he seemed to calm down, became rational again. The change seemed to puzzle him.

"What happened there?" he said, his voice more a whisper in puzzlement.

"I think you took control of yourself," said Johnathon. "That was excellent, well done. That will do for today." He nodded at the guard who unlocked Jackson and led him away.

"Did you get what you wanted?" asked Johnathon as Ben and William returned to the room.

"I certainly got something," said William. "What actually happened? What did you do?"

"As he got onto the violence, his brainwaves became red, jagged, sharp. I concentrated on trying to change the colours to blue and yellow which I have found to be most effective and smooth out the jagged edges."

"It seemed to work," said Ben.

"For now," said Johnathon. "I doubt the change will be permanent, I'll probably need several sessions."

"But you've been successful many times," said Ben. "I see that several of your patients have been moved from the maximum-security wing to minimum-security and there's been no recidivism so far."

"I'm pleased with all of it," said Johnathon. "Finding that wild talent has been a great gift."

"You'll do another session now?" asked William.

"Not yet. This is a seriously exhausting business. So two of us work together, taking it in turns. I'll go and have a rest while my colleague, Phyllis takes the next prisoner."

He walked out of the room while William and Ben remained. A few minutes later, a woman was shown into the room. She looked in her sixties, grey hair, smartly dressed in a blue trouser suit.

Introductions over, Ben and William watched from the next room as the process was repeated with a man in his forties with a long history of violent outbursts, several attacks on bystanders and one death from a single-punch on a young man in Kings Cross for which there was no motive and no warning.

Half an hour later, the session ended and the prisoner was led out.

"How did that go?" Phyllis asked. Her face looked drawn and fatigued.

"I think I got what you did," said William. "How about you?"

"I managed to smooth things out, change the emotions. That was my third session with that man, I think one more and he can probably move to minimum-security."

"You do amazing and valuable work," said Ben. "Your colleagues all over the world have reduced the prison population significantly."

Phyllis smiled. "I've very proud of it and grateful to have developed this talent. Now, if you'll excuse me, I need a cup of tea and a lie down."

By the end of the day, William had six recordings in his system.

"That should be enough," he said as he packed up the gear. "We've got fifty-three recordings in total, should be enough for me to analyse and see just what happens."

They nodded at the guard and were led out of the maximum-security wing, to the front of the prison and back into the open air.

* * *

"It's taken me some weeks, but I've finally got what we need," said William.

"It's been that long since I saw you last," said Ben. "And then both of you just rushed off to your labs without more than a mumble. Better explain."

"I analysed fifty-three recordings of our best operators effecting changes in the emotional and mental structure of some serious criminals," said William. "It took a lot of work, but finally I was able to structure them in the same wave format as in the energy bolts that leave the body at the point of death."

"And then?" Ben looked calm, sipping his coffee, relaxing in the armchair, but there was some tension evident in him.

"And then it took a while longer, but we found that these waves could be merged with those of the energy bolt."

"And then we released those modified bolts of energy to join the core entity," said Karen. "There were only a few, so they would have no effect on the entity."

"This sounds extraordinary, but what do you plan to do with this new technology?"

"Ben, I'm sure you know," said Karen, smiling gently. "We're going to play galactic psychiatrists with the rogue galaxy."

* * *

"The first problem," said Karen, "is to capture as many of the energy bolts as possible from dying individuals in the rogue galaxy. William designed a device that does it successfully with humans, there's no reason to doubt that it will work with any species."

"That means going down to several planets there and taking numbers of the boxes with us. That sounds risky, given the hostility of the Mentors there." Ben frowned as he thought about it.

"We've thought about that," said William. "As you know, this galaxy has always signalled to you when a new species reaches enough intelligence to need mentors. It didn't happen when the alien ship arrived, but now we know why."

"It's always been a mystery how that happened," agreed Ben. "That is, until we identified the existence of the entity at the core."

"But we've paid two visits to the Rogue galaxy and our arrival didn't get signalled to the Mentors there," said William.

"That's true!" said Ben. "So we could probably land a ship somewhere and unload a number of William's devices into a store somewhere and depart without being seen. But taking some hundreds of the bolts from dying individuals, that would take time and our people would be detected eventually."

"Thought of that, too," said William, smiling broadly.

"Why am I not surprised?" said Ben.

* * *

The air outside was cool and pleasant as Ben's ship landed in the centre of the small town.

"The last time this ship was here, we faced a hostile army of invaders from the Rogue galaxy," said Ben. "Our two agents did a remarkable job modifying their minds to become peaceful settlers. This little town looks like it was a successful operation."

"That looks like the town hall," said Karen. "Hopefully, we'll find some sort of authority there."

"It's the only urban centre on the planet," said William. "So that's probably right. Let's go and see. Personal shields on, translators tuned in."

The short walk to the biggest building in the town was observed by many of the locals but no threat or hostility was observed. They entered the town hall to find a spacious area with high ceilings. Several of the local people were there.

"Hello!" said Ben. "We thought we'd pay a visit and see how you were getting on."

"You are most welcome," said one, a tall man wearing an ornamental chain round his neck. "I am Chasek and I was elected leader of our community. And we would like to request some assistance from you."

"Not a problem," said Ben. "What do you need?"

"Some farming machinery. Ploughs, tractors and some engineering facilities to build more."

"I'll send the request to my home as soon as I get back to the ship. We'll also send some engineers to assist in the set up and running of a manufacturing plant."

"That would be wonderful."

"In return, there is some assistance we would like with one of our projects."

"Of course! How can we help?"

"Two things. May we take some DNA samples from a few people? It would help us learn more about you and be prepared to help should illness strike at any time. We would be able to create some medicines for any possible problem."

"Of course, that seems something that would help us. And the second?"

"We have only limited language translation capabilities at the moment. Could we record the speech of a number of individuals so that we can enhance the systems?"

"Again, not a problem. Please feel free to proceed with both plans."

"Many thanks. We'll return to the ship now so I can send the request for machinery and engineers back to my home planet."

"That gets us started on the project," said Ben as they sat back in the ship's lounge. "Once we have the DNA, we can grow some bodies of the locals and we can develop the language education systems to full functionality."

"The DNA should also provide us a great deal of the history and culture of the people so that we can educate our agents fully," said William.

"We'll need to identify their home planet, too," said Karen. "One species will be enough for the plan."

"Then let's get to work," said William.

* * *

"This will be the most dangerous mission we have asked of you," said Ben to the room of apprentices and journeymen mentors. "It will be the first time we have sent any of you to another galaxy and the work you will do is nothing like that which you have done so far. You will work on a small planet a long way from the centre of the authoritarian regime which the Mentors there have created, but that regime would be hostile to what you are doing, should they be able to discover it.

"Unlike previous missions, the transfer to an alien body will take place here and then you will travel by spaceship through a series of hyperspace jumps, the only route we have found so far, to another galaxy."

A hum of interest ran around the room.

"Going with you," continued Ben, "will be a number of electronic devices for a purpose I will explain later. You will need to be on the planet for perhaps a month, depending on how successfully you will be able to deploy those devices. At the end, we will be able to return you to your own bodies in the normal way, an instantaneous transfer."

* * *

"I want go on this assignment," said Karen

"Me too," said William.

Ben sighed. "Somehow I thought you'd both say that. Honestly, it's far too risky to chance losing either of you, but at the same time, having you there to ensure the systems are properly deployed would be a major advantage.”

“So when are we off?” asked William.

“Two weeks,” said Ben.

* * *

Karen opened her eyes and slowly took her awareness down through her body, sensing heavier than usual arms, thicker waist, longer torso and heavier, muscular legs. *My God, I'm in an alien body*, she thought to herself.

Carefully, she tested every muscle, flexing fingers, toes, moving her hands, then arms, lifting her head and looking around. A short distance away, she saw a bed with another alien body resting on it and wondered if that was William. As she watched, the person went through the same testing out process that she had conducted.

Carefully, she eased herself up into a sitting position and increased the movements of her arms and hands, gradually feeling more control grow. She looked down at her new body and saw it was dressed in something like a flight suit worn by pilots, much as the entity in the other bed wore. As she looked, it also sat up and stared at her.

“William?” she tried to say but found that her vocal cords could not cope. Trusting to the training she had received by high speed transmission from the computers, she tried again, leaving it to her reflexes. This time, she spoke in the language that had been given before her transmission to the new body. The sound was different, but recognisable.

“William?”

On the other bed, she saw him go through the same attempt, failure, analysis and adoption of the current approach.

“Of course it is, little sister,” he said, the alien words clear to her.

"I have to admit," she said, "this is one experience I never expected to have."

The door to the room opened and in walked Ben and Mary.

"How are you coping?" asked Ben. "Can you stand up yet?"

"About to try," said Karen. She realised she had spoken in the alien language, but Ben nodded.

"Translators in effect," he said. "I heard that in English."

Karen put her hands on the aide of the bed and pushed herself to her feet, just as William did the same. For a few moments, she felt unbalanced, then muscles she didn't know about took effect and she steadied. Again, she ran an internal check of the new body, sensing bones structured differently, muscles applying forces new to her and her eyesight was much sharper than before.

She looked over at William and saw that he was studying her in the same way she was examining him. There were sexual differences, she realised. William's body was a little taller than hers, arranged in different proportions with wider waist, shoulders and arms.

"The ship is loaded with twenty of William's boxes," said Mary. "There are ten of you on this mission. As we have said, take two each, the ship will drop you in five different cities in one country on the planet, working in pairs. You will need to find the equivalent of a hospice and arrange to leave your devices anywhere in the building you can. We were told by the aliens we had met earlier that they are termed "Death Houses" and it is customary for the very old to move there for their last few months, so there should be no difficulty in finding one."

"Check your bags," said Ben. "You have enough of the country's currency to last you some weeks, you will need to find accommodation. Our local aliens say that low-cost motel-type lodgings are common."

"And that device round your necks will provide instantaneous communication with the ship," said Mary. "When you have finished, touch that, we'll snap you back to your bodies here immediately."

"What happens to the alien bodies we leave behind?" asked William.

"They are programmed to dissolve into dust," said Ben. "So make sure you are well away from the towns and other people before you call home."

"Can we see our bodies?" asked Karen.

"Are you sure?" said Ben. "That can be a distressing experience."

"I'm curious," said Karen.

"That's spooky," said William. He and Karen stood a few metres away from the series of transparent cocoons in the ward dedicated to the purpose. Each body was fully enclosed and lay on its back.

"Everything functions normally," said Ben. "And all the mechanisms keeping the heart beating, blood flowing, skins kept fresh and so on, they all have triple backup systems. There's a small army of technicians monitoring them at all times.

"I can't see any connections," said William. "How is all that happening?"

"All contained in the beds," said Ben

"I didn't realise I was so small," said Karen.

"It' always a shock to look at one's own body," said Ben. "It's also very rare, because normally you are transmitted to the new body on its own planet and you are never in the same place. Can I suggest we get going? This can have a bad effect on you."

"Agreed," said William and took Karen's arm. "Let's go, little sister. We have important work to do."

Karen didn't speak but followed William out of the ward.

Chapter Thirty-Five – Foreign Mission - 2066

"This is a very unusual request," said the manager of the Death House. "I don't want to cause any more stress on my people here than they already face."

"They won't know anything about it," said William. "But it's important scientific work. There have been several reports by electronics engineers of sensing energy leave the body at the time of death and we are trying to verify them."

"You will leave these devices hidden in some room, not in the sleeping quarters of the residents?"

"Exactly," said Karen. "They need not know anything about it."

"And just what will these things do?"

"If there is any electronic or energy event as the person dies, the device will simply record it. We don't need to know anything about the person, or even who it is. We are just looking for an energy surge."

"Then you will get plenty of data here, if that is what happens. On average, we get three or four deaths every day."

"The devices will be self-powered for about a month," said William. "That will be enough for our analysis."

"In that case, I'll show you where you can place the boxes."

The manager led the way from his office, down a corridor and opened a door to a small room. It looked about half full of boxes, stacked almost to the ceiling.

"These are the personal effects of the residents," said the manager. "We store them here and when the relatives of the deceased come, we hand them over. Your devices will not be disturbed here."

"Thank you," said Karen. "We'll just switch them on, check that they are working correctly and leave you. We won't need to return because the results will be transmitted to our offices at the University."

The manager nodded and walked out of the room.

For a few moments, Karen and William busied themselves making sure the two systems were powered up and ready for work. They didn't have long to wait for a live test.

The first one beeped at them and they watched the monitor. A flash of energy appeared and moved rapidly around the electromagnetic enclosure as if seeking a way out. After just a second, there was a second beep and a smaller flash.

"Energy bolt appeared," murmured William. "Automatic generation of the secondary energy bolt containing the emotion-affecting wave directly into the first one, the two are now merged."

A third beep sounded and the electro-magnetic field that had captured the energy leaving the dying person somewhere in the building faded.

"Okay, little Tachyon, fly home to Mommy," said Karen.

A few minutes later, they returned to the manager's office.

"We can leave you now," said William. "We'll leave the systems in place."

The manager looked up from his desk and nodded. "Do you really think something leaves the body as a person dies?"

"We're sure of it," said Karen. "But just what it is, we don't know."

As they walked out of the building, William said, "That's our job done. Want to go home?"

"You're kidding!" said Karen. "We're on a planet in a galaxy that isn't ours! I want to be a tourist for a couple of days."

"No problem," said William "Though the food here is bloody horrible! I can't wait to get back to steaks, fresh fruit and sushi."

"You're boring, Big Brother."

"But a real genius," said William.

Chapter Thirty-Six – A Baby Cries – July, 2066

Penny's sleep was disturbed. The dream was bizarre, almost a memory of the first few months after the birth of her daughter Jessica when she would wake up to the sounds of the child crying and had to get up to feed her.

She woke with a sense of fright. She sat up, almost automatically turning sideways, sitting up and reaching for her slippers before she woke fully. Jessica was now forty, an accomplished surgeon in Sydney with her own teenage children.

Beside her, Avram stirred and woke up. They had always been so close mentally and he had sensed her disturbance.

"Going somewhere?" he murmured and stroked her back.

"That was weird," she said, realising she was trembling lightly. "I could have sworn I heard a baby crying and I woke up, just about ready to go and feed baby Jessica."

"Hey, don't tell me you just had a subliminal wish to have another baby!"

She turned round and lightly smacked him on his shoulder. "Silly man!" she said with a smile. "I think we're both a bit past that!"

"Just as well," he replied. "Never could cope with that midnight feeding and nappy-changing stuff. So, tell me more about the dream."

"Not really a dream," she said and lay back on the bed, turning to him and putting her arm round his shoulder. "But it was so lifelike, just a sense of a baby calling out in distress and needing comfort."

"It's odd how our memories play tricks on us," he said. "Our minds seem to travel in time quite easily."

There was no answer and Avram smiled as the sound of her breathing became deeper and slower. He had always envied her ability to fall asleep so quickly He thought back to Jessica's childhood and the astonishing intellect and almost telepathic abilities she had demonstrated. Within seconds he was also asleep.

* * *

The next night it happened again. This time, Penny was almost out of the bedroom before she woke up and stopped with a small cry of shock. Already half awake from her movement, Avram got up and put his arms round her.

"Another crying baby?" he asked.

She clung to him, breathing rapidly.

"Much louder, this time," she said into his shoulder. "What the hell is the matter with me? It sure as hell is not frustrated maternal instincts and this has never happened before."

"Let's go and sit down, I'll make you a cup of mint tea and see if you can calm down."

Ten minutes later, sitting side by side on the settee in the lounge, she closed her eyes and inhaled the aroma of the tea.

"The options seem to be that I'm having frustrated maternal instincts or something else. We both know the first is just twaddle, so the second could be that I'm actually frightened of something myself and just believing I'm hearing a child cry out."

"Hard to imagine what you're frightened of," said Avram. "Given the sort of experiences you have had the last forty years, I have no idea what could frighten you."

"You may be right," she said. "Hell, I've turned back mobs of people intent on killing us, I've stopped a crowd of armed aliens doing the same and travelled a decent proportion of the galaxy. What's there to be frightened of?"

"And you've been married to me for forty years. That should terrify any self-respecting woman."

She touched his hand. "Couldn't have done any of that without you," she said."

"Well, there's a third option," he said.

She looked sideways at him.

"You really were hearing somebody or something cry out," he said.

"This house is highly sound-proofed and secure," Penny said. "I don't think we'd hear that sort of noise level from outside. And there's no baby inside the place."

"Probably right. I tell you what, give it another night, if it happens again, we'll take the problem to the geniuses at the office. Somebody might be able to throw some light on this."

She put her cup down on the coffee table. "Sounds like a plan. Otherwise, we have to consider the possibility that your dearly beloved wife is on track to becoming stark, staring, batshit crazy."

"That sounds like fun," he said and rose to his feet, pulling her up alongside him. "Back to bed, young lady," he said.

"That's a better plan," she said and followed him back to the bedroom.

* * *

The third night, it happened again

"I think we need external help," said Avram, the anxiety showing in his eyes.

"I think you're right," she said.

* * *

"Did it really sound like a baby?" asked Karen.

"I'm not sure," said Penny. "It had that sense of fear and helplessness, but the baby-like sound may have been my imagination trying to make sense of it."

"Anything more than that is stranger than we might imagine," said Garry. "But we've all worked together for some decades now and we've seen some amazing things, so I'm not prepared to discount any possible answer to this."

"One thing I can think of," said Mary, "is remembering when Jessica was just about five and you found her reading some advanced book, astronomy I think. She told you then that you had diabetes, something you had no idea of."

"An ability she probably inherited from her parents, even though you had never realised either of you had it," said Karen.

"Where are you going with that?" asked Avram.

"Penny, you were the first to find that ability to affect other people's emotional structures," said Karen. "And today, even in your eighties, you still have it stronger than anyone else we've known."

"I think so," said Penny. She reached over and took Avram's hand. "Like Avram said, where are you going with this?"

"Back when you two and Ben first encountered the alien invaders, you hadn't been able to influence them," continued Karen. "But the second time, you told us how you had felt a wave of support from some source, how you abilities seemed increased by some influence and that time, you were able to change the invaders' emotional state."

"Which we thought must have been the core entity somehow influencing her," said Avram.

"But as Karen has shown," said Penny, "that entity is relatively a new-born infant and was just reacting to the fear of what it experienced as an infection."

"That's the key," said Karen. "Penny, you are the only human we know who has had some sort of communication with that core entity. We know it's just a new-born babe by its own timeline and it can't express itself coherently, but it can do what a human baby can do, cry out when it's frightened or hungry."

"And you think..." Penny looked startled.

"Yes, I do," said Karen. "The core entity is frightened of something, it's crying out and you're the only person who can hear it."

The room was silent for several minutes as each of them absorbed the implications of Karen's suggestion.

"But what can be frightening it?" Penny asked finally.

"Look at what we've done recently," said Karen. "We sent several thousand bolts of energy into the Rogue galaxy's core entity. They were modified with a wave version of the emotional changing ability we got from some current practitioners and we hoped that they might start to affect the entity's mental difficulties, though maybe not for a century or more. What if they've already started to have an effect, the rogue entity has sensed the change and it's frightened? And then what if it's crying out in distress and that's being heard by our home galaxy's entity which echoed the fear?"

This time, the shocked silence lasted even longer.

"Good grief!" Alana said into the silence. "Have we any way of proving this?"

"It's just an idea," said Karen apologetically. "I really don't know."

Garry broke the tension with a loud laugh. The others looked at him in astonishment.

"I've known a Karen Petrova of one sort or another for over fifty years," he said, struggling to contain his merriment. "One thing I learned from the first one is that her craziest ideas were always based on inspired genius. She was never wrong. Even when we started Blueprints with no pointer as to what we were looking for, Karen knew we'd find what we did. Everything she ever suggested turned out to be right. So when the second Karen Petrova makes a suggestion but says she doesn't know if she's right, I call bullshit! I'll bet the universe she's dead right! Our home entity is calling Penny for help."

The amusement spread around the room as the tension died. When it stopped, Garry asked the obvious question.

"So what are we going to do about it?"

"I have an idea," said Karen. The smile on her scarlet lips was wide.

"I thought you might," said Avram. "Let's hear it."

* * *

"We've found five therapists with the sort of patients that we're looking for," said Karen.

"I bet there are a hell of a lot more," said William. "It still amazes me how many frightened people there are in the world."

"No doubt," said Karen. "But these five have eighteen patients in total. That clever little box of yours should work the same way as it did before."

"Very likely," William said. "Shall we proceed?"

"Absolutely. The first one is here in Newcastle, she's got three patients, so let's start on our doorstep. We'll have to rent a car, we can't get all that stuff in my Ferrari or yours."

* * *

"We don't need to be in the same room," said William. "But we do need to have that box in there with you while you work."

"No problem," said Christine Worrall. "I'm so thrilled to be working with the Karen Petrova Foundation. After all, this career I have resulted from the work you did back in England."

"Who is your patient?" asked William as he took his electronics device from its case, switched it on and checked the start up processes.

"Jenny Parson," said Christine. "She's eighteen, only daughter of a violent father and a completely incompetent mother. She spent the first few years of her life being beaten regularly and then sexually abused before she ran away last year. She was found in the streets just a week ago and this will be our first session."

"You have a video-camera hidden in the corner?" asked Karen. "She won't see that and know she's being watched?"

"No chance. Now, put that device under the coffee table, I'll put a tablecloth over the table, that will hide it. Jenny and I will sit in the two armchairs across from each other and I'll try and work my magic on her. What is that thing, anyway?"

"We're trying to record the mind process you conduct as you work," said William. "We've been looking at this for some years, but this new box is showing good promise in seeing what you do."

"Wow," said Christine. "Okay, let's get started.

Two minutes later, Karen and William were sitting before a large tv monitor in another room as Christine settled herself in one armchair. The door to her room opened and a nurse walked in, holding the hand of a thin, dark young woman. At the sight of Jenny, the woman reacted strongly, gasping in terror and trying to run back out of the room. The nurse held her in a close embrace and murmured something to her that was inaudible to the watchers. When she let go, Jenny just moved to the corner of the room and huddled close to the wall, her face on her knees and her arms over her head.

"Really terrified, poor child," murmured William. "What sort of monsters were her parents?" He looked down on the mobile phone-sized device in his hands. "We're getting something," he said. "Christine is certainly radiating something."

The scene didn't change for over twenty minutes and then Jenny lifted her face from her knees, dropped her arms and looked at Christine.

"Who are you?" she asked. Her voice was barely above a whisper.

"My name is Christine. Would you like to come and sit in this nice comfy chair instead of the floor? Then I can pour you a cup of tea and we can have a chat."

"You won't hurt me?"

"Heavens, no! You're in a safe place here."

"I'd say Christine has worked some of that magic on the kid," said Karen. "You're sure you recorded the waves?"

William grinned at her and said nothing.

"I think that was pretty successful," said Christine after Jenny was led away by the nurse. "Her mind was a horrible shape of jagged edges, blind terror, red points like knives. I've never seen such a dreadful mess."

"But you managed to make some changes?" asked Karen.

"I did, but I'll need a few more sessions with her."

"You have two more patients?"

"I do. You want to stay and watch again?"

"If we can."

"Sure. Okay, go back to your room, the next one is coming in."

Over the next two hours, Karen and William watched as Christine sat silently while she tried to smooth out the fears of her patients. The next one was a middle-aged man, thin and bony, his face almost a skull with huge, dark, terrified eyes. He had once been trapped in an underground cave for four days before being discovered and rescued and had somehow survived the blackness, the rats and the terror. But he needed a lot of work to be returned to normal.

The third and last patient was a young man in his twenties who had begun to experience appalling nightmares two years earlier, many of them had infiltrated his waking hours and he spent much of his time screaming and sobbing, shaking like an unbalanced wheel.

Both patients showed some improvement after thirty minutes with Christine and were taken back to their rooms.

Christine could hardly stand up.

"I'm totally buggered," she said with a weary smile.

"I can imagine," said William.

"Did you get what you wanted?" she asked

"Yes we did," said William. "Sincere thanks, you do amazing work."

"Okay, shove off," she said. "I'm falling asleep."

As they closed the door behind them, they could see that she was indeed asleep in the armchair.

"Tomorrow, Port Macquarie," said Karen. "Four patients to watch."

"And just as stressful to watch as today," said William. "I never knew that some people could be such wrecks."

"At least we've been part of something that is able to help them," said Karen.

"Too right," said William. "But I need a drink."

* * *

"By the time we had seen all the therapists, we had wave records of eighteen treatments of terrified patients," said Karen. "My big brother's clever little box had recorded them and converted them to a form suitable for the next stage."

"So you are essentially repeating the process you followed before?" said Penny. "You recorded the efforts of a couple of therapists at a prison working with violent prisoners?"

"Exactly," said William. "Then we continued that process, we sent out some of our apprentices around hospices all over the place and left the gear with them on a permanent basis."

"So as of now, we have caught eight hundred energy bolts as they left the body, merged them with the new treatment waves that would modify the panic and calm the patient," said Karen. "Then we released them immediately and they set off to the Big Momma by the black hole. We left the devices at the hospices and the process of capture, merger and release will continue indefinitely."

"And you think this work? Our core entity will calm down?" Penny looked anxious.

"It worked with the Rogue and far quicker than we believed possible," said Karen. "So yes, it's a fair chance that you will start getting a proper night's sleep again."

"I'll prescribe some heavy-duty sleeping pills for the next few days," said Avram. "Hopefully, she'll sleep through the baby crying."

The rest of the group nodded with murmurs of support and Avram and Penny returned home.

Two weeks later, the crying stopped.

Chapter Thirty-Seven – An Invitation – 2067

Garry looked up from his desk as Ben walked into his office.

"Ben!" he said. "Good timing! I don't come to the office much these days, a man of my age has so much other stuff to do."

"Not a coincidence," said Ben. "I need to talk urgently to you and Mary. And I think you should include Alana, Avram and Penny."

"This sounds serious," said Garry. "And judging by your expression, it really is. What is it that needs the oldest members of the Foundation to get together?"

"Would you call them in, please, Garry?"

Garry looked briefly at Ben and picked up the phone. None of the others was in the building as all had essentially retired from Foundation matters in recent years, leaving the apprenticeship training program largely to Ben and the mentors on other planets. It took just over thirty minutes before the group was assembled in the small conference room used for such events. As each of them entered, they all had the same query.

"Garry, what's so important that the oldies fraternity has to be summoned from their bingo, needlework and television soap operas?" asked Mary, the first to arrive to see Garry sitting alone.

Garry smiled. "You were more likely engaged in matters involving Australian national intelligence," he replied. Alana walked in at that moment.

"Aha!" she exclaimed in mock anger, "I've found you two in a compromising situation! I always knew it! What's happening?"

"Ben needs us," replied Garry, taking her hand as she took a seat next to him. "And it really does seem critical."

Avram and Penny came in at that point, studied the group and raised their eyebrows. "Are we declaring war on somebody or winding up the Foundation?" asked Penny. "Avram and I were sitting on the deck with a bottle of champagne, looking at the sea when your call came through. Do you know how difficult it is to put the cork back in a champagne bottle?"

"My apologies to all of you," said Garry. "Ben needs to talk to us. We're the oldest members of the Foundation, so it must be critical."

"It is," said Ben, walking into the room and taking a seat at the conference table. He looked each of them in the eye for a brief glance as if ensuring he had their attention.

"When we started this apprenticeship program, I told you that Humanity was just one of a small number of species being considered for the role of mentorship of the dozen or so planets in the galaxy that had intelligent life forms with their own civilisations, cultures and levels of maturity. I told you that you were being evaluated and the process of evaluation would probably take some hundreds of years as your people and those of other species worked their way from apprentices to journeymen. That's how long it took my people to be selected, after which there was a long period of training from our own mentors before we were able to take on the role. And I had told you that our mentors had died out after a long period of declining birth rates."

"Yes, this is what you told us over thirty years ago," said Garry. "Has something changed, or has a decision been made to remove Humanity from consideration?"

"Some things have certainly changed," said Ben. "You may have wondered why I was the one introducing you to the Galactic Mentorship Council when I was just the planetary lead mentor here. Why not the most senior mentor, the one supervising all the planetary leads?"

"That did occur to me," said Penny. "But I assumed it was some form of protocol. Actually, I was more intrigued by why you were supporting Karen's and William's projects to affect the core intelligences in our galaxy and the Rogue. I thought that one would be surely the job of the senior guy."

"And you were right," said Ben. "It was."

"So you were promoted at some point?" said Avram. "But you didn't tell us?"

"About ten years ago," said Ben. "I didn't think it was necessary to tell you because the emphasis of my duties was here on Earth, with this Foundation. Here is where I have spent almost all my time, as you know."

"That's interesting," said Alana. "Are you telling us that we are perhaps the leaders in the evaluation process for mentorship? That seems unlikely, given that nearly all our own people are still only apprentices, just a very few journeymen."

"I'm not telling you that," said Ben. "What I am telling you is that the Management Committee of this galaxy has decided that the human race should be asked to take on the role."

The silence lasted for a full minute as each of them tried to absorb the enormity of what Ben had said.

"Why?" asked Garry, finally.

"A number of factors," said Ben. "You achieved some of the required standards earlier than other species by some centuries. I had already told you that your developments in the arts were far greater than any others and this is an essential characteristic for what it tells us about a race. The next rapid development was the almost total elimination of religions and mythical beliefs. This has left you free of fear and authoritarianism and again, it happened at an astonishing rate. I consider our work in getting two great religious leaders together and seeing them develop rational, humanitarian philosophies instead of the old fear-inspiring myths and legends has been one of the greatest successes of the mentorship programs on any planet."

"That was part of your efforts on Earth?" asked Mary. "You deliberately set out to eliminate religion from our cultures?"

"We have found it essential, everywhere," said Ben. "Religions have always clouded clear thinking, corrupted rational analysis and tried to control people through fear of some form of divine retribution if they didn't behave according to the wishes of the few in control. Mentors must have powerful critical analysis abilities and pure objectivity in conducting their missions. Religions counter that ability. And you achieved the same with politics and international relations."

"That was inevitable, once all secrecy had gone when anyone could read anyone's DNA," said Alana. "I don't think we set out deliberately to do that."

"No, but that's what has happened," said Ben. "A long time ago, nations' leaders began exchanging their DNA with each other before top-level meetings as a gesture of openness. There can be no surprises anymore."

"But as the first Karen Petrova once suggested would happen, despotic governments used that ability to search for opposition by conducting mass DNA readings of their citizens," said Mary.

"Yes, they did," said Ben. "But the same weapon was used against them by more democratic nations. They obtained samples of those dictators' DNA and uncovered secrets that when revealed to the world resulted in a quick removal for a variety of reasons. The result is that nobody dared try to rule by force because they faced total destruction through their own shame at some point. Several emperors were shown to have no clothes and disappeared soon after."

"But surely, you have achieved similar results with other civilisations?" said Avram. "Maybe not as fast as with us, but still you achieved them? Do none of the other contenders for this role have advanced arts cultures? Have none of them grown beyond religions?"

"Yes, we have," said Ben. "At least three of the contenders have achieved these goals, but humanity has a significant edge in the rapidity and the degree to which they were achieved."

"Okay, this is all stunning," said Alana. "It's most gratifying to hear that the human race has achieved great things. But this cannot be enough to nominate us as the next Mentors so early in the program. You said it could take a couple of centuries while we acquired much more experience in dealing with alien species and learning how to influence them in positive ways in their route to maturity. Why now, Ben? Why the rush?"

"You are quite correct, Alana," said Ben, smiling at her. "There are two reasons for the rush. The first is the unique characteristic that humans have developed. It first appeared as a weak form of telekinesis that your researchers developed as far back as the early days in England. Nobody else has ever developed such an ability."

"But you did," objected Penny. "Remember, way back at that golf game, you found you could move a golf ball with your mind. You're not from Earth, so how come you could do it? And have any others of your species developed it?"

"It's true, I did and I was shocked to discover it. Since then, we have been experimenting back home with hundreds of subjects. Not a single person has ever been able to reproduce that talent. We wondered if it was a characteristic of human DNA, we took samples to my planet and people spent hundreds of hours studying them but nothing happened. We had our apprentices and journeymen on Earth do the same, no effect. I seem to be the only one who got it and we still don't understand how. Maybe it was just the extended exposure to human DNA that this body has experienced for many decades, but that's not the critical fact."

"What is?" asked Penny.

"It's that the telekinesis was only a minor side-effect of a far greater ability."

"Ah! The ability to modify emotional behaviour," said Penny. "Yes, I can see how that is super-critical in this situation and it certainly has proved invaluable on a few occasions."

"And that is a huge understatement when you look at the work of Karen and William in affecting the emotions of two galactic core entities," said Ben. "How can we place a value on that achievement?"

Again, a short silence hung over the table.

"Okay," said Mary, "I can see why we have been nominated, but that doesn't explain the rush."

"And that's the other factor," said Ben. "As I have told you, our mentors died out after a long period of declining birth rates. It last two centuries and one day, the last one died. That was when we took over their role. Our birth rate began to decline about sixty years ago. But in the last thirty years, there has not been a single birth anywhere on my home planet. We can find no reasons for it, no medical answers can be seen, none of the usual factors of pollution, poisons, nothing. It's almost as if some external force is killing us off. And we think it's the influence of the galactic core entity. Somehow, it has recognised that my people have no further role to play in the future of the galaxy and we are quite certain that our early decision to nominate humanity was also influenced by that entity.

"You have about fifty years to take over the mentorship of the dozen or so civilisations we look after."

* * *

"So what happens next?" asked Garry.

"Next must be your decision to accept the job," said Ben.

"But who can make that decision for the human race?" asked Alana. "Who is possibly qualified to speak for seven billion people?"

"First, you won't be making that decision for the whole world," said Ben. "The number of people actually involved in the mentorship programs and the training of apprentices is minute and the rest of the world has no need to know, even if they could handle that knowledge. On my own world, the number of people involved barely reaches a thousand, most of them are agents working on alien worlds. Only ten people are on the management committee to which I report. They have a small number of support staff. No more are required."

"Alright, but as I asked, who can possibly make that decision?" asked Alana.

"Who do you think?" asked Ben. "This group here has been involved with the Foundation almost from its very first days. Who is better qualified to make the decision to help bring the galaxy's civilisations to maturity?"

"Don't be silly, Ben," said Mary. "We're all over seventy years old, we're not in a position to decide the fate of worlds, you need the world's best scientists, philosophers, academics to handle this."

"Actually, you are at the peak of your intellectual abilities," said Ben. "And please note, all the journeymen on all the planets have confirmed that they are ready to accept the leadership of the humans because of that ability to effect emotional change in others. It makes the task many times easier than it has been. And before you take over, you can take the time to select the world's best scientists, philosophers, academics as you said, to comprise the management committee for Earth. I suggest Karen Petrova and William Askins as the first two."

He looked around the table.

"I think it's time to meet my superiors," he said.

Chapter Thirty-Eight – The Job Interview – 2066

"Their images will already be waiting for us when we enter the holographic suite," said Ben. "Shall we go in?"

Garry, Mary and Alana nodded and he opened the door.

As they entered, Garry saw a ring of images forming a semi-circle before four armchairs. They stopped just inside the room and studied the group. Garry counted ten, just as Ben had said there would be. One was a very old woman, three were elderly men, four were women he estimated to be in their early forties and the last two were tall, athletic young men. All were studying the Foundation group with as much interest as the group was studying them.

"A little intimidating," muttered Garry. "I've never had a job interview like this one before."

"We've already been offered the job," said Alana in a low voice. "I think this is more a matter of our deciding if we want it."

"Would you take your seats?" asked Ben from where he was standing by the four armchairs and the others did as asked, Ben at one end, Garry at the left hand end with Alana next to him, Mary sitting next to Ben.

The old woman at the edge of the group in front of them opened the proceedings.

"We are so delighted and very honoured to meet the representatives of the human race," she said. Her voice was a pleasant contralto that didn't match her appearance.

"Thank you," said Garry. "This is an extraordinary experience for us, as you will understand."

"We do, of course, just as you will understand that this is similarly extraordinary for us. While we are familiar with the work that Ben and his teams of mentors have been doing within the galaxy and the developments of your group ever since Karen Petrova and her husband began their work, we have never had the experience of meeting our successors before."

Finally, Garry relaxed and sensed the same reaction in Alana and Mary. He smiled. "We hadn't thought of it that way," he said.

The old woman returned his smile. "You realise from your meetings with the Galactic Mentor Council that these are not our natural forms and our words are being translated into English by the holograph system."

"Ben has explained that to us fully," said Garry.

"Of course. So let us get down to the basis for this meeting," said the old woman. "Ben has also explained to you that for a number of reasons, we want you to take on the job of Galactic Mentors to the twelve species around the galaxy that we are looking after and assisting and leading the teams of mentors, journeymen and apprentices that do the work on the planets."

"Madam, he has," said Garry. "But we are quite overwhelmed by the suddenness of this request, and even more by the scale of the task. It seems that we have very little time to prepare ourselves should we decide to take on the responsibility."

"To be honest, Garry, we are also overwhelmed by the same things." The old woman looked sad. "This sudden and rapid decline in our birthrates and the clear message we seem to be getting from the semi-sentient intelligence at the core of our galaxy that our time is up has distressed us all."

"But at the same time, that is a source of great encouragement," said one of the young men at the centre of the group. "The fact that the core intelligence seems to trust you means that you will have infinitely more assistance in the job than we or our predecessors had."

"But it's only a new-born baby," said Alana. "We cannot talk to each other and it can hardly know what it's doing!"

"Agreed," said the young man. "But it has already responded to the calming influence of those extraordinary people, Karen Petrova and William Askins. We liken it to the behaviour of a new-born baby feeling trust and closeness to its mother, without being aware of the nature of the relationship or be able to express wants and needs."

"My God," said Mary. "Karen and William are the parents of an entire bloody galaxy!"

Garry and Alana couldn't help themselves and burst into laughter.

The Committee members smiled in sympathy. "Yes, it really is a grotesque idea," said the old woman. "But it has some basis in reality. It's one of the key factors in our request to you to take on the assignment. Remember also that you already have the willing support from all the other species that were under consideration for the role we have asked you to take. All of them understand that you must be the new Mentors and you will get nothing but support from them."

"One thing that has bothered us in discussing this," said Garry, "is how the rest of our world will react to this development. I really do not feel any certainty that the human race is ready to know about the role we'll be playing or that we have the maturity to deal with it."

"A fair point," said the elderly man seated by the old woman. "But not a problem. Few people on our planet know of the role we have played for so many thousands of years. This committee exercises great care in selecting our replacements and doing our work. You will need only perhaps ten members, two of whom will join the Galactic Mentors' Council. The support staff will be equally carefully selected and few people outside your immediate family and this Foundation need know of your work."

"But how on Earth can we learn about all your work, all the details of the civilisations you are helping, all the cultures, languages, technologies, everything in so short a space of time?" asked Mary. Her distress was high.

"With the assistance of the greatest library ever created," said one of the other women. Garry thought she looked no more than forty, a petite frame, pretty, long, auburn hair and beautiful eyes and wondered what her real appearance was. "All the information of everything we have done, all the civilisations we work with, all their technologies, languages, cultures, all are stored there. And as you have seen, we have learning tools that can give you an alien language or a complete history of the society in just a few hours. We will give you the access tools for your use at any time."

"That's another benefit you will get," said the old woman. "The hugely advanced technologies that we have will also be given to you. Our spaceships, for instance. We have a fleet of over a hundred and the technology to build more. You will get full training in the handling and navigation around the galaxy. There are new power sources, enough to provide free power to your whole world without pollution. Then there is this holograph technology. All of these can be slowly introduced to Earth without it seeming to have been derived from elsewhere. The vast majority of your people need never know where it all came from. You could probably introduce it all through this Foundation. Set up a design and invention company and nobody would be surprised at the stream of genius flowing out! After all, you already have that reputation."

"When we were in your situation and first took on the mentor role, there was a massive flowering of our world," said another of the men in the group. "As you have already done, you have set yourself up for wonderful progress, having eliminated many of the factors that cause conflict. Now it can grow even faster and with the technology we will give you, Earth can finally fulfill an ancient dream and start to colonise suitable planets as you find them. And believe me, there are many to choose from."

Alana, Mary and Garry looked at each other.

"That's one hell of a sales job they've done," said Alana. "How can we possibly turn it down?"

"Damn right," said Garry.

"No argument from me," said Mary.

They turned back to the ring of faces before them.

"I feel very strange about claiming to speak for the human race," said Garry. "But we understand that we must take on this task. My friends and colleagues here, plus Karen Petrova, William Askins and their mother Galina Askins will discuss it and decide just what roles we will take on, but it seems likely that initially, all of us will comprise the Management Committee until we can find some suitably qualified people to bring in."

He sat back, feeling out of breath as if he had just run a race or climbed a mountain.

"Thank you," said the old woman. "I know that I speak for my colleagues when I say we are delighted and relieved at your decision. From here on, Ben will guide you in the transition process. We know that you will be most successful and many civilisations that might have died will now survive and prosper under your guidance."

All the committee members raised their hands in farewell and suddenly the holograph room held nothing but the four people who had entered.

"We'd better get to work," said Garry.

Chapter Thirty-Nine – The Universe in Crisis – July, 2066

Penny woke up screaming.

It was a full-throated scream of such fear that her body shook and she curled up in a tight foetal position, her teeth leaving blood on her hands where they jammed against her mouth. The pain in her hands woke her up just as Avram came sharply awake.

He rolled over to her side, sat up and wrapped his arms around her.

"Penny! Penny, sweetheart, wake up, wake up, what has happened?"

She clung to him, her violent trembles vibrating against him, weeping loudly. Avram held her tight, stroking her back until after some minutes she calmed down and stopped crying.

"Penny, what on Earth was that all about?" Avram murmured.

"Oh, God, Avram, it was like when I woke up before, thinking I heard the baby crying. But this was much worse, it seemed like she was screaming in terror and I was terrified."

"Still frightened? Now you're awake and our daughter is grown up, how are you feeling?"

"All I can remember is a sense of utter horror. I'm still shaking, even though I know it was just a nightmare."

"One hell of a nightmare, kid," he replied. "Can you recall any details?"

She lifted her head from his shoulder.

"Just fear," she said. "Just like the last time but far worse."

"We all concluded that somehow you were sensing the fear of the core entity. You obviously have the greatest connection to it. Was that it again?"

"Oh lord, if it was, the poor thing is frightened out of its mind. And... Avram, I can still feel it, there's a massive sense of terror and helplessness."

"And you're not going to be able to sleep, are you?"

"Not a chance."

"Then it's a good thing that I'm a doctor, because I'm going to give you a serious sedative. Can you stand being alone for a few minutes while I get my bag?"

She nodded, but as he stood up, she folded her arms tightly around herself and rocked gently back and forth, shoulders hunched as if afraid of being hit.

Despite the high-strength sedative, Penny's sleep was still badly disturbed for the rest of the night. When she finally woke up, her face was white and her eyes dark with fatigue. Avram had sat up the whole time, watching her and occasionally taking her pulse and he was in no better shape.

"We'd better call the group together," said Avram.

* * *

"I'm getting calls from all the mentor teams on every planet," said Ben. "They're all reporting the same thing, waves of fear and anxiety among their populations, the teams themselves are experiencing the same thing, just about everybody is afraid of something, but nobody knows what."

"It does sound like a repeat of the last episode," said Alana. "Penny is somehow experiencing something of the emotional disturbance of the core entity, but this time it's so much more intense that everybody in the galaxy is sensing it."

"I know I am," said Mary. "I woke up in the night feeling quite worried and I'm still feeling it. I couldn't keep my breakfast down. Is everybody else here feeling the same?"

"All of us," said Garry, looking round the group.

"We'd better call the Galactic Mentors' Council together," said Ben. "I suspect this affects us all. And I have a horrible suspicion that we're the cause of the problem."

* * *

Garry studied the holographic images of the Galactic Mentor Council as one by one, they flickered into view in the holograph suite.

"Oh look," he murmured to Ben and Mary. "The Rogue Mentor is here."

"Suggesting they're badly frightened, also," said Ben. He looked out at the semi-circle. "Thank you for responding so quickly to my call," he said. "This seems to be the biggest crisis we have experienced in our entire experience and it looks like we are all affected by it."

"What have you done?" shouted the Mentor from the Rogue galaxy. "We know you people have been in our territory, we know you did something on one of our planets, we've found all those devices you left in the Death Houses, but we can't work out what they were. Do you realise the damage you have done with your meddling?"

"Actually, Madam, we don't," said Ben. "We are aware of great distress within our own galaxy, apparently resulting from a sense of fear within our core entity, but we don't know what else has happened."

"Then you should know," said the Mentor. Suddenly, she looked tired, not outraged. "For a few weeks after your spies had invaded our territory and planted those weapons in the buildings all over the one planet, everything was normal. We were sure that perhaps a time of stability had come. But now, this has all gone wrong. The anger throughout our galaxy has shot up, wars are breaking out, riots and violence are happening on many of our planets and every single person is in a state of distress. This is what you have done."

"Oh dear Lord," muttered Mary. "Their core entity must have sensed we had tried to affect it and it's reacted violently. Ben, we've really miscalculated here and now we've got blood on our hands."

"I think so," Ben said. His face was white. He turned to face the Mentor again.

"We must accept responsibility," he said. "What we were trying to do was exactly the opposite of what happened. We had identified that your core entity was emotionally unstable and was causing distress to its equivalent in our own galaxy. We have a mechanism for affecting emotional states and we used it to try and help you. I deeply regret that we made the situation worse."

The other Mentor's anger had returned.

"Yes, you did and you will pay for it. We are sending out thousands of warships and they are looking for pathways to all your galaxies. They will find them and they will make you pay in blood for your crime."

"Can I ask the rest of you," said Ben. "Have you experienced any problems in recent days after our work in that galaxy?"

The other Mentors nodded.

"Quite a lot," said one. "Our own mentors and journeymen have experienced some distress themselves and they are reporting varying levels of anxiety in the general populations. They have been unable so far to explain this."

"Well now they'll understand," said the Rogue Mentor. "The orders have gone out. Prepare to be hurt."

Her image flickered out of existence.

"You think all this has been caused by our efforts to change the emotional state of the entity in that galaxy?" asked another of the council.

"It looks like it," replied Ben. "And the last comment by our departed member is worrying. As you know, we found a couple of ships that had somehow crossed the gap between their galaxy and ours. One was destroyed by a force affecting our ship's computer and we have since considered that it was our core entity somehow expressing a reaction to its fear. We examined the second one and found the track through hyperspace to the Rogue galaxy and that's how we got there and tried our healing process, but we got it wrong."

"Then it seems critical that we all conduct searches through our home galaxies in case they manage to repeat their exercise and send invading forces," said another.

"Agreed," said Ben. "And if you find them, you must seize them and do what we did, examine their computers and find the routes they took."

"As you know," said the other Mentor, "we did the same research you did and we have all found semi-sentient but intelligent entities at the core of our galaxies. It's clear that they were all reacting to the distress of the Rogue but to lesser extents because of the distance, perhaps or maybe because they have different levels of maturity."

"That is interesting," said Ben. "But does anyone have suggestions for what we do next?"

"It seems obvious to me that what we did clearly had some effect on the emotional state of the Rogue," said another mentor. "But we under-estimated how much stronger should have been the forces we sent. I can only recommend that we do the same but at a much more intensive level."

All the Mentors expressed approval.

"I think we're at war," said Garry.

Chapter Forty – The Universe at War, 2066

"We found two ships from the Rogue galaxy," said the Mentor from one of the other three galaxies.

"None," said another.

"Just one," said the last Mentor. "And like my colleagues, we captured it without difficulty and dived deep into the computer. Now we have a route, a bit untidy but a definite route through a number of hyperspace jumps back into the Rogue galaxy. So now that we have the devices that your extraordinary electronics genius designed, we can repeat the process you executed some months ago."

"This is excellent work," said Ben. "So as you explained, you will build hundreds of the devices, send them with a number of agents to every populated planet in the Rogue galaxy and absolutely flood their core entity with emotion-modifying energies. We put our genius to work some time ago and he has enhanced that emotion-modified by several factors. We'll join in the exercise."

"How will their Mentors react, do you think?" asked the first speaker.

"We must all be careful," said Ben. "They will have no difficulties in detecting our influx and will try and prevent our actions. I recommend that you send armed agents along with the others and be prepared to be attacked. We have consulted our United Nations Security Council and they have agreed to send members of our armed forces along. I am going to advise their Mentor Council that if they attempt any further conflict, we will destroy their capital city."

"That's horribly extreme, isn't it?" asked one of the others.

"I see no options," said Ben. "It's no exaggeration to say the health and safety of five galaxies is at risk. And we don't know if there are other populated galaxies we haven't yet encountered."

The others nodded.

"Let's get started," said one and in turn, each of the images flickered out of existence.

* * *

December, 2066

"So far, it's been smooth sailing," said Ben. "I think my warning to the Rogue Mentors had an effect. Our agents worked at more than thirty Death Houses, sending energy bolts of just-died people to the core entity. We had transported fifteen groups of agents to the first planet and installed the devices there and we had no interference until one of the last. That's when we ran into a problem..."

"I gotta say, these weapons are pretty nifty," said the SAS Sergeant, holding up the alien gun in admiration. "I think I still prefer our standard Thales Lithgow F125, I like lots of bullets pouring out when I pull the trigger, but these things are great – no recoil, no noise and I can vary the power from stone dead to knock-out punch."

"I still don't like 'em," said the Corporal. "Too bloody science fictiony for my taste."

"Then let's hope we don't have to use them," said the Sergeant. "Andy, how much longer will we need to be here?

It gives me the creeps working in something called a Death House. Why couldn't they call it something easier, like a retirement home?"

"Can't explain that," said the Journeyman mentor. "Anyway, we need another two hours to install the last four devices. The others are all checked out, they're collecting the energy bolts as people die, merging them with that emotional modifying energy and sending them off to the Big Momma in the middle of the galaxy. Once we're done here, we can go home, this was the last installation site on our schedule."

"About bloody time," said the Corporal. "I just can't believe we're on a planet in another galaxy. Can't wait to get back to Bondi Beach and a spot of leave."

"Stop grumbling, Jerry," said the Sergeant. "Get the men deployed and keep your eyes open. Nobody's got stupid yet, but you never know."

But even as the Corporal moved outside, there was a yell from one of the soldiers on guard and the entire troupe of men leapt into action. Yellow beams flickered across the upper level of the building, melting the concrete and bringing chunks of masonry thundering to the ground.

Well-trained combat soldiers rapidly took protective positions and returned silent fire with lethal accuracy. It took only three minutes for the assailants to be knocked unconscious and the battle ended.

"Cover us," ordered the Sergeant and eased himself out of the defence position, nodded at the Corporal to accompany him and with his gun at the ready, advanced on the positions from which the attack had come.

Several unconscious soldiers lay there. The Corporal carefully picked up their weapons and moved them well away.

"Bloody amateurs," said the Sergeant. "All the military skills of a kindergarten class." He put his fingers to his lips and blew a loud whistle. The remaining troops slowly emerged and cautiously examined the dozen or so attackers, gathered up the weapons and stacked them with the rest. The Sergeant walked back to the building.

"You guys alright?" he asked.

"Why, did something happen?" said Andy, the Journeyman.

The Sergeant grinned cheerfully. "Too bloody cool for a civilian," he said. "When can we get out of here? Those kiddies out there will start recovering in about two hours."

"That'll do it," said Andy. "I'll call the ship down."

"I hope they have lots of beer in the fridge," said the Sergeant.

Chapter Forty-One – Second Crisis – 2067

March 15, 2067

"It isn't working," said Garry. His face was white and he looked far more aged that his actual eighty-two.

Not that any of the others of the Foundation Management looked any better. Ben was mostly unchanged but the lines of worry in his face were deep. Alana seemed composed but the tension in her body was almost a spring, ready to release violently. Mary had lost so much weight, her clothes seemed to hang on her like an oversized dress on a child.

"I've had to keep Penny in an induced coma for some weeks now," said Avram. "I moved her to the hospital and she's being fed by tubes. If I hadn't, I know she'd have probably killed herself. She's feeling the core entity fear more than anyone. I feel it badly too, but not as severely as she does. As it is, I need a heavy sleeping pill to get to sleep at night and I still wake up a few times, feeling terrified."

His face was tightly drawn and the bones stood out from his cheeks and jaw almost like a victim of starvation.

"We were so sure this would work," said Karen. "For a time, our first effort did have the result we wanted, the Rogue entity seemed to calm down. And now I have to live with the fact that my brilliant ideas have caused the deaths of thousands in riots across worlds in five galaxies and there's no sign of a let-up."

The grief in her face was like an ancient painting of a martyred saint. For the first time anyone at the Foundation had known her, she had not made her face up and the normal bright scarlet lipstick was missing. Her eyes were dark with fatigue and there was a slight tremble in her hands.

"I'm just as much to blame," said William. He too had lost significant weight and looked seriously ill. "I designed the machines that set off this horror. I just never thought it through."

"You have to stop blaming yourselves," said Ben. "The first approach by you and Karen obviously did have the right effect. The Rogue entity did calm down, it stopped emoting fear like a terrified infant and the other Galactic entities all followed. When the infant got frightened again as it realised we'd done something to it and sent foreign agencies into it, it was the perfectly rational solution to repeat the treatment only on a larger scale."

"But we increased it by several thousand percent," protested William. "We sent hundreds of thousands of energy bolts merged with the emotional modifier into that thing and instead of calming own, it went berserk. It's caused distress in all five of our galaxies and people are going crazy. I can't begin to imagine how many people have died in the upheavals."

"There was no way of knowing that would happen," said Ben. "And if we'd done nothing, the problems would have persisted and we'd probably be in much the same situation we are now."

"What do the other Galactic Mentors say?" asked Garry.

"They report the same as we have experienced," said Ben. "A couple of weeks of no change after all the agents had returned home and then a sudden outburst of distress, anger, violence on all planets containing civilisations, obviously affected by the distress and tantrums from the Rogue entity and the resulting distress in the other Galactic entities. All intelligent species were affected by this. The death rates are horrific."

Karen burst into tears. "How can I live with this?" she whispered.

"Karen, we'll get through it," said Ben. "Even a galactic scale infant will get tired of its tantrums."

"I don't know," she replied, gasping her words through the sobs. "These things have a huge timescale. What if it takes a few centuries to calm down?"

The others had nothing to say.

Karen stood up and walked out of the conference room.

"Better keep an eye on her, William," said Alana.

March 17, 2067

"Karen's in hospital, her condition is critical," said William, his voice sounding harsh from the loudspeaker in the conference room.

"William! What the hell happened?" Mary's voice was high pitched in panic.

"Last night, she called me from her apartment. She sounded terrible, weak and frightened. She said she had to say goodbye."

"Oh my God," exclaimed Garry. "She tried to commit suicide?"

"She tried. I raced round there, I've always had a key to her place and I found her on the bed, completely comatose. I called an ambulance, they got there bloody quickly and she was in the Emergency Room at John Hunter Hospital in a few minutes. They pumped her out, but it's touch and go. Any later, we'd have lost her. She's still not out of danger."

Mary burst into tears and Garry hid his head in his hands. Alana looked as if carved in stone

"Avram's here too," continued William. "He was sitting with Penny when Karen was brought in and he's had a look at her. He's fairly hopeful, says Karen is so fit and healthy, not even the overdose she took will kill her. He even tried to joke about it, said it was the first time anyone called Karen Petrova had ever failed at anything."

"Thank God for that," murmured Garry. "Mary, Alana and I will be there in a short while."

March 18, 2067

"Dearest Penny, I hope you're sleeping well," said Avram. He sat by the bed, holding Penny's hand. "You're missing the worst time in the Foundation's history, the first time we've hit real failure, miscalculation, bad judgement, the first time anything has ever really gone wrong since the first Karen was killed."

He studied Penny's face. It looked calm, her complexion quite normal. The mask over her nose and mouth nearly hid the sound of her breathing. Tubes inserted into her arm led from containers on a rack by the bed.

"I do miss you so badly," Avram said, tears appearing in his eyes. "And now Karen is in the Emergency Room in intensive care. She felt so guilty about what has happened, she tried to kill herself, but I'm pretty sure she'll recover. Whether she'll ever come to terms with what has happened is another question."

He laid his head down by her hand and tried to stop weeping. After a short while, he fell asleep, having slept very little the last few days.

And woke up with a start, feeling his hand being squeezed. He sat up and looked at Penny. Her eyes were open and she was gazing at him.

"What the... Penny, you're supposed to be in a coma! What's happened?"

She gestured at the mask to get him to remove it. Utterly stunned by what was happening, knowing as a doctor just how impossible this was, he gently removed the mask from her face.

She was smiling at him.

"Penny, how can this be happening? Are you really awake? How can you be awake...? This is impossible."

"Shhhh," she whispered. "Avram, it's fine. I'm fine."

"But what's happened?" His voice was trembling from the shock.

"I just talked to it," she said softly. "It can't talk back, it's far too young, but I know what it meant."

"You talked...? The core entity? You talked to it?"

"I really did," she said and touched his face. "It was just like when Jessica was an infant. I talked to her and I knew she understood and somehow she told me what she wanted, even before she could talk."

"But.. what did it say?"

"First thing was to say that the problem is resolved. All the other galactic entities have joined together and they've told the Rogue to grow up and behave itself, or words to that effect. It will take a while, but it looks like they've learned something of the Mule abilities a few of us have got."

Avram took a deep breath, leaned over and kissed her. She responded gently.

"And the second thing?" he asked.

"It told me to wake up. Now, get these damned tubes off me and get me my clothes. I want to go home."

Chapter Forty-Two – A Final Question – 2067

"It's slowly returning to normal," said the Galactic Mentor Council member. "It's been a month since you told us about Penny reporting that somehow she had communicated with your core entity, but within a few days of that, the distress and fear in the whole galaxy began to wind down."

"Just as here," said another member and the others all nodded in agreement.

There was a sudden flicker of movement in the holograph suite where Ben and the others had gathered for this meeting and another image appeared. A stir of surprise ran through the other members.

"We are delighted you decided to join us," said Ben.

The Council member from the Rogue galaxy looked weary and severely unhappy.

"It was an obvious requirement," she said. "Your previous intervention caused horrible results, but this time you appear to have succeeded. Our galaxy is returning to mental health."

"And your people?" asked Garry.

"My people, too," said the Councillor. "On all fifteen inhabited planets, we have at last realised the madness that has affected us for centuries. We have recalled all our ships from their efforts to reach the other galaxies. We understand what you did and something of how you did it."

"We cannot blame you for all this," said Ben. "We remain baffled by what mental illness affected your core entity, but at last we have found a way to treat it."

"What has amazed us all," said one of the other Councillors, "is how the entities in all our galaxies seemed to become aware of the problem and joined together to treat the sick one. There's another development also. Several of our mentors rapidly developed what Ben's people call the "Mule" ability to affect somebody's emotional state. It has never been found before in all these thousands of years and yet suddenly it has appeared."

"In ours, too," said another Councillor. "At least six of our mentors found this talent. And while not to the extent that Penny experienced, some of them also sensed communication with their core entities."

The Councillor for the last galaxy nodded with a smile. "The same with us," she said. "Two of our people established some sort of communication but they feel their core entity may be a little bit more grown that yours, Ben. You indicated that your entity seems like a new-born baby, ours gave our mentors the impression of being a little bit more mature, not yet talking, but showing more self-awareness."

"That is extraordinary," said Ben. "It still remains incomprehensible to us how they all cooperated and made the emotional change in the sick entity and it's a source of absolute astonishment that this "Mule" ability seems to be one they all have."

"One day, you will have to explain to the rest of us why you gave it this name," said the last speaker. "But for now, with the crisis declining, we should address the issue of the next Galactic Mentor race for your galaxy."

"And this is welcome news," said Ben. "My Galactic Mentor Council unanimously agreed that the human species should take on the role. As I have told you, my race which has held the responsibility for many thousands of years appears to be about to disappear, probably within fifty years. So the training of humans to take on the role must be concentrated into a severely restricted time period."

"That is potentially dangerous," said another speaker. "My people have been in this position for over a thousand years but once we had been nominated as successors, we took two centuries to reach the maturity and skills needed."

"I agree," said Ben. "This is unprecedented. But we are all aware now that the core entity somehow affected the decision process, just as it has somehow developed additional communications with human trainee mentors. I'm certain it will give a great deal of help to the new mentors."

"So you will give them access to the Universal Library?"

"We will, of course, quite soon," said Ben.

"The Universal Library?" asked Alana. "Just what is that, Ben?"

"We told you about it before," said Ben. "But let me remind you. It's a data base of every experience, all knowledge and every development of the mentors in all five galaxies," said Ben. "It also has a complete history of every intelligent species on all worlds in all those galaxies. You will be able to access all of it through technologies we will make available to you. Millions of people will be able to spend their lifetimes researching this database, though mostly it is designed to give the mentors the knowledge, understanding and skills they need to do their job."

"That's startling enough," exclaimed Mary. "And what else do we get?"

"You get training in the care, maintenance and operation of the spaceships," said Ben. "That will be the role of the finest technicians on Earth. You get complete knowledge of the holographic technology, the language translation computers, the consciousness-transfer mechanisms, literally everything we have. The human race will advance technically a few hundred years in the next decade, just as all the other Mentor races did when they were given this knowledge."

"And I think there is a new field of science that all of us need to work on," said another member. "This last crisis has resulted in a fairly primitive way of travelling between galaxies. So far, the routes we found between our own galaxies and what we called the Rogue galaxy only resulted from a series of random hyperspace leaps. But now that we know it can be done, we must be able to find more efficient and reliable routes between all five of us. The possibilities are endless."

"And maybe we'll be able to make contact with other galaxies," said another. "Our community of five may expand."

"The Universe will surely change," said Ben. "But for now, my main task is to get the human species started on the most intensive training program ever devised."

"Something else has occurred to me," said Alana.

Every face of the images around them and those of her own group turned to her.

"It was said that your core entities all seemed to have some familial connection," Alana continued. "Does this mean they are related? Are they from a common source? If so, I have one final question.

"Who and what are their parents?"

** The End **